THE ETERNAL WARRIOR

BOOKS BY ARI MARMELL

STANDALONE NOVELS

The Eternal Warrior

The Iron Devils

Arkham Horror: Litany of Dreams

Darksiders: The Abomination Vault

The Goblin Corps

Gehenna: The Final Night

OBELISKS

Dust

Ashes

THE MICK OBERON SERIES

Hot Lead, Cold Iron

Hallow Point

Dead to Rites

In Truth and Claw

NOT FANG, NOR FIRE

Ash & Ambition

THE CORVIS REBAINE SERIES

The Conqueror's Shadow

The Warlord's Legacy

IRON KINGDOMS CHRONICLES

In Thunder Forged

WIDDERSHINS ADVENTURES

Thief's Covenant

False Covenant

Lost Covenant

Covenant's End

MAGIC THE GATHERING: PLANESWALKER

Agents of Artifice

ANTHOLOGIES

Tales of the Lost Citadel

Operation Arcana

Madness on the Orient Express

Writing Fantasy Heroes

When the Villain Comes Home

Foreshadows: The Ghosts of Zero

Tales of the Far West

Broken Time Blues

Human Tales

SHORT STORY COLLECTIONS

Strange New Words

A VALIANT UNIVERSE NOVEL

THE ETERNAL WARRIOR®

ARI MARMELL

BLACK STONE PUBLISHING

www.valiantentertainment.com
Published in 2025 by Blackstone Publishing
Cover artwork provided by Valiant Entertainment
Cover layout by Candice Edwards

Printed in the United States of America

First edition: 2025
ISBN 979-8-8747-4845-6
Fiction / Superheroes

Version 1

Blackstone Publishing
31 Mistletoe Rd.
Ashland, OR 97520

www.BlackstonePublishing.com

THE ETERNAL WARRIOR®

PRELUDE

If he lived for a thousand years, Colton would never get the sting of gasoline out of his nose.

It permeated his world, baked into everything by the crushing heat. The cracked stone and brick of the buildings. The concrete of the streets, the packed dirt of the roads. The fabric. The Kevlar and ceramic inserts. Even the pungent rubber of the tires.

The gunpowder. The blood.

What the fuck am I doing here?

In Dhi Qar province, a trio of US Army Humvees tore through the byways of a suburb, practically a village in its own right, on the edge of Nasiriyah. Private First Class Colton Beltran, unaware just how tightly his gloved hands grasped and twisted the stock of his M4 and deaf even to the roaring engine over the chatter of his own thoughts, jostled with every dip in the road until his teeth nearly ground themselves to powder.

Tonight was far from his first hostile engagement. More experienced soldiers assured him it got easier. Of course, they'd assured him of that after the first one, too, and so far nerves still told him otherwise every damn time he—

Sudden pain in his left arm, between the armored segments, made him jump. A quick glance revealed Private Kolowitz's bright eyes, round with alarm, gleaming from beneath his helmet. Colton realized what he'd felt was the sharp jab of an elbow. Before he could question why, though, a deep-voiced question sounded from the seat in front of him.

"Something you want to ask, Private?"

Colton cringed at Nash's voice. His commanding officer reminded him—reminded everyone—so completely of the sergeant from *Aliens* that Colton once accidentally called him "Apone" during the first month of his tour.

It was a mistake he'd learned not to repeat, even though Nash had admitted with a faint grin that Colton wasn't the first to make it. Admitted *after* the fifty extra push-ups and half a dozen extra laps.

"Sorry, Sarge, I'm not sure . . ."

Then, and only then, did Colton realize that just maybe he'd muttered his question aloud.

Well, shit.

"That is, just wondering what we're doing here, sir!"

"Pretty sure I saw you at the briefing, Beltran. You sleep through it?"

"No, sir!"

Some briefing. Rousted in the middle of the night, told that Intelligence had identified an insurgent hideout outside Nasiriyah that needed to be dealt with. Okay, sure. Not a unique circumstance, barely a year out from the "liberation" of Iraq.

But why them, rather than the squads on night duty? Why the urgency, greater than any Colton had seen since Saddam's capture? If this group had already killed a few American servicemen, as they'd been told, why hadn't Colton heard about any losses in the last few days? What kind of intelligence asset was command protecting, that they were feeding the men such limited information?

And why the *hell* was Major Nathan Wheeler taking personal field command of an operation that consisted of only a two-team squad?

It didn't make any sense. Colton was pretty well accustomed to working with limited intel and an incomplete picture—that was a soldier's lot—but this *really* didn't make any sense.

Nor was he the only one to feel that way, it seemed. When Sergeant Nash spoke again, his voice was . . . Well, Nash's voice didn't *do* gentle, but this was as close as he ever got.

"I was at the same briefing you were, Beltran. I don't know anymore'n you do."

Colton didn't doubt him for an instant. Nash would absolutely keep information from his men if ordered, but he would never lie to them about *having* it.

Not that Sarge being in the dark made Colton feel any better. After sharing a worried look with Kolowitz, he turned his attention to the darkened world outside the window.

Wasn't much to see. The moon was low, the night thick. A few dim electric lights and some flickering fires indicated windows (or possibly holes) in passing buildings, mostly squat stone tenements, but otherwise the neighborhood seemed a grim and lifeless blur. What little activity might normally be visible at this hour had ceased, citizens no doubt taking shelter at the sound of approaching engines.

Of course, the enemy would hear them coming, too. But stealth would never have been an option from the ground, and since the use of a drone or air attack had been ruled out—for reasons that fell into that broad and ever-growing abyss called "need to know"—the next best choice was speed.

With the rough growl of rubber on earth, the Humvees

skidded to a halt outside one tenement among nearly identical buildings. Several tattered banners hung from an upper balcony, and artillery damage to the topmost floor, probably dating back to the Battle of Nasiriyah, gaped open to the elements.

Colton's fellow squad members poured out of the first two vehicles, while Major Wheeler and his driver stepped from the third. If Sergeant Nash reminded Colton of Apone, Wheeler looked like the cookie-cutter field officer from every action movie who got in the hero's way, more concerned about protecting his own little fiefdom than smaller issues like "listening to experts" or "lives."

Not fair. You don't know the man, and this isn't a movie.

A sharp nod from Wheeler, and Nash turned to his men. "Stack up! Pak, hit it!"

Corporal Pak stepped forward, shotgun at the ready. A single blast took the lock and latch completely out of the door, and the follow-up kick did the rest. Pak swung out of the line of fire as the door flew open, tossing an M84 into the darkness beyond as he moved.

Adrenaline flooded through Colton at the flash-bang's detonation, washing away the nerves. He was inside before he knew he was moving, spreading out along with the rest of the squad, weapon raised, surveying the room through the spectral green hue of night vision goggles.

Nothing. Nobody. Other than some rickety furniture and torn curtains, the room was empty.

Colton felt like he'd been caught in the stun grenade's burst. Hyped up as he was, this felt like the one circumstance he couldn't handle.

Everyone seemed just as bewildered. Well, almost everyone. Nothing ever seemed to rattle Nash, and Wheeler . . . Wheeler just looked pissed.

"Check the room," the sergeant ordered them. "Watch for IEDs."

That made sense. Only reason the insurgents wouldn't be waiting in ambush was if they'd rigged the place, right?

Colton didn't find anything, though. Neither did anyone else. "Clear, Sarge!" Pak reported.

In a night of nonsense, this ranked high up there. Why weren't they defending themselves? The enemy *had* to have heard them coming . . .

Assuming the enemy was here at all.

Someone in Intelligence had a *lot* of tap dancing to do if they weren't.

"Major?" Nash asked.

"I want this entire building searched. Every floor, corner, and fucking cupboard. You find *anyone*, assume hostile."

Nobody came out with a direct question, but the whole squad traded looks and a few mutters. Nasiriyah wasn't enemy territory; it was an Iraqi city, full of Iraqi civilians. Whole reams of protocol, above and beyond even the normal rules of engagement, governed the soldiers' every move. What Wheeler was suggesting, if taken too literally . . .

Even Nash scowled now. "Major, with all—"

"Don't 'due respect' me, Sergeant. I know the situation here. You don't. If I could tell you, you'd understand, but I can't. So you're just going to have to trust I know what I'm doing and follow your orders."

Wasn't a whole lot even Nash could say to that, but the normally implacable sergeant radiated obvious displeasure as he told his men, "You heard the major—get searching! Alpha Team, spread out. Bravo Team, top floor. Meet in the middle."

"Bravo Team" meant Colton, among others. He dutifully trudged up the stairs, following Corporal Pak. They tested every step, cleared every corner, searched every room, even the ones covered in rubble and open to the night sky.

What they found in those rooms was a whole lot of room. No hostiles, no civilians, no IEDs, nothing to suggest the battered top floor remained in use as anything more than a ceiling for the next level down. Everything but the insects had moved on to better quarters, and even the dust felt lonely.

Nor had they had any greater success by the time they met with Alpha Team near the stairwell between floors two and three.

"Anything?" Wheeler asked.

Nash glanced at Pak, who shook his head. "You'd need a microscope to find a rat turd, sir."

The sergeant repeated the report to Wheeler, in slightly less colorful terms. "All right," Wheeler said. "Just the door, then."

Door?

Colton didn't ask aloud—he was sure of it, this time—but Nash clearly saw the question written across all of team two.

"There's a door behind an old wall hanging back on ground level. Guessing it's a cellar or something. Got Bailey and Major Wheeler's man watching it."

As they all trooped back downstairs, Colton overheard Nash and Pak in whispered conversation, the corporal asking his commander why he hadn't alerted them to the presence of an unknown basement.

"Would've. Wheeler wanted it kept off comms."

"The hell is he up to, Sarge? What are *we* into?"

Nash's lack of answer was louder than the M84.

Yet not quite so loud, it seemed to Colton, as the shouting that soon followed.

He'd taken rear guard as the squad proceeded downstairs, so he'd barely set foot on the steps before it began. Multiple voices: several in English that were familiar to him, several more that were not.

"On the ground! Tell them to get on the ground!"

"Daniels! Daniels, get over here!"

Colton made it to the cellar as fast as he could while covering everyone's six, finally turning to see what was happening.

Three men stood against the far wall, one dressed in a dishdasha robe, the others in modern suit vests and slacks. All three wore keffiyeh, and all three carried beat-up rifles—two AK-47s and a Korean Daewoo K2—though the weapons were deliberately held down by their sides rather than raised to fire. Two of them spoke loudly and emphatically in Arabic, even as Wheeler ordered them to drop their weapons and lie down on the ground.

Private Daniels, far more fluent in Arabic than anyone else in the squad, had scurried forward at Nash's call and struggled to hear and translate despite the cross fire of voices.

"They want us to leave . . ." he began in his unpleasantly nasal tone.

"No shit they want us to leave!" Wheeler snapped at him. "Tell them if they don't drop their weapons, we—"

"They say . . . They say they're not insurgents." It would've been unthinkable for a private to interrupt the major, but Daniels clearly *wasn't* thinking, focused entirely on drawing meaning from the cacophony. "They don't mean us any harm."

"Oh, bullshit!"

"They're just trying to . . ." He stopped, lips moving silently as he wrestled with the translation. "To protect some . . . relics? Cultural art, or . . . or something."

Wheeler was far from the only one who wasn't buying it. "You see any art in here, Private Daniels?" Pak demanded.

The younger soldier shrugged. "Just telling you what they're saying, sir. Besides . . ."

He didn't gesture, precisely. Like most of the squad, he held his weapon trained squarely on the trio of purported insurgents, and he wasn't about to shift his aim. His gaze, however, encompassed several large chests to one side, which certainly could have held artwork. Or blankets, clothes, dishes . . . hell, a dead walrus, for all Colton knew.

It was the men themselves who most held his attention, though. *Old* men, all three of them, their faces made of weather-beaten wrinkles and cotton-hued beards. The elderly certainly could be insurgents, he'd seen that firsthand, but *only* the elderly and nobody else here? And these three . . . This didn't feel right.

Not that he lowered his M4.

"Daniels," Nash ordered through clenched teeth, "tell these men that if they're really not our enemy, they've got nothing to worry about . . ."

Was Colton losing it, or did Wheeler's lip quiver in an angry twitch at that?

". . . but if they want to prove it, they need to drop their weapons and let us take them into custody. *Now!*"

With only a slight halt to his words, Daniels translated. The foremost of the trio looked back at his companions. A flicker of sadness, a firm set of the jaw . . .

Oh no. Please don't—

Three guns rose rapidly, and over half a dozen carbines opened up. The old men died without getting off a single shot.

Silence fell throughout the cellar. Colton swallowed hard, willing himself not to vomit. Daniels and Pak moved in to check the fallen, but this was a formality and everyone knew it. Two were dead before they hit the floor, and the third—the man in the dishdasha—followed them after only a few seconds of choking and spastic clutching at Daniels's arm.

"Why?" Colton knew the voices of every member of his

squad, but in that moment he couldn't identify the speaker through the ringing in his ears and the static in his mind. "Why'd they do that, Sarge? They had to know they couldn't—"

"They're fucking fanatics," Wheeler interrupted. "That's all the 'why' they need. What I need is for you all to get searching."

Colton and several others didn't register the order, still staring at the dead men. He'd killed before during his tour, multiple times, but he'd always comforted himself with the knowledge that every life he'd ended belonged to an enemy who'd have happily seen him dead in turn.

No matter how hard he tried, and he absolutely tried, he couldn't make himself believe that here.

Sergeant Nash, on the other hand, heard the order loud and clear. "And what exactly are we searching for here . . . sir?"

The extra pause was short, subtle, probably not even noticeable to anyone who didn't know him well. To his men, though, it was practically a shout of disdain and disrespect toward the officer in charge.

For a breath or two, it seemed Wheeler might not answer, or else offer something useless like "Anything" or "You'll know when you find it." Eventually, however, he came to a decision.

"A door."

"Say again?"

"A door, Sergeant. I have reason to believe there's more to this place."

"Is that anything like the reason we had to believe these old guys were insurgents?" Kolowitz muttered—a hair too loud, as it happened.

"Stow that shit, Private!" Nash barked at him. "Everyone get to searching! Kolowitz, we're gonna have a chat back at base."

Kolowitz winced but snapped off a "Yes, sir, Sarge!" before moving to tap along the far wall.

Colton wondered if his friend realized that Nash had just saved his ass. Whatever discipline the sergeant had in mind, he'd no doubt just circumvented far worse from Wheeler.

Since nobody else was doing it and Nash hadn't tossed out specific assignments, Colton moved to the chests. Just might be a trapdoor underneath, assuming Major Wheeler wasn't smoking something regarding this whole secret-door crap. Felt more like something out of a D&D game than an actual assignment, but orders were orders.

Colton wasn't about to try moving the chests without checking inside first, though. Getting careless, assuming a room was clear because the rest of the building had been, was a damn good way to lose a limb or worse to an IED.

Daniels joined him, and the pair checked carefully around the edges for catches or wires before preparing to open it up.

"He spoke to me," the other man whispered, right as Colton was about to lift the lid.

"Say what now?"

"The old man. When he was dying."

"You don't think you maybe should report that?" Then, when Daniels didn't agree or even react to the notion, Colton asked, "What . . . what'd he say?"

"I mean . . . he was choking, and real quiet, and I'm still not *completely* fluent . . ."

"Daniels . . ."

"I think . . . ? I think he said, 'Better to die clean.'"

For no reason he could have begun to articulate, Colton felt a brief chill.

The chests held no explosive surprises. Beneath layers of folded fabrics, Colton and Daniels found scraps of faded text, hard and brittle, stored between panes of picture-frame glass. Whether they were old or rare enough to qualify as "cultural treasures" could certainly be debated, but they hardly seemed worth dying over.

"They're not," Wheeler insisted when Daniels shared that observation. "I told you, this isn't all they're hiding. Keep looking."

Nothing under the chests. Nothing special about the back wall where the men had been standing, nor anything as the soldiers worked outward from there. Minutes turned to hours, the soldiers' tension rising with every additional moment spent in what they'd been told was an enemy stronghold, let alone in the same room with the slowly cooling bodies of the men they'd just killed.

Colton broke off his own efforts long enough for several long swigs from his canteen, then climbed a couple of steps back up the stairway, looking for a new perspective on the room. Nash opened his mouth, perhaps to order him back to work, then shut it again at the look of concentration on the private's face.

Okay, the three old men had been against the far wall. Not the most tactically advantageous spot if they'd planned an ambush, but since they'd tried talking first, it made sense. Make yourself obvious, plainly nonhostile.

Except . . . they hadn't been *exactly* opposite the stairs, standing instead a little ways over to the right of anyone who entered. Not enough to take them out of the line of sight, but clearly not centered.

The squad had begun their search in that spot since the men had obviously chosen it deliberately. And found nothing.

Colton's mind raced. *If they weren't guarding something . . . were we meant to* think *they were? To draw attention from somewhere else?*

But they'd covered practically the whole room now, tapping on walls and checking the floor, frustrations mounting to the point they were snapping at one another.

Of course. That was the point. To frustrate the searchers by the time they'd looked everywhere in the room, fray their patience and make them . . .

Make them overlook anything just *outside* of the room.

PFC Colton Beltran turned and bent over the steps, poking at them with his M4. He found the concealed hinge on the fifth one up.

"Sarge!"

Flipping the wood up on that hinge revealed a catch beneath it, which in turn loosened the entire lower section of the staircase, allowing it to slide into the left wall. Beyond, a separate staircase, far narrower and carved from stone, plunged ever deeper into the earth beneath Nasiriyah.

"Form up!" Nash ordered. "Beltran, take point. And good job!"

Colton beamed with pride at his own cleverness.

It wasn't an attitude he kept for long.

The claustrophobic stairs had taken them impossibly downward, like something from the start of a horror movie, and when they'd finally opened up . . .

"How? How is this fucking possible, Sarge?"

Nash had no answer for his men. Even Wheeler, who clearly knew far more than he was telling, stood speechless.

They'd abandoned night vision, unable to comprehend what they saw through the electric-green tint. The squad stood now in a sphere of dull illumination, the immediate ruddy glow of night vision–safe flashlights giving way to the more infernal red of a dozen flares. They'd hurled those sizzling lights as far as they could, and still they couldn't see to the edges of the vast chamber in which they found themselves.

Uneven stretches of rock suggested this had once been a natural hollow, though smoother sections of wall and a mostly even floor were proof enough it had later been modified by human hands. The air sat heavy with dust and the scent of untouched ages.

Half a dozen thick columns supported the ceiling, columns adorned in mosaic patterns of jagged lines and overlapping diamonds.

Colton was no historian, but he'd gone through an artsy phase in high school, and he'd always had a pretty sharp eye for detail. This style he recognized immediately as pre-Islamic. Perhaps even pre-Persian.

What the hell have we found?

"All right," Wheeler snapped, shaking himself out of his own near stupor, "enough gawking! Sergeant, have someone check the door. I want it open!"

Door?

Only then did Colton manage to tear himself away from the age and enormity of the cavern—a cavern that shouldn't exist here, historically or geologically—and spot the ponderous stone portals that occupied a substantial portion of the far wall. The double doors loomed over the soldiers, far taller than any man could ever require, unbowed by the weight of millennia that lay atop their squared frame.

Colton must have *really* been distracted by the rest of the place to miss those. And he'd been on point; if any hostiles had been hunkered down by those doors, he'd have led his squad straight into an ambush. *Eye for detail, my ass.*

It took almost no time for Pak and Kolowitz to give the massive portals a once-over. Beyond a few triangular carvings and the wear of ages that even the depths of the chamber couldn't fully prevent, they were unmarked stone without obvious latch or mechanism.

Wheeler scowled. "Figure something out, or we're gonna have to blow it open."

Everyone stared, respect for rank and procedure very nearly forgotten. Even Nash had reached the end of his rope.

"Major! There's no immediate threat here. We have to report this, have it cataloged—"

"Were my orders in any way unclear, Sergeant Nash? Do you need me to repeat them?"

"What's clear are the regulations! A cultural find like this—"

"Do you. Need me. To repeat. My orders?"

Nash stepped to within a single pace of Wheeler, fists clenched, and Colton wondered if he was about to see some full-on insubordination, if the sergeant was about to refuse a direct command.

And then every soldier present discovered that Nash had been wrong about one vital detail:

There absolutely was an immediate threat.

It came from the flare-tinted shadows between two of the great columns as if spat out by the darkness itself—nearly invisible in the flickering gloom, save for an occasional dull reflection at the edge of a flashlight's beam, a peculiar colorless glint. It moved in a twisting, serpentine path, visible mostly by the dust it kicked up in its wake, and it moved *fast*.

The massive chamber reverberated with its cry, a hideous shrill hiss somewhere between a teakettle and a dying infant.

Daniels went first.

He'd barely even turned to face the oncoming enemy when the impact lifted him from the grit-strewn floor. Kevlar split. Ceramic plates strong enough to stop bullets cracked and shattered. Flesh tore.

Colton still couldn't even see what had hit his friend, as if it had been the shadows themselves that clawed him open. Daniels hit the floor and rolled, screaming in agony—a scream that turned just as swiftly into a wet, choking gurgle. The skin around his gaping wounds turned inky black. The gush of spilling blood slowed as the already dark crimson grew darker, oilier. The fluid stiffened, not congealing so much as becoming gelatinous, even gummy—stretching, swaying, dangling in rubbery strands.

The pink froth at the corners of Daniels's mouth followed suit. His eyes glazed and bulged, swelling in their sockets as they partially hardened. When he finally stopped thrashing, when one last choke squeezed from his throat along with his final breath, Colton could only be grateful that at least his friend was dead.

Nobody waited for the order to fire. The thunder of multiple carbines flooded the chamber. Fragments of stone burst from dozens of impacts across the walls, pockmarked the priceless historical art on the columns.

Yet even the guns couldn't drown out the high-pitched shrieking of the thing they faced. It snaked through the dull edges of the light like a living bullwhip, so that few of the bullets struck their target. The ones that did had precious little effect, occasionally throwing the enemy off its stride for a step or two, but nothing more. No blood flew, no flesh burst, if the entity was even made of flesh at all. If it felt any pain, it showed none. Its movement never slowed, its constant wail never wavered.

The next to die was Kolowitz, his end as terrible and agonizing as Daniels's. Colton could do nothing to help his friend but to scream his fury and to continue firing his weapon. Both proved equally ineffective.

Corporal Pak, standing near enough to Kolowitz that he now wore some of the dead private's blood, flipped down his night vision goggles despite the illumination of the red-hued flashlights and flares. Perhaps he thought those might offer him a better view of the nigh-invisible threat than the naked eye alone.

Whatever he saw drove a sharp, throat-rending scream from his chest. He collapsed to the floor, seated like a child with his legs stretched out before him. There he stared straight ahead, gibbering and laughing and sobbing until the entity took his face from the front of his skull with a single broad swipe.

Then it was Colton's turn.

By a stroke of fortune, some particular angle of not only the flashlight on his own weapon but those of the panicking soldiers around him, he saw another gleam off the shade-wrapped skin as it moved. Part of him registered motion, speed, angle, well before his conscious mind understood what was happening. Despite the enemy's astonishing pace, Colton stepped partway from its path, his mad flailing and desperate turn saving him from a gaping chest wound like the one that had claimed Daniels.

Unfortunately, even with that brief warning, he couldn't possibly have moved swiftly *enough*. Those claws or tendrils or blades or shadows, whatever slashed and tore from the dark, opened an array of lacerations across his left forearm.

The agony washing over him was unlike any pain Colton had ever known. The gashes felt somehow *wrong*. Dirty. Burning and freezing simultaneously, not just physically but spiritually. He might willingly have sacrificed the entire arm if losing it would take those wounds with it.

He knew, in the portions of his brain not already succumbing to panic and pain and whatever corruption now ate away at him, that he had only seconds remaining. He'd seen the contagion spread through Daniels, through Kolowitz, murdering them as surely as any weapon.

Gibbering animal instincts screamed at him to stop it, to get it out. So it was not quick thinking so much as primal frenzy that drove Colton to grab the last flare from the pack at his side, snap it into ignition, and jam the searing end directly into the wound.

The world went white. He couldn't see, hear, think . . . *be*.

Nothing for an eternal instant but shock and a pain so intense he couldn't consciously register it.

Something smacked against his knees, then one shoulder, bringing him back to himself—if only just. Colton realized he was lying on the floor. That it was the impact of the fall that had brought him back to himself, that he'd passed out for some few seconds.

Yet in those seconds, something had changed. The thunder of the guns had fallen silent, the hysterical screams of his fellow soldiers now transformed into bewilderment. The high-pitched shriek of the entity had grown ever so faintly muted, perhaps puzzled or confused.

Or, for the first time, perhaps concerned.

And Colton heard another shout, a cry of exertion in a voice he didn't know, followed by the meaty sound of heavy impact.

Colton forced his eyes open.

A stranger stood between the surviving soldiers and the living darkness. He wore no military uniform, no armor, only tunic, trousers, and boots of local make, all in dull grays and browns. Dark hair hung far longer than any army would permit, swept back in a simple tie to keep it out of his way and out of the grasp of any enemy. In his hands he held . . . In the chaotic lighting, Colton couldn't say precisely *what* he held. Some manner of axe or hammer, something far too primitive to find on any modern battlefield.

The young soldier saw no motion in the gloom, yet the stranger circled to one side as if matching an opponent's steps. When he spoke, however, it was clear—despite his attentions remaining fixed upon the threat—that his words were meant for the assembled squad.

"You should have heeded the old men."

Dust flew, reflected light glinted, and the darkness roiled as the partly unseen thing charged this new enemy. The warrior reacted in kind, lunging directly at it rather than making any effort to dodge aside.

The arm that had casually swatted Daniels into the air, if "arm" it was, swept toward the stranger in a blow mighty enough to shatter limbs. The man caught the attack, allowing it to land against the palm of his left hand and the haft of the axe in his right. How it didn't break both his arms—how, for that matter, the man had the reaction time to intercept the thing at all—Colton couldn't imagine.

Instead it carried him up and back. The stranger let himself be lifted slightly off the ground, then swung himself upward with a grunt, using the thing's own arm, or its equivalent of an arm, as a gymnast's bar to launch himself higher.

For an instant he hung in the air, then swung his weapon as he began to fall. Colton heard the scrape of a mild, glancing impact; while unsupported several feet in the air, the stranger lacked the leverage to deliver any substantial blow. Still, the darkness shifted just enough to give the watching soldier the impression that it had thrown up both its hands in a desperate attempt to ward its face or head from the attack.

This thing may not have cared at all about an M4's bullets, but *this* weapon, it feared.

The stranger landed in a shallow crouch and swung again, bringing the weapon up in a swift half-crescent arc.

An arc the entity could not possibly intercept with both arms raised to protect against the earlier attack that was, Colton recognized now, merely an elaborate feint.

The weapon didn't scrape this time; it *crunched*. The pitch of the thing's wail rose until Colton's eardrums threatened to burst . . .

Again the stranger swung his weapon, this time in a simple,

brutal overhand chop. A second crunch. A strange, almost wet thump, as if someone had dropped a sack of jelly from a great height.

Then silence.

The newcomer's boots crunched on the occasional loose pebble as he approached, halting to gaze down at the young soldier. This close, the man looked . . . Actually, Colton wasn't entirely certain what he looked like. Middle Eastern or Mediterranean by feature and complexion, but not precisely Iraqi, not precisely anything he could identify. Lean, sharply muscled but more wiry than bulky, more Bruce Lee than Dwayne Johnson.

Colton saw as well that the weapon he carried was indeed an axe of ancient make, the blade carved from bone rather than metal. The strangely glistening substance spattered across it wasn't the blood of any living being he could imagine.

He knelt, taking Colton's wrist and turning his injured arm for a better look, ignoring the hiss of pain the movement elicited. "Good. I think you stopped it in time, Private . . . ?"

"Uh, Beltran."

"Mm. Smart move with the flare, Beltran." He rose, turning his attention now toward the others, and Wheeler in particular. "Not nearly so smart, the rest of you. You've no business being here. Leave."

"Just a Goddamn minute!" the major snapped back, raising his weapon. "Who the fuck do you think you are? You're not in charge here!"

"No. You murdered the men who were in charge here. Good men who begged you to leave."

"And what makes you think we'll listen to you any more than we did them?"

The stranger couldn't have asked for a better cue if he'd planned it himself. As if in answer to Wheeler's bluster, a low grinding rumbled through the chamber. In a shower of rock dust, the great double doors began to open.

As the ruddy illumination leaked into the space beyond, chipping away at a darkness that might well have lain undisturbed for thousands of years, Colton saw the first in an array of massive stone tablets. The writings across it formed rows of simple lines, a long-dead language he couldn't have hoped to interpret. He could make sense only of the roughly carved figure at the top, a robed and heavily bearded man reaching up to grasp what appeared to be the disk of the sun itself.

Then his view was blocked by a faint movement and an all-too-familiar glint of light reflecting somehow off the shadows themselves. Then another, and another still.

Pointing in response to Wheeler's question, the warrior said, "That would be what makes me think you'll listen. Unless you care to wind up like your dead companions."

"Major!" Nash shouted, already kneeling to help Colton to his feet.

For a terrible moment, Colton thought Wheeler might actually order them to stay, even when faced with multiples of whatever it was that had already slaughtered three of the squad.

Then, "Fuck!" The major spun, racing for the exit. "Fall back!"

As Sergeant Nash half carried him back up the stairs, the last PFC Colton Beltran saw of the stranger was the man approaching the opening doors, axe hanging from a shockingly relaxed grip, walking into the mind-rending scream of those unseen things as casually as if they were a summer breeze.

ONE

The dream. Again, the dream.

Always different, yet always the same. Always another time, another place. Now it is Egypt, though far from the modern desert of that land. Thick grasses and mud of a Nile-adjacent marsh squish beneath his feet as he walks, his sweat- and blood-covered body warmed by the overhead sun.

He sees nothing around him to indicate that this *is* Egypt, at least no sign that any modern person would recognize. He knows it to be so, all the same.

With each pace, his feet change. Now, work boots and blue jeans, worn by long hours of labor. Now, simple wrap sandals on browned skin. Back again, and back again.

He knows who he is, or at least he thinks he does. *Jack.* His name is Jack . . . isn't it? Jack does not belong here, yet he belongs here. Two lives in one body. The dreams are always like that.

He's never dreamed this far back. It's fascinating.

Ahead of him, a large broad-leafed plant boasts a spot of glistening blood. He pushes aside a frond (his arm is bare, marred by bruises and shallow lacerations; his arm is covered in the sleeve of a flannel shirt; his arm is bare).

Concealed beneath, staring up at him with wide white eyes, a soldier of the enemy. He wears a sleeveless leather tunic and kilt; he's lost his leather cap in battle.

He opens his mouth, no doubt to scream or beg for mercy. The Dreamer raises his mace, a simple wooden haft with a weighted copper head, and crushes the man's skull. (The corpse is fresh, bloody and mangled and still twitching; the corpse is ancient, hollow and gaunt, preserved by the hot and arid land.)

From behind him, a voice. "Any survivors, Sumerian?" The words are Ancient Egyptian. The words are English.

"Not anymore," he replies, turning.

The man who approaches him wears the same reinforced tunic and skullcap as the many soldiers who stretch out across the marsh and the grasses behind him—some injured, some tending the injured, and some milling about as the frenzy of battle slowly seeps from them. Unlike them, however, this man wears them with discomfort. No warrior, this one.

"Meriiti," the Dreamer—Jack? The Sumerian? Both?—greets him.

The functionary frowns at him. "Not the answer I hoped for from you. Djer King would have men left alive to question." Meriiti gestures back at the battlefield, now a veritable carpet of corpses and broken weapons. (The corpses are fresh. The corpses are ancient.) "These are not soldiers of any *sepat* or nation known to us. They fight under a strange banner. Some are not even Egyptian."

"Yes," he replies, "and of course no power of Egypt has ever employed foreign soldiers."

Meriiti offers a shallow smile. "Point taken, Sumerian. Still, there are far more outlanders among their number than among ours. Djer King would know who they are."

"Holy Djer needn't worry. I know them." The Dreamer is surprised, yet even as he speaks the words, he knows they are true.

"Do you?" For a moment, Meriiti, too, is nothing but a desert-dried corpse before he is once again a living man.

The Sumerian nods. That symbol—a double-headed mace, each head that of a lion—will never leave him. He will forever remember it, forever despise it.

For now, he says only, "I've battled them before."

After a moment, when it becomes clear he means to say no more, Meriiti nods. "Very well. We should return to Djer King, tell him what you know." Another pause. "And you should repeat your tale to the sorcerers as well."

As they begin to walk, the Dreamer sighs. (The ground is marsh, thick with life. The ground is desert, gritty with sand.)

"Should I? It hardly seems relevant."

The king's functionary shrugs. "Perhaps it is not. But they've told you that the more they know, the better their odds of success. You're the one who asked this favor of them."

Another sigh. "I suppose it can do no harm. Though I doubt whether any mortal magics can undo what's been done to me."

"I confess, I don't understand you, Sumerian. Most men would challenge the gods themselves for what you are so eager to be rid of."

"As would I have, before I had it. But I'm tired, Meriiti. Of loss, of this world, and of the duties laid upon me by this 'boon.' I've lived centuries already. I cannot imagine wanting to continue any longer."

"Well, so be it. We will go to the sorcerers after we see the king and let them wind these new parts of your tale into the spell they are scribing. Who knows, Sumerian? Perhaps, if the gods will it, your long journey nears its end."

The intended reply is interrupted by the call of a bird,

perched somewhere in the trees. It begins abruptly and continues unabated—constant, regular, unchanging. The Dreamer who might be Jack feels his irritation rising and starts casting about him for the source, or perhaps a stone to hurl. And still the call continues.

Chirp.

Chirp.

Chirp.

Chirp.

Chirp.

TWO

Beep.

Beep.

Beep.

With a frustrated snarl and a grumbled word that might not have even been English, he rolled over, twisting the blankets, and slapped the top of the old alarm clock hard enough to shake the bedside table.

I've really got to start using my phone for this like everyone else does. He had no idea what tone or song he would choose, but anything would be less annoying than that bird . . . uh, beep.

After long seconds of wrestling with the covers wound cocoon-like around him, Jack Eren rolled upright to sit on the mattress's edge. He ran calloused fingers through a ragged beard and allowed himself one moment to let the dream fade before stumbling toward the shower—and thank God he didn't *really* live in a time before hot running water—which would kick off what promised to be a long day.

—

"Getcha anything else while you're here?"

Jack shook his head with a polite smile. "No, thanks, Mrs. Hennesy. Just tell me what I owe you."

"C'mon, Jack, you know better. Sent Henry the invoice when the order came in. He's already paid online."

"I sometimes wonder who runs that damn place," Jack said, bending down to the pile of burlap bags, casually hefting one over each shoulder.

The wrinkles spread across Linda Hennesy's face didn't fade when she smiled, but they did adopt whole new intricate patterns. Watching the change was like looking through some peculiar skin-kaleidoscope. "Oh, it's Henry. You just *own* the place, but everyone knows who runs it."

"Careful," he warned. "You're not the only feed store in Fabry, you know."

"Sure. I'll just call Rich and tell him to expect you next month." Still smiling, she stepped around the counter toward the feed.

"That's not necessary," Jack protested, shrugging to indicate the two he already carried. "I can do the whole thing in a few trips—"

"Jack Eren, until you throw us over for Rich's store, you're a paying customer. Now hush."

"Yes, ma'am." And he did, saying no more about it even as she clearly struggled with the single bag, taking longer to carry it out to his truck than it took him to deliver the two, go back, and deliver two more.

"Whatever's in the water up on that ranch, I want some," Linda told him through deep gasps.

"What makes you think we ever drink water?" Jack dropped the last bag in the bed of his truck—a fifteen-year-old Frontier, a *real* work truck, not one of those yacht-sized modern monstrosities usually bought by people who just wanted to *look* tough and impressive—and slipped in behind the wheel. "Tell Mac hi for me. When you can breathe again."

"Get out of here, smart aleck."

Jack drove from the parking lot of Hennesy's Farm and Feed, his fourth errand of the day, turning west. The other way would've taken him to the main highway, such as it was, and made for a faster trip home. It would also, however, have taken him through the heart of Fabry, Montana, and while Fabry might only be a small town of fewer than two thousand souls, he still preferred to avoid it when possible.

He wasn't antisocial, not exactly. And the people of Fabry were friendly enough now that he'd been here well over a year, even if he'd gotten some odd looks and a few cold shoulders when he first moved in. He stood out, a man of traditionally Middle Eastern complexion in a community mostly pale as printer paper. Not a racism thing, as it turned out, or if it was, it was at least well hidden; just an obvious marker that he was an outsider.

Not anymore, not since buying the Callahan Ranch and making himself a constant, if not exactly common, fixture in their lives and businesses. Now most of the folks here welcomed him well enough.

He'd never grown close to very many of them, though, and he preferred to spend his time in the company of those he really trusted. Something about this place . . . He found nothing wrong with it, but he still wasn't sure he belonged.

So, since he'd already spent the whole day dealing with this shopkeeper or that, the long and lonely way around it was.

A few minutes of absent thought, and fiddling with the radio to see if any of the south Montana stations were reaching this far today, found him approaching the Gas and Gulp: Fabry's only gas station not actually inside the town proper, and the only business on this route other than a tractor lot between him and the ranch.

One hand resting casually on the wheel, he debated popping in for a cold drink. It'd certainly be welcome.

Then again, the sun was already low, the shadow of his Nissan stretching far ahead of him on a road painted in the late afternoon's golds and oranges. The time—

Quit lying to yourself. It's got nothing to do with the time, and you know it.

His reluctance was named Anne Patterson, the Gas and Gulp's manager, who might or might not be working this evening.

In a way, Anne was a lot like Fabry itself, or at least his relationship with her was like the one he had with the town. She was welcoming enough, maybe more than enough. He'd spent a decent chunk of time with her, and he was fond of her, but she didn't feel . . . right.

He didn't feel like they belonged together, even when they were. He was single, unattached, yet every time he and Anne crept around the edges of anything serious, he felt as if he were doing something wrong.

It wasn't something he'd been able to explain, or really *wanted* to explain, but he knew the conversation was coming.

Just not tonight.

The accelerator sank under Jack's foot, the truck picking up speed to bypass the station . . .

He registered everything in a flash. He'd always been observant, quick, for as long as he could remember.

Three cars in the lot, which was about two more than normal for this time of the evening on a weekday, and a couple of them clearly hadn't stopped for fuel or food. The bright-green Sierra had massive scrapes along its right side, with the rear door crumpled badly inward. The Explorer, a newer model in glossy navy blue, had a busted headlight and slight crumpling in the hood on the left.

Right. Mystery solved. Just some folks dealing with the banal aftermath of a minor accident. Trading insurance, maybe making some calls, standing around looking at the damage as if sufficient staring would undo it. The usual. Move on for the night.

Except he didn't. Jack found himself guiding the truck into the parking lot before he fully realized he hadn't already passed the place by.

He felt himself go alert, tension flooding through him followed by a surprising calm. He hadn't experienced this in a long while, but he knew better than to question it. He'd noticed something more, something his conscious mind still needed a moment to register . . .

There it was.

Three men, all white, all in their twenties or thirties, all similarly dressed in T-shirts and jeans. Two of them—the two drivers—gestured at each other in intense discussion. It was the third man, though, a shaggy-haired blond guy in a Kid Rock tee, who'd drawn Jack's attention. He was standing at the open passenger door of the Explorer, watching the other two talk.

That was all. Standing there.

Yet there was a tension in his stance, a wariness and a worry Jack couldn't pinpoint, couldn't even say how he'd noticed. He knew only that it bothered him. A lot.

Jack circled around the two cars, pulled into a spot near the front door, and climbed out, making a show of putting his hands on his lower back and stretching, using the opportunity for another look around.

Yeah. The passenger maintained enough self-control not to glare at this new stranger—he was, Jack interpreted, still hoping to avoid attention—but the man *really* wasn't happy Jack had just shown up.

He couldn't just stand here indefinitely, not without making it blatantly obvious that he was trying to eavesdrop. Instead, he made a point of wandering around to check the feed bags in the back of the Frontier and then ambled over to the entrance.

The charade didn't give him enough time to overhear specifics, but he understood the gist of it now. The driver of the Explorer was trying to convince the other guy that the accident wasn't worth calling the cops or the insurance companies over. That he couldn't afford to have this on his record. That he'd be happy to just hand over cash, more than enough to cover any potential damages.

Right. That's not suspicious in the slightest.

The other driver, the guy from the GMC, clearly didn't find the offer any more aboveboard than it sounded to Jack, and while he'd maintained his composure so far, his patience with the first man's cajoling looked to be nearing its limit.

Through it all, the blond passenger's shoulders drew more taut, obvious even beneath his shirt, and his jaw clenched ever harder.

Jack pushed open the glass door covered with ads and specials, entering to the sound of the electronic chime.

"Hey, hon!" The cheerful greeting echoed over the tile floor and through the rows of overpriced and mostly nonessential goods, drawing a sliver of his attention to the woman behind the counter.

"Evening, Anne." She no longer felt like his most immediate concern.

"Anything I can help you with?" She kept any obvious double entendre out of her tone, but he knew it was there all the same. Any other night, his concerns over the seriousness of their relationship notwithstanding, he might have been tempted.

"I think just a drink tonight," he replied, opening one of

the refrigerated cases and retrieving a peach-flavored Lipton. It meant turning his back on the storefront—and on the drama playing out beyond the glass. Apparently, he grabbed the beverage and spun back around a bit more intently than he'd meant to.

"Don't suppose you heard what's going on out there?" she asked more seriously, having noticed where he directed his own attention. She waved one hand toward the lot, the other running just a bit nervously through her almost electrically dyed blond locks. "I mean, an accident, obviously, but . . ."

"They're discussing the matter."

"Discussing?" She sounded dubious.

He didn't want to alarm her. This still might all be nothing. Was *probably* nothing. "I don't think it's an argument *yet*," he hedged.

Both could see, though, that the drivers' gestures had gotten sharper, more animated. If it wasn't an argument yet, it was about to be.

"Hey, Jack, um . . . you're not . . . I mean, could you . . ."

"I'm not going anywhere." He returned her relieved smile and began aimlessly wandering the aisles, always keeping the parking lot in view.

"Think I should call the Highway Patrol?" She frowned at her own question. "I'm not looking to stick my nose in or get anybody in trouble, but . . ."

It probably wasn't a bad idea, but something in Jack didn't care for it. Involving the authorities almost never made things better; best to handle it alone . . .

That brought him up short, blinking. *Where the hell did* that *thought come from?* It wasn't as though he had much experience with any trouble the authorities would care about.

He startled himself again when he found himself asking, "Lonnie still keep his old Springfield in the back office?"

"How'd you . . . ? I took you back there *once*!" At which point, the reason behind the question finally sank in. Anne's breath caught. "You don't think—?"

The door chimed, admitting the two drivers—now full-on shouting at one another—followed by the lighter-haired passenger. The first two men were fully occupied getting up in each other's face, but the third's attention flickered around the store, taking in Jack, Anne . . . and the absence of anyone else.

Everything felt suddenly slow, instincts Jack didn't know he had now screaming at him—yet he hesitated, uncertain why the need to act had come over him.

Anne reached for the phone.

The passenger's features tightened as if someone had yanked on the back of his skull. With a motion smooth enough to suggest he'd practiced it at least on occasion, he yanked a 9mm semiauto from the back of his waistband and fired three shots over the counter.

Thankfully, whatever practice he'd put into the maneuver wasn't enough. All three rounds struck the back wall rather than the manager. Anne screamed and dropped out of sight behind the counter, but she had nowhere she could go from there.

The passenger advanced, closing to make sure his next shots were more accurate. His companion, the driver, was shouting a litany of expletives at him—mostly consisting of variants and permutations of "fuck"—without any effort at stringing them into coherent sentences.

He also, however, pulled a gun of his own.

For the barest instant, Jack berated himself for not having noticed those two were carrying. He absolutely should have seen it.

Why? Why should I have noticed? What am I now, Batman?

He didn't know why. He just knew he should.

Then the driver raised the weapon he'd just drawn, and Jack's body took over.

He dropped into a crouch, ducking low enough to keep out of the gunmen's view, denying either of them a clean shot. He tossed the iced tea to his right hand, reaching out with his now-empty left to snag a bottle of cheap convenience store wine off the shelf. He rocked forward, weight on his toes and the balls of his feet, already starting to spring.

The blond passenger stepped into view near the counter. One more pace would allow him to lean over it for his point-blank shots at Anne.

Jack hurled the Lipton. The small bottle cracked painfully against the man's wrist, eliciting a sharp shout and ruining his shot. Only sheer luck kept the pistol in his fist.

It wouldn't help him.

In the split second it took him to recover from the unexpected impact and begin to turn, Jack dashed in, closing the distance with blazing speed, flipping the wine bottle to his right hand and wielding it by the neck.

A swift underhand blow shattered the passenger's elbow. Even as Jack withdrew the bottle, spinning it for a second strike, his left hand snaked across his chest to grab the pistol, yanking it down out of his opponent's hand and in the process bending the arm further against the broken joint until it hung entirely the wrong direction.

So swiftly did Jack spin into his second strike, the man had no time to scream with the agony of the first before the bottle came round again and crashed into his skull, shattering with the impact.

Connected with the side of the bottle, not the base. Depressed skull fracture, but not as deep as it would've been. Severe concussion and intracranial bleeding, but decent chance of survival and partial recovery if he's treated quickly. Elbow treatable with multiple surgeries and internal pins, probably regain about 75 percent functionality.

How the hell did he *know* that?! And why was *that* what he was thinking of? It felt as if he were sitting back somewhere, watching it all happen on a screen, or maybe through a window.

"Fucking freeze, you fuck! Hold it right fucking there!"

Jack was already facing the shouting driver, but this guy apparently had a different sense of tactics than his partner. He'd grabbed the owner of the Sierra, whose mouth hung agape in shock, one arm around his neck while the other pressed his gun to the man's head.

"You fucking come any closer, I'll paint this fucker's head all over the fucking Pop-Tarts!"

Huh. There actually *were* Pop-Tarts on the endcap of the next aisle. *Good eye.*

Broken bottle still to hand, Jack kept still, ready to dive aside if the pistol turned his way, or into the gunman if the opportunity arose. The driver's gaze darted wildly, doubtless seeking escape from the situation his partner had just escalated beyond salvation.

In the silence, Jack heard running footsteps and the slam of the office door.

Then the creak of it opening once more, and the clacking bolt of the well-used .30-06.

A split second to glance over his shoulder, to assess. Anne held the Springfield like she knew what she was doing, tight against her shoulder and cheek welded properly to the stock. He also saw, though, the faint tremor of the barrel and the wild whites of her eyes.

She may have used a rifle before, but never in circumstances like these. No way she'd actually take the shot, certainly not with a hostage in the way.

Up to me, then.

"Do it," he ordered.

He knew she wouldn't, but he also knew the driver didn't know that; his attention would shift to her, if only for a second.

That second was enough. In another burst of speed, Jack was across the store . . .

Or would have been, had his right foot not skidded completely out from under him when it hit the puddle of spilled wine.

He toppled into a spinning rack of key chains and jerky, sending it clattering away. The impact was enough for him to right himself instead of hitting the floor along with it, but the stumble cost him precious time.

Clumsy! Stupid and clumsy! He was *better* than this! Again he didn't know *why* he thought himself better, but he knew it to be true.

With no better option, he corrected his angle and lunged into a new attack . . .

The gun fired.

Not, thankfully, at the helpless hostage. Jack's charge had once again drawn the gunman's attention.

Burning pain blossomed through his left arm, and he felt as if he'd been kicked by an elephant. His body jolted in mid-step, enough to set him stumbling once again, and the entire limb fell limp at his side . . .

Jack felt the world recede. If he'd been watching himself move through a window earlier, now that window had pulled away, growing ever more distant. Some other person, other part of him, other voice, had taken control.

Biceps and ligaments torn. Bone fractured, probably not badly. Massive loss of flesh and blood.

Mild inconvenience.

He found himself dropping into a crouch as he turned, letting the momentum of the bullet carry him into a full spin. He kicked out in a perfect leg sweep, taking the ankles out not from under the enemy, but from under his *captive*.

The owner of the Sierra hit the ground with a startled cry, dropping clean out of the other man's grip, leaving him gawping without his human shield.

Jack observed as whoever was in control continued the spin farther still, straightening back upright as he came around to face the gunman once more. An abrupt stab, angled outward and upward.

A thick wetness washed over his hand, warm and sticky and somehow familiar. Both men looked down at the broken bottle Jack had embedded into the enemy's solar plexus—angled expertly under the sternum—then up again at each other.

Feeling nothing save the vague lingering sense that he *should* be feeling something, Jack watched unblinking until the spasms stopped and all life faded from the other man's gaze. Only then did he yank the bottle free and let the corpse fall.

The gun lay on the tile, several paces away. Jack had knocked it aside with his injured arm even as he'd thrust the bottle through flesh, and hadn't even noticed.

Feet squelching in the mingling solution of blood and wine, Jack walked almost robotically to a far aisle. Anne stared at him, lips quivering, from behind the counter; the hostage—well, former hostage—doing much the same from the floor where he'd fallen. Jack ignored them both, instead making straight for the store's tiny selection of menstrual hygiene products.

There he tore into a box and removed a couple of tampons, which he swiftly used to stanch the open wounds in his left arm. Not the best tool for the job, but accepted first aid practice, and definitely more effective than the flimsy gauze bandages that were the only other available option.

Ignoring the sound of Anne calling his name, or maybe he wasn't ignoring it so much as he still lacked sufficient control over himself to answer, Jack left the Gas and Gulp and made for his truck.

THREE

Night had fallen by the time Jack's Nissan crunched over the dirt and pulled up to the barn he and his hired hands had converted to a garage. The waning moon skulked behind a layer of overcast, so the world around him consisted only of puddles of illumination: the headlights of the truck, which he dismissed with a click, and the lights spilling out of the windows of the main house.

A lot more lights, he couldn't help but note, than was normal. Most of the hands should've gone home already, and the few who lived on-site ought to be either gathered in the TV/game room or already as deeply asleep as the cattle.

As he stepped from the barn, a small throng of men poured from the front door of the house, their shouts instantly silencing the evening's usual chorus of crickets and frogs and God knew what else.

In the lead, as Jack would've expected, was Henry Luckenbill. A short, stocky man who didn't seem to own a single item of clothing or even a pair of glasses that wasn't badly work scuffed, Henry had been his chief hand since Jack bought the place.

Even now, when he was obviously as concerned and curious

as everyone else, Henry's shouted "All right, you guys, knock it off!" silenced every voice present.

Then, in a slightly softer tone as they neared, he continued, "Boss, the entire damn world's been calling and texting you every thirty seconds for the last hour. Anne, the freaking cops, even— *What the fuck?!*"

Jack followed his friend's shocked stare downward, then half lifted both hands. In the dark, Henry and the others had only now gotten close enough to spot his blood-caked sleeves.

"Had a bit of an evening," Jack said, then stepped past them toward the door.

"A bit of an—! Boss, whose blood is that?"

"Depends. Which arm?"

He'd taken a few more steps before realizing Henry wasn't beside him any longer. He turned to look back at the ranch hand, who'd stopped still as if he'd walked into a minefield.

Which was fine with Jack. He really didn't want to talk about it, not least because he hadn't the faintest idea of *how* to talk about it.

Instead, he said, "Damn it, I forgot the truck's full of feed or I'd have parked over by the storage shed. Since you're all still here, would you mind unloading?"

"Unloading . . . the feed? Boss, you can't be serious right now! What happened to—?"

"Or doing it in the morning's fine, if it's not going to set tomorrow's schedule back any. Thanks."

His tone was apparently final enough that Henry didn't try to stop him again. He heard the muttered questions and guesses start up before he even reached the door, continuing until he closed it behind him and cut them off.

He didn't have to hear them clearly, though, to know what they were.

Man, who even is he?

Where'd he come from?

You think he got in a fight?

You think he killed someone?

He's killed someone before.

You don't know that!

Well, I know he was military!

No, you don't!

I do! I told you, my brother served, I can tell . . .

You can't tell shit!

I think he's on the run from something.

Like what?

I dunno. Something bad.

Well, no shit, something bad! How many people you know are on the run from something good, *you fucking potato?*

He didn't blame them for their curiosity, even if he wasn't about to assuage it. He'd told them almost nothing about himself, not when he hired them on and not in all the days since. He treated his people well, tried always to remain at least approachable, if not full-on friendly, so none of them had any reason to complain. Still, it only made sense for them to wonder even on a normal day, let alone an evening like this one.

He'd have to tell them something. Tomorrow. He'd figure out what to say tomorrow—and what not to.

His mind shied away from following that thought like a terrified horse, so dramatically it was almost a physical sensation. Jack didn't like thinking about the past.

No, "didn't like" wasn't strong enough. He had that same reaction every time he so much as considered it. He never felt quite like he *couldn't* remember, more as if he simply *wouldn't.*

He just felt happier, more content, knowing only about as much about his life prior to the past two years as Henry did.

What happened tonight, though, the strange bits of

knowledge, the sense that someone else was behind the wheel, that was new. That, he'd have to think about.

Tomorrow. A whole lot of almost everything could wait for tomorrow.

Jack kicked off his mud- and blood-covered boots in the entry hall, then padded through the main room. Uneven brick and long wooden planks formed most of the walls, against which leaned an array of shelves. A variety of chairs and a couple of tables, mostly matching but not entirely, stood atop a threadbare rug boasting patterns that its creator might have imagined, if they'd squinted really hard, to look Cheyenne.

All the decor and most of the furniture had been here when he'd bought the place. He hated the bulk of it, but it never seemed worth the cost of replacing.

The stuffed heads and antler sculpture, though, *those* had come right down the day he'd moved in. He'd never much minded the idea of hunting (*or killing*, a small part of him commented, thinking back on the day's events), but the thought of doing it for *trophies* kindled a simmering rage.

And you're thinking about all this to avoid actually thinking, Jack.

Growling softly to himself, Jack made for the winding stairs to the second floor, lured by the siren's call of a hot shower.

Which he'd get to right after he pulled the tampons out of his arm.

He stood over the sink in the steam-slick bathroom, a towel wrapped around his waist, and studied his injury. He'd wiped a spot clear in the mirror to get a look at both sides, but what he saw didn't make sense.

Both wounds, the smaller entry and the larger exit, had already scabbed over. Jack was no doctor but felt like a gunshot wound wasn't supposed to just "scab over" at all, and if it did, it sure as hell should take longer than a single evening.

Yet that's what he was looking at.

It still ached, but it was a dull pain, not the sharp burn of earlier. He didn't yet have full strength in his left arm, but he could move it, use it, without much impediment.

Although it hardly seemed necessary, he carefully disinfected both spots with rubbing alcohol and wrapped his biceps in lengths of bandage from one of the ranch's many first aid kits. It would've felt strange—and certainly *looked* strange—not to.

You've done this before.

Which was ridiculous. When would he ever have been shot before?

You've done this a lot.

Shut up.

He'd gotten himself into a clean pair of jeans and halfway into a rugged work shirt when he heard another commotion from downstairs. Pounding on the front door. Loud conversation between Henry and a few other hands on one side, unfamiliar voices on the other.

The bathroom's frosted window flickered alternating shades of red and blue.

Honestly, he'd expected them earlier. It was why he'd gotten dressed to go out again, rather than for bed.

A quick rush to get shoes on and grab his wallet, then Jack ran his fingers through his hair and beard and headed downstairs.

"Henry? Phone please." He'd forgotten it here when he went out for the day's errands, as he so often did; just couldn't get used to carrying the damn thing. Then, after catching it,

"Evening, Officers. I'm going to take a wild guess that you're here looking for me."

The ninety-minute drive to Butte in the back of the Highway Patrol Charger didn't precisely ingratiate Jack to the two officers taking him in.

He was never anything but polite, but he'd raised their suspicions when he refused medical treatment for his injury or even to let them look under the bandaging, only insisting that he'd already dealt with it and that he guessed it "wasn't nearly as bad as it looked earlier." He'd also refused to talk about what had happened; he knew he was in for a long night of questioning, and he had no desire to go over everything more than he had to.

As such, most of the ride was split between either a sullen silence or forced casual conversation from the two cops in front, while Jack sat in unspoken exasperation.

Eventually they stopped in front of a squat stone structure that just screamed "government run," then hustled him through a lobby that was mostly empty at this time of night and into one of the back rooms of the Montana Highway Patrol's District III headquarters.

There he waited, mostly studying the handcuffs that he felt almost certain he could break despite how unrealistic a premise it seemed, for almost half an hour.

When the door finally opened, it was to admit two people, a man and a woman, both wearing rumpled suits.

"Mr. . . . Eren?" the woman asked, glancing down at her notes. "I'm Detective Mastriano, Montana Investigations Bureau, Major Case Section. This is Detective Ruiz."

They took their seats across the table from Jack, who nodded.

"You were present during an incident at the Gas and Gulp off Horseman Road this evening."

Again he nodded. Then, when the two detectives glared at him, apparently expecting more, Jack said, "Yes."

Ruiz scowled and spoke for the first time. "You killed a man and then left the scene!"

"Well, yeah. It wouldn't have done any good if I'd left the scene *before* killing the guy."

When Mastriano's expression hardened and Ruiz looked about ready to detonate, Jack raised a palm in supplication. "Look, I'm sorry. I do take this seriously, and I'll happily answer any questions. But I don't think I can tell you what you really want to know."

"And what's that?" the woman asked.

"At this point, you've already talked to Anne and the other man who was there. You've checked the security footage. You know everything I did, I did in self-defense or to protect others. I'm not under arrest, and these"—he raised the cuffs—"are only because you have no idea who I am or how I did what I did. And that's what you're getting around to asking me."

He let his wrists fall with a clatter of chain. "And that's what I can't tell you. I'm not anyone special. I'm not Rambo or John Wick. I don't know how I pulled any of that off. I just acted on instinct."

"Some fucking instincts," Ruiz muttered.

"As for me leaving . . . I was out of it. Wasn't thinking clearly."

Mastriano leaned back in her seat. "And you want us to believe that's it? You *instinctively* took down two armed men with a wine bottle?"

Jack shrugged. "It's the truth."

It was a truth he repeated multiple times over the next

couple of hours. The detectives came at it a dozen different ways, drawing details from him that he was honestly stunned he even remembered. Yet his story never changed, and—as he'd pointed out—they already had corroborating testimony.

In the end, while Mastriano and Ruiz may not have been happy with the idea that they had a guy in their jurisdiction who came off as Captain America in a fight but couldn't tell them how or why, it seemed they'd come around to believing him.

"All right, Mr. Eren," Mastriano finally told him. "We may have more questions for you, but in the meantime, you're free to go." Ruiz came around the table and unlocked the cuffs while she continued, "Like you said, you did what you had to do in a bad situation. I don't anticipate you'll be charged with anything."

Jack rose, rubbing his wrists, less because they genuinely hurt than because it seemed the thing people always did after handcuffs came off. The two detectives were leaving when Jack asked, "Do we know why?"

"Pardon?"

"Why any of this happened. Why the guy started shooting."

Mastriano and Ruiz exchanged a look and a shrug. "Fentanyl and meth," she told him. "The back of the Ford was full of it. Way Patrol figures it, those two were probably small-time dealers coming up the I-25 corridor. Got into the accident and panicked once they realized they couldn't talk the guy out of calling the cops."

Ruiz scowled. "Dumb thing to kill over."

Or die over. Probably best to keep the thought to himself, though.

It took Jack about a minute, leaning against the lobby wall by the vending machine, to call Henry for a pickup. It took Henry about an hour and fifteen minutes to make the ninety-minute drive to Butte.

Jack decided not to ask how many traffic laws the ranch hand had broken on the way.

Henry popped out of the pickup before Jack had even made it down the station's front steps. "Check it out. You're famous."

Oh no . . .

The image rotated to follow the angle of the phone Henry turned toward him. Jack stared at the web page for KBZL, one of several news stations devoted to the city of Bozeman and to south Montana in general. Beneath some clickbaity headline touting "convenience store carnage" and a photo of the Gas and Gulp storefront was a breathless article about yesterday's mayhem. The details were more or less accurate, at least in the broad strokes. A general sequence of events. The same basic summary of the smugglers' motivations he'd already heard, no doubt taken verbatim from an Investigations Bureau public statement. Some quotes from Anne, along with a new picture of her.

None of that was the problem.

No, the problem was the name Jack Eren. Right there in the article, second paragraph. And the photo further down, past the store, past the manager, the one he had to scroll to get to.

This one wasn't recent, wasn't as sharp. His hair and beard were shorter. It'd been taken over a year ago by a local paper, back when he'd closed on the purchase of the Callahan Ranch. They must've pulled it up online since they had nothing more recent of their "hero."

"Guess there's no help for it, boss," Henry continued, starting the truck back up and pointing them west along the darkened highway. "You're just gonna have to learn how to be around people. Tolerate them, maybe even *talk* to them! I know this is a tough time for you, but me and the boys and the grace of God, we'll help you get through it."

Jack watched the patches of dark on dark that were the

landscape passing by in the lightless night, his mind racing, and scarcely heard a word of Henry's friendly ribbing.

True, Jack had never been a social guy. Other than his occasional and brief forays into town and the kinda-sorta romantic interludes with Anne, he preferred to keep only the company of his employees at most and treasured his moments of solitude. Solitary, however, didn't necessarily mean secretive. Everyone in town knew him, or at least of him, thanks to the ranch. This new article shouldn't change anything. A few people beyond the gravity of Fabry would read his name, see his face, and then they'd forget again an hour later. So what?

Why, then, did his fist clench when he thought about those news sites and the people who would read them? Why did the hair on the back of his neck threaten to staple itself to the headrest for the entire ride home?

FOUR

The setting sun hurled the last of its anger against the black reflective western face of Rimmels Tower, one of a huddle of modest skyscrapers in the heart of downtown Chicago.

Even through the heavy tint of those windows, the glare was mildly painful, which was why—well, the first of several reasons why—Cassandra didn't like being stuck at work this late.

The boss wanted her report on her latest endeavor, though, and Valerie Coswell was a good enough boss, and Cassandra's position a good enough job, that she wasn't about to protest.

Valerie's office, the heart and brain of Coswell Security Consultants (suite 37-A), was enormous, bigger than Cassandra's first apartment had been. Like the rest of CSC, it was carpeted mostly in maroons and grays with a tasteful array of potted plants, fancy but simple furniture, and various awards and testimonials. One couldn't have designed a more emblematic "we are a serious business with no nonbusiness thoughts" layout if one tried.

That, however, was the point. CSC's range of clients was varied, and their reputation spoke for itself.

The two women sat, not at Valerie's desk, but across a small table from one another. Their chairs were thickly upholstered with leather, comfortable enough to sink into, and the single malt they shared was richer still.

They wore almost matching dark pantsuits, the boss's in purple, Cassandra's in burgundy. They hadn't planned it; they just shared similar tastes in clothes, even though Cassandra was tall and all angles, nearly six feet, while Valerie's build more resembled Velma from Scooby-Doo.

"Hold on," the boss interrupted, leaning forward over the table. "Back up. Broadbent *gave you* his books?"

"Yep." Cassandra swirled her drink, grinning. "Soon as I pretended it was Rutherford under investigation and not him, he pretty much threw his whole laptop at me."

"Even though there was more than enough in his own records to nail his ass."

Again, "Yep." Then, "Guess he thought if he wasn't our suspect, I wouldn't look at his numbers."

"So he's a moron."

"Pretty much."

A moment of silence, save the clinking of ice on glass.

"All right, spill it."

Cassandra's lip quirked. "Am I being that obvious?"

"I notice things. I do run a private investigations agency, you know."

"I'd heard that." Cassandra put her glass down, idly scratching at her left arm through her sleeve. "Look, Val . . ."

"Uh-oh."

"I know Postmodern Solutions is a big client . . ."

"A big client who just paid us a fortune on an embezzling case," Valerie added.

"Yeah. But . . . look, I didn't just find evidence of Broadbent skimming. They've been shorting close to half of their employees. Sometimes by a lot. Like felony levels of 'a lot.'"

"Cassandra . . ."

"Don't."

Valerie rose, wandered over to her desk, and poured herself a second glass. "We promise a certain level of confidentiality. If we turn around and burn a major client right after working for them, CSC is dead."

"I know, but . . ."

"If, on the other hand," Valerie continued, "someone dropped an anonymous word on one of the federal whistleblower hotlines—after, say, a few months had passed—that wouldn't have anything to do with us, would it?"

Cassandra slowly nodded. It wasn't satisfying—she wanted to deal with it now, and there was no guarantee the Feds would take an anonymous report seriously, or find what she had, or decide to move on it if they did—but if that was as much slack as the boss could offer, she'd take it. She raised her glass in acknowledgment.

Valerie returned the gesture. "Now go home. Take a couple of days to unwind before you have to pack."

The glass froze halfway to Cassandra's lips. "Oh, come on!"

"This isn't news. I told you if the Postmodern job was wrapped up in time . . ."

"So I'm punished for being efficient?"

Valerie's eye roll was almost cartoonish. "For fuck's sake, Cass, it's a *conference*, not a punishment."

"You say tomato . . ." Then, when her boss clearly wasn't amused, "Peter Garrison's going, right? He's more than capable of handling any presentation we're supposed to give."

"I want both of you there. What's the big deal?"

Cassandra sulked in her chair, knew she looked childish,

and didn't much care. "I hate those people. There's nobody who can manage that perfect mix of evil and boring like insurance executives."

"Insurance investigations are half our business!"

"So? I'm seventy percent water. Still hate the ocean."

"Cassandra. You leave on Friday."

Her shoulders slumped—which, at Cassandra's height, was a lot of slumping. "Fine. But I'd almost rather be back under fire again."

FIVE

Night had once again fallen on the Callahan Ranch—had, in fact, fallen several hours ago—and still Jack, Henry, and the others scrambled to finish the day's labors.

Today had been better, at least. For the first few days after the Gas and Gulp incident, the ranch had seen just enough outside interference to torpedo Jack's entire routine.

Reporters from local news stations, small-town newspapers, even the hosts of a "weird crime" podcast who posted on YouTube and boasted an audience of almost hundreds.

Highway Patrol troopers and Major Case Detectives with follow-up questions.

Anne, on three separate occasions, during none of which Jack felt even remotely like socializing. Or "socializing."

And on three other occasions, random trespassers, looky-loos hoping for a glimpse of their newly revealed local badass.

Every time, long enough to completely throw off the work schedule. The hands had been great about it, never complaining about the disruptions or the extra hours, but Jack was heartily sick of it all. He valued the comfort of routine. He valued privacy.

Above even that, it was growing ever harder and more frustrating to keep pretending his arm was worse than it was. Even if the bullet had only grazed him, as he claimed, the limb should still have been in pain, still have been weak.

It wasn't. It barely even bore a scar anymore, and he continued bandaging it every morning for no other reason than to hide that fact.

Just one more mystery to add to the list of—

"Boss?"

Jack pulled himself back to the moment and looked up from the line of barbed wire he held in heavily gloved hands.

Henry gestured with a pneumatic staple gun toward the fence post at which he'd been working. "Think we're done here."

"All right. Pack it up, everyone!"

Henry gathered the tools while a younger hand by the name of Sergio coiled up the remaining length of barbed wire. Both dropped their burdens off in the back of a near-prehistoric Chevy pickup so beat up, consisting of almost equal parts duct tape and metal by weight, that it wasn't legal to drive beyond the boundaries of the ranch.

Jack and Henry slipped into the cab—it had no doors for them to open—while the others piled in the back, and they were off, rattling and bumping and clattering toward the main house.

Nobody said much. Everyone was exhausted, Jack knew—or rather, everyone but him. For whatever reason, no matter how late the hours or how hard they all worked to catch up, he felt fully energized from the moment he woke up until he finally fell asleep. Maybe it was leftover adrenaline from the fight? That made no sense, but he couldn't come up with any other explanation.

By the time they got back, pulling up to drop everyone off at the front door before Henry went to park the truck, Jack had decided that none of tomorrow's tasks were urgent. He slid out of the truck, was just opening his mouth to tell everyone to come in or wake up a couple hours late the next morning . . .

From the pool of shadow around the corner of the house, well away from the crooked beams of the truck's misaligned headlights, came a taut *twang.*

Jack was in the mud and rolling before he even registered the sound, let alone what it meant: *crossbow*. Behind him, a wet impact led instantly into a short, sharp cry.

"Get down!" He sprang partly upright just long enough to grab the nearest ranch hand—a young man named Mateo, his newest employee—and drag him prone from his frozen stupor.

A glance under the truck revealed Sergio lying flat on his back on the opposite side of the vehicle, bleeding from around the bolt in his chest and the corner of his mouth. Henry struggled to drag the fallen man behind the wheel for extra cover.

More crossbows fired, puncturing thin steel and old rubber. The pickup sagged as tires deflated.

Coming up into a crouch, Jack lunged around the front bumper, putting the engine block between himself and the attackers. Another glance over at Sergio; it didn't look good. He was about to start losing people.

His people.

As had happened in the convenience store, a thin veil seemed to settle over Jack's mind, separating him from the chaos around him and allowing someone else to step into that gap.

Or maybe it wasn't someone else at all.

Keeping low, scrambling on hands and feet, Jack scuttled to the back of the truck, past the choking Sergio and the wide-eyed Henry. With a quick leap and one hand on the metal, he vaulted up and over, landing flat in the bed of the pickup. A trio of crossbow bolts hurtled through the space he'd briefly occupied in his flight.

Reaching one hand up and hauling with a strength he didn't know he had, a strength he *shouldn't* have had, Jack pulled loose the massive toolbox that sat mounted behind the rear window frame. He flipped open the latch and tilted the box, letting most of its contents clatter to the metal around him. He grabbed one heavy claw hammer and stuck it through his belt, then grasped the now-empty toolbox in both hands.

Wait for the next volley . . .

Another sequence of *smacks,* bolts on the body of the old Chevy.

With a shout of fury, Jack jumped over the edge of the truck bed. Holding the toolbox before him like a shield, he pounded over the dark grass toward the nearest crossbowman, never once questioning how he'd pinpointed the source of the attacks.

A bolt from one surprisingly fast reload slammed into the toolbox, even punching partway through, but between the thickness of the metal and the deflection of the angle, it came nowhere near Jack's skin.

If they'd bothered with actual guns, they'd probably have had me.

The man lurking in the bushes alongside the house tossed his crossbow aside and rose, drawing some sort of long knife or short sword from a sheath at his side. He was dressed in loose-fitting garments and a face wrap of deepest blue, perfect for night camouflage, somewhere between a black-ops soldier and a comic-book ninja. Blade in hand, he stepped forward to meet Jack's charge.

Jack hurled the toolbox straight downward, crushing half the bones in the man's foot.

The intruder stumbled with a cry of pain. Jack's left hand rose to catch his enemy's wrist, ensuring the sword didn't come anywhere near him, while he struck with the right.

A fist to the gut, angled up and under the ribs. A twist to slam an elbow into the man's jaw as he doubled over. A yank with the left hand, taking the blade and bringing it down into the back of the attacker's skull.

The whole sequence took less than two seconds.

Slow. Too slow. I'm moving too slow.

If he could've stopped and stared at himself, he would have. It was a ludicrous thought, yet he knew it was true. Quick as he'd been, *astonishing* as he'd been even to himself, it wasn't up to par.

Whatever "par" was.

He followed the dead man to the ground, dropping in case another volley of bolts followed from the others, but apparently the intruders had scattered when he closed. Jack reached out and snagged his opponent's crossbow, hauling back the mechanically augmented string and dropping a bolt into place.

"Henry! Get Sergio and the others inside and stay there! Anyone comes near the house who isn't me, shoot them!" He'd long ago given Henry the combination to the gun safe.

"Boss, what about—?"

"Don't worry about me! Go!"

He came to one knee, crossbow leveled to cover his friends as they scurried to the front door, Henry and Mateo carrying Sergio. Nobody took a shot at them.

That makes me the target, not any of them. Somehow, he wasn't remotely surprised.

Henry stopped once more at the door. "Boss . . ."

"Get inside and *stay*!"

Scowling, Henry obeyed.

Silence, what Jack was sure would be a very temporary silence, fell over the ranch.

All right, you fucks. If he was the target, then he needed to move this away from the main house, away from the others. *Let's do this.*

Jack broke into a dead sprint, feet slapping in the dirt, kicking up a short spray with each step. From new hiding spots, crossbow bolts flew, punching through the air in his wake as he pounded toward the nearest cover.

He hit the door of the storage shed at full speed, turning his shoulder into it at the last second. Hinges, latch, and the wood itself all gave under the living battering ram, spilling him into the shed without so much as a hitch in his step. He spun to one side, moving out of the now-empty doorway and the line of fire of any pursuers. All around him, an array of supplies, of tools.

An arsenal.

The closest of the shadowy assailants leapt through the doorway with a cry, armed with a Japanese wakizashi. Seeing his target, the invader lunged, bringing the blade down in a trained kenjutsu strike.

Jack caught the incoming arm in the crook of a massive pair of gardening shears. Fabric and tissue parted with the impact alone, and when he twisted the tool, the blades tore away flesh and muscle to scrape on bone.

The wakizashi fell from nerveless fingers, and any scream the man might've emitted died stillborn as Jack hurled his weight against him, driving his attacker's arm back and one tip of the shears into a lung.

More approaching footsteps, sacrificing stealth for speed. Jack let the body fall and launched into a low lunge, catching the incoming man around the waist. With a grunt of exertion—though far less exertion than he'd anticipated—he straightened, throwing his latest target over him and into the far wall. An array of tools fell, knocked loose by the impact, forcing the man to pause and shield his head.

By the time he began to rise, Jack had grabbed a coil of barbed wire from a spool that was twin to the one he'd been working on minutes earlier. He dropped a loop around the other man's neck, planted a knee in his back, and not only yanked back but started *sawing.*

A gurgle, a wet tearing, and then the *thump* of another body falling to the floor.

That's three.

Unfortunately, however convenient it might've proved for Jack, the rest weren't so foolish as to keep charging into the equipment shed one by one. Smoke began to curl from the wood of the leftmost wall, and he knew one of them had set the small structure alight. Doubtless they were waiting with blade or bow to cut him down as he emerged.

Jack pulled the hood off the man he'd just garroted; they looked nothing alike, but in the dark and the chaos they didn't have to. He then retrieved a pitchfork from where it had fallen in the struggle, sank it into the corpse's back, and thrust the macabre makeshift puppet through the doorway.

He was running again before the trio of bolts, instantly protruding from the lifeless flesh from three separate directions, finished vibrating.

SIX

Ducking around the now brightly burning shed, Jack broke line of sight with two of the shooters. The third he'd hoped would lose track of him in the shadows beyond the fire, but no such luck. Despite his speed and his deliberately swerving path, a sharp pain in his back, some ways below the shoulder blade, nearly knocked him from his feet.

Cursing, he dropped low and changed course. After what felt like an eternity of sprinting, ignoring the insistent stabbing and growing wetness across his back as best he could, he saw wooden fence posts up ahead.

The closest cover he could reach from the shed that didn't take him right into the enemy's cross fire: the cow pasture.

He jumped, vaulting the fence, and dropped to a crouch behind the nearest post, watching for pursuit in the dark of night.

They were coming, but a ways back. He'd handily outdistanced them. His brow furrowed as he thought about how far he'd come at a dead sprint, yet the only shortness of breath he felt was due to the pain. He wasn't fatigued in the slightest.

One more mystery on the heap that is the past week. Deal with it later.

Speaking of dealing with things . . .

It took him three tries to find an angle from which he could reach the bolt, and even then it was a near thing, but he finally managed to twist and pretzel himself enough to get a grip on it. Best not to pull it out, agonizing as it was; he had no means of stanching the blood or bandaging the wound, and he'd gotten a close enough look at the arrowheads to know the bolt wouldn't come out clean. Instead, clenching his jaw to prevent any accidental sound, he braced himself against the fence and snapped the shaft free.

Mentally cursing and shouting at the pain, he slipped deeper into the field, moving once more at a low crouch. Only a few trees and some shallow rolling of the terrain provided a modicum of cover, but he used it well. He paused behind one of the trunks, watching the shapes move behind him as more of his attackers jumped the fence. He dashed to the edge of a rise that couldn't even generously be called a hill and slid down through the grass on his belly.

Up ahead, a portion of the Callahan herd sprawled over the pasture, the white portions of their hides like ghosts in the darkness. A few of the Herefords stood, only dozing, but most had lain down for the night. Moving carefully so as not to startle any even if he woke them, Jack crept among the animals. Several large dark eyes fluttered open to watch him with sleepy curiosity, but the cows and their calves all knew him well. Only some gentle shifting marked his passage.

The intruders couldn't say the same. A growing protest of waking cattle spread from one side of the herd. It was no fear response; Jack and his hands treated them well and never performed their slaughtering where the others could hear or smell, so these animals knew no reason to consider any person a threat. Rather they were simply dismayed at finding their slumber interrupted by strangers.

Regardless, their complaining told Jack where to find the nearest foe.

He crawled, peeking over the flanks of a sleeping heifer. Indeed, there was one of the enemy now, a brutal hunting knife in each fist, peering with some bewilderment at the slowly rousing beasts around him. While certainly not afraid of the cows, he seemed wary, uncertain.

City boy.

Jack rose behind him like a phantom and drove the clawed head of his hammer through the man's temple with a single sharp swing, then slowly lowered him to the ground so as not to alert the others.

It was only the faintest disturbance in the air and the softest rustling of fabric that warned him the cattle here had been reacting to not one intruder, but two.

Jack dove, but not quite fast enough. He avoided what might have been a crippling blow, or worse, but the second man's blade still carved a furrow down one side of his back. Again the sharp pain, the quick wet warmth, and Jack felt a soft grunt escape despite his tightly clenched teeth. He skidded across the grass on his chest, further tearing his shirt.

Now the cows began to grow alarmed, disturbed not just by the unusual activity but by the ever-increasing scent of blood. First one, then several more, rose and began milling about, not yet ready to run but unable to remain still.

Over his shoulder and behind him, the latest of the attackers advanced on Jack, wielding a wakizashi very much like his counterpart back at the work shed—and Jack no longer had his hammer, which still protruded from a corpse's head a few yards away.

Instead, then, he reached out, scooped up a reasonably fresh cow patty, and heaved it straight into the approaching man's face.

Very few forms of training, as it happens, teach a combatant how to react when their eyes and their airway are abruptly full of feces.

He fell back, gagging and choking, blade waving to keep anyone or anything from getting too close. The distraction lasted only a moment—the mask that wrapped part of his face protected him from the worst of the sodden missile—but it was plenty of time for Jack to regain his feet, to focus past the new pain in his already shredded back, and to ready himself.

Both men tensed to throw themselves at one another. Both men paused at a sudden irritable snort from nearby.

Enkidu had awoken and come to find out what was disturbing his herd.

One of several studs that lived on the Callahan Ranch, the Hereford wasn't particularly large as bulls go. He certainly wasn't a very temperamental example of the breed. Neither of those made it any less unnerving to see the horns on that white-and-brown head appearing out of the darkness.

The man masked in fabric and cow shit froze, uncertain what to do, how to react to the imposing animal. Jack advanced, cracked an elbow into the side of the other man's skull to disorient him, then grabbed him by the face and slammed his head back into Enkidu's left horn.

The impact jolted the surprised bull's head to the side. Enkidu lowed in protest.

"I know." Jack pulled the twitching corpse free and dropped it, stooping to retrieve the wakizashi. "Sorry about that."

Another low, vaguely accusing and put out.

"I know," Jack repeated, then laid a hand softly on the bull's head. "You're a good boy."

Snort.

Jack moved on. The cattle would remain agitated until he could get these corpses out of here, but right now that didn't seem his most immediate concern.

He felt his back tightening up, the pain radiating through every muscle. He'd already been moving too slowly, and this would only make it worse. He hoped he didn't have too many more of these people, whoever they were, left to deal with.

And it occurred to him only then that he wasn't hearing the commentary of that strange other-him anymore. While he certainly had questions, the situation no longer felt especially strange. That honestly made him more nervous than anything else going on.

Far back the way he'd come, the fire's glow was starting to die. The shed must have been mostly consumed already. Thankfully it was surrounded by dirt on all sides, so the flames probably wouldn't spread.

The garage. Get to the garage, maybe I can end this. The roof would provide a strong vantage point; other than the main house, the former barn was the tallest building on the property. The interior offered many places to hide, and if he started up one or two of the cars, made it seem like he was trying to make an escape, he might just draw in the rest of these assholes. Risky, but easier than wandering in the dark hoping he found them before they found him.

He approached from the open field behind the garage, slipping through the shadows where no lights or other buildings stood. If any of the enemy were watching, their attention would probably be fixed on the open front of the structure, where the vehicles could pass. Coming in through the smaller entrance in back would more likely avoid them, but it meant dealing with the old and rickety door. He dithered briefly, then decided he could manage carefully enough to prevent any potential click of the latch or squeak of the hinges.

Stolen blade at the ready, he slowly turned the knob, pushed the door inward.

Nothing.

He crept inside, past the riding mower, an old tractor, the empty slot where the Chevy normally sat, an even older truck long stripped for parts. Up ahead remained only the Nissan, at which point he'd be visible to anyone lurking near the front outside.

One last glance around, debating whether it was worth the potential noise of breaking out a ladder or if he could reach the roof access by climbing the walls . . .

The headlights on the old tractor snapped on, bathing the interior of the barn and shining a signal beacon into the night. Jack dove aside without waiting to discover if he was under attack, and indeed yet another bolt flew through the spot he'd just vacated. Two of the intruders leapt down from where they'd lurked in the vehicle, drawing swords. Cursing himself for not checking for just that when he entered, Jack went to meet them.

They separated as he neared, intending to flank him. Rather than allowing it, Jack changed course abruptly, racing instead between them and back the way they'd just come. He heard a startled curse as the pair moved to pursue, but he was already ducking back behind the tractor—and then, the instant he broke line of sight, dropped to his belly and slid between the rear tires.

From there, a quick flick of the wakizashi severed the tendons in the back of an intruder's ankle and indeed took the entire foot halfway off. Jack rolled free even as the man collapsed with a scream, stood, and took an extra second to stomp hard on the back of the fallen attacker's neck to ensure that, crippled or not, he'd never rise again.

Now facing the second man one-on-one, Jack went on a

straightforward offensive. Swords clanged together once, twice, before Jack landed a bone-breaking stomp to the inside of his enemy's knee. A thrust caught the man's throat in mid-stumble, and Jack was already turning away, blood raining in an arc behind him.

Yet this latest altercation, swift as it was, had given the rest of the attackers time to respond to the light from the garage. More of them appeared in the barn's main entrance.

How many of these fuckers are *there?!*

Even facing such ludicrous odds, and as equally ridiculous as the thought might be, Jack couldn't help but think he should have been able to take them. *Should*—if he weren't at so much less than his best, weren't so damn *slow*.

But he was. His opponents charged.

Falling back now entirely on instinct and muscle memory that came from God knew where, Jack met them as they approached. His blade struck in short thrusts and close cuts, his knees and elbows seeking unguarded flesh, fingers jabbing at throats and eyes. Indeed, even in his current state, he killed three of them and permanently maimed a fourth before sheer numbers brought him low.

Flesh tore along his arms and shoulders, short blades taking tiny bites out of him. His leg collapsed as one of his attackers hit him with his own medicine, stomping the inside of his knee. Jack knew from the feel of the impact that the limb wasn't broken, but it certainly wasn't in good shape.

Eventually they backed off a step or two, leaving him on his hands and knees, battered and bleeding.

He remained strangely unfatigued despite it all, but even if he could focus past the pain, the many wounds sapped too much of his strength. If they gave him long enough, he might just have a surprise or two remaining for them, but . . .

A gunshot drew everyone's attention once more to the main entrance.

"Let him go!"

Henry, Mateo, and two of the other ranch hands—a married couple named Jessica and Chris—leveled hunting rifles at the invaders. "Not gonna tell you twice," Henry continued, his tone grim.

No, God damn it! I told you to stay in the—

Another four intruders materialized from around the corners of the barn near the ranch hands, even as several of those inside dropped to their knees or spun aside while reaching for various small weapons at their belts.

The ranch hands cried out in shock. Guns fired. Knives flew, and dark-clad men charged.

Desperate to help his friends, Jack scrambled at the nearest fallen body, grasping for any weapon, any tool, that could possibly do him any good right now.

Instead, a careless grab yanked aside the top of the corpse's dark-blue tunic, revealing a small tattoo between collarbone and shoulder.

A shaft surmounted by the silhouetted shape of twin lion heads, joined back-to-back.

He'd never seen it before.

His breath caught in his throat.

He was *sure* he'd never seen it before.

His pulse pounded in his neck, in his temples. His fists clenched.

Into his mind came a word. A name. A name he'd never heard, as surely as he'd never seen that symbol, but a name that would not fade, that made his blood boil and the bile rise in the back of his throat.

Nergal.

Nergal.

Nergal . . .

SEVEN

"*Nergal! Nergal! Nergal!*"

Above the clash of battle, the crackle of countless fires, the screams of the killing and the dying, and worse than killing and dying, that constant litany still carries. It echoes through the narrow, winding streets, bouncing off the walls of baked mud and clay. He cannot shut it out, cannot refuse to hear.

Rain falls lightly around him, turning the air heavy and the road to muck. Yet it is not nearly heavy enough to douse the many flames, and it is spilled blood more than water that thickens the ground beneath him.

This is like his dreams in many ways (the part of him that is still Jack cannot help but note), yet subtly different. He does not see the land and the people shift from then to now, as he has before. Yet, as before, he understands everything he hears, everything he sees. It feels natural. Familiar.

He belongs here.

At Jack's feet—though he is not Jack—lies a corpse, fresh, still spasming, armored in a reinforced feathered kilt and a leather cloak adorned with copper disks. In Jack's hand is the narrow-bladed bronze axe he used to put that corpse where it now lies. He bends over the body, spits, and delivers one final blow. Not to kill, for that task is well complete, but to split the brand on the dead man's upper arm.

The brand of the lion-headed mace.

Another raider dead, five that he has accounted for, but they are five out of what seems an infinite horde. And still, throughout the district, perhaps throughout the city entire, they shout their dreadful cry.

"*Nergal! Nergal!*"

Jack-Who-Is-Not-Jack cries out as well. "Janna! Aram!"

No response. If any of his family are near, they cannot hear him through the din.

Still calling despite the risk of drawing more of the raiders to him, he lurches through the rain. Each step brings a hiss of pain between his calls, and his free hand stays pressed tight to his side in a losing struggle to stanch the bleeding.

He may have won his clash with the man he's now left in the road behind him, but not without cost.

Sloshing. Splashing. Constantly shifting his blood- and rain-slick grip on his weapon.

Around a corner and up ahead, he sees a quartet of raiders, gore-encrusted bludgeons lifted overhead, burst through the doorway of one of the cramped homes at the far end of the street.

He knows that house. It is the home of Urbau-Mumu, potter and tinkerer, father of five, and close friend of Ivar.

Ivar. The eldest brother. Older than Aram, older than Jack-Who-Is-Not-Jack.

Ivar, who sent his own children away to hide when the raiders first appeared. To hide in the home of Urbau-Mumu.

He runs now, screaming. In warning? In fear for his family? In mindless, animal rage?

From inside the house, other screams answer his own, screams of terror and of pain.

A massive weight slams into him from behind, tackling him to the soft earth, thrusting a dagger into his side. The agony scarcely registers. Still he struggles, trying to crawl forward, empty hand reaching for the house as though he can grasp the doorway and drag himself nearer.

The raider on his back raises his blade to strike again.

From within the house, one last shriek. "*Sheshabba!*" *Uncle!* A call to him in a voice, a child's voice, he knows far too well. A call to him for help that will not come.

A call that trails off in a wet, ragged gurgle.

Again he screams, sobbing, but he can no longer hear even his own voice.

Not above the chant that fills the world.

"*Nergal! Nergal! Nergal!*"

Between one blink and the next, the world as he knew it returned.

Jack looked up, fighting his own thoughts, trying to push the strange imagery of the ancient world aside. Later. He'd figure out what it all meant, or if he was just going mad, later. Right now he had to anchor himself in the here and now, in reality.

Not that reality seemed all that real.

One of the intruders lay dead on the ground, and another crouched against the barn wall, clutching at a badly bleeding thigh. Henry and the others had landed a couple of their shots.

But Chris lay sprawled in the dirt, eyes wide and unseeing, a throwing knife lodged in his throat, a second in his ribs. Jessica was on her knees beside him, weeping, oblivious to her own injury where a third blade protruded from her side. Henry and Mateo stood rigid, stripped of their rifles, surrounded by men with swords.

One of the enemy, identical to all the others so far as Jack could tell, advanced to stare down at him. "Ready to surrender? Or do you need to see more of your people die first?"

Five. Only five enemies capable of fighting remained. At his best—though yet again, he couldn't say how he knew—Jack could've taken them all. Perhaps even as he was now, with just a moment to catch his breath and adjust to the pain of his fresh wounds, he could still pull it off.

But not before the hostages, his friends, paid the price.

Gut churning and teeth grinding at near-tectonic levels, Jack unsteadily stood up with his hands raised.

The man who'd spoken crooked a finger. One of the others stepped briefly from the garage, returning almost immediately with a large rucksack they must have left right outside. From within, he pulled a set of dark iron manacles. Thicker and far heavier than modern handcuffs, these either were modeled on or actually *were* restraints from at least two centuries prior. A matching set of leg shackles followed; these guys clearly meant to take no chances with him.

The instant his hands were locked behind him and his stride limited, the apparent leader made another gesture, a sort of chopping motion at the wrist.

Jack knew as soon as he saw it that he'd been betrayed. He shouted, trying to force himself forward despite the restraints, a glimpse of his struggles on the muddy streets of that ancient city once more flashing through his mind.

The men surrounding the captive ranch hands raised their weapons . . .

Theirs, however, were not the blades that fell.

A new figure, garbed in the same midnight hue as the other intruders but slighter of build than most, swept through the entryway. Blades flashed in the tractor's headlights, a series of patters sounded as blood hit the dirt, and two of the enemy guarding the hostages fell.

The rest of them froze, if only for a heartbeat or two, in shock. Jack did not.

He jerked his head back, flattening the nose and splitting the lips of the man who'd just fastened his manacles. The resulting stagger, accompanied by a ragged gasp of pain, gave Jack room to move. He spun, the weight of the leg irons barely slowing him, and threw his body into a jumping kick with both feet. Ribs cracked under the impact, and both he and his opponent fell. Jack rolled just enough that he didn't land on—and break—his wrists, still locked behind his back. A violent flex of his legs, an arch of his back, and he flipped back up to his feet, an acrobatic exploit he'd never have believed himself capable of.

The man whose face and chest he'd just battered stayed down.

Several paces away, the newcomer brandished both weapons: daggers, Jack now saw, broad and slightly rounded, an ancient Mediterranean and Persian style called *akinakes*. Even as the two surviving raiders scrabbled for their own armaments, the stranger—a woman, judging by shape and movement—flipped the daggers in her hands to hold them by the blades and hurled them, one at each.

They weren't designed or remotely balanced for throwing, these blades. One glanced harmlessly off its target, striking pommel first, while the other wobbled harmlessly past.

Both men flinched, however, moving aside or raising a hand in protection, and that instant of distraction had been her goal. Swiftly and smoothly, she produced a Beretta M9 from behind her back. Whatever aversion the raiders had to modern weaponry, she clearly didn't share it.

Two shots.

Two more corpses.

Then finally, silence, save for the frightened panting of the hostages and Jessica's soft sobs.

The woman holstered her weapon, calmly went to retrieve her akinakes, and only then turned her attention toward Jack.

Nodding, presumably to herself, she removed the hood and mask, revealing a face dark of complexion and surprisingly young for what was obviously a skilled killer. If she was older than her mid-twenties at the most, Jack would've been shocked.

"All right. Let's get you out of those cuffs, Jack." She drew close, then halted again a step or two away. "Or do you prefer 'Gilad'?"

The first cracks had formed at the Gas and Gulp, the adrenaline and the struggle and the pain of his wound. They had widened when those injuries healed so much faster than they should have.

More cracks had appeared over the course of this night as he'd battled against a veritable army of intruders, suffered and delivered ever-bloodier damage, tapping into skills and instincts that came from God knew where.

Now, at the sound of that name—of *his* name—the dam burst.

Dirt roads winding through the uncomfortably narrow spaces between homes of baked mud.

Stone columns covered in brightly hued geometric patterns.

Deserts and marshes, squat public structures and towering pyramids, gleaming in the sun.

Dense jungle, thick with biting mosquitoes and air so humid one could almost drink it.

Glass skyscrapers reaching to heights beyond what even the gods of prior ages could aspire to.

Men, women, children. Allies, enemies, strangers, friends, a sea of faces ebbing and rising like a storm-driven tide.

Aram, Ivar, Vexana, Janna, Leena, Kalam, Mitu, Xaran, Dayo, Eveleen, Ko, Sophie, Timeus—an endless litany of names that make his blood burn and his tears flow.

Clubs. Maces. Axes. Swords. Spears. Knives. Bows. Muskets. Flintlocks. Winchesters. Colts. AKs. Uzis. Shotguns. Mines. Grenades. Teeth. Claws.

Pain. Blood. Blood. Pain. Corpses—piles, mounds, carpets, mountains of corpses.

Death. Not only others', but his own. Time and again.

Relief. Rest. Guilt. Duty.

Fields of horrors, vicious and indescribable things spread across rocks and mountains, terrain found nowhere in the real world, and towering above and beyond it all, an iron door. The *Iron Door, portal from what isn't to what is.*

Caught in the deluge of five thousand years of memories, Jack Eren fell to his knees with a throat-rending scream . . .

And Gilad Anni-Padda woke up.

Atop a hill, some few hundred yards beyond the boundaries of the Callahan Ranch, stood yet another figure dressed to blend with the surrounding night.

Through a powerful night vision scope, he watched as events unfolded across Jack Eren's property. Through multiple devices locked to specific radio frequencies, he listened in when angle or obstacle or wall kept him from seeing.

He scowled, furious and frustrated, as his oldest friend in

the world interfered at the moment when success of the primary plan seemed assured.

Digging into a pouch at his side, he pulled out an old cell phone, modified against electronic eavesdropping and linked to no legal names, and stabbed a finger at the only number committed to its memory.

"Namenzida," he demanded as soon as it was answered. "Now."

"I'm here." The familiar voice came over the line almost immediately. No doubt he'd been waiting for this call, probably standing right beside whoever he'd had answer. "Report."

The observer couldn't keep the tremble of fury from his own voice. "Everything was going as well as we could have hoped—until Halba fucking intervened."

"Details, Aradlugal. 'Report' means details."

Temper still on the verge of boiling over, Aradlugal repeated everything he'd seen and heard, everything that had happened on the ranch.

All of which earned him a reply that consisted entirely of, "Hmm."

"That's it? That's what you have to say?" Aradlugal had to restrain himself from dashing the cell to pieces on the earth beside him. "We could've had him! All we had to do was go in with a few automatics and riddle the truck before he even got out! We could have—"

"How many times do you need us to go over this?" Namenzida demanded over the phone. "There are reasons we prefer not to use—"

"Bullshit! They're all bullshit! Nobody would've heard the shots! This ranch is in the middle of nowhere! And it didn't stop Anni-Padda's people from using guns, did it? Or Halba? And as for *tradition*—"

He couldn't hide his disdain at the word, but his leader didn't permit him to continue.

"I've been patient with you because I know what you're dealing with, and the difficulty it's causing you, but you will *show respect*!"

Aradlugal took several long, deep breaths. He pressed the fingers of his free hand into his temple, trying to rub away what had become a near-constant agitation as if it were a headache. "Of course. My apologies."

Namenzida's return to a calmer, friendlier tone was the only indication he'd even heard the apology, let alone accepted it. "Besides, we want Anni-Padda alive. Turning his car into scrap with him inside isn't the best way to accomplish that."

"But why?" Now Aradlugal worried he was whining, petulant, but he couldn't help himself. "All we had to do was keep the body under observation. He'd be back soon enough."

"We don't know that. We don't know how long it might be. We don't even know with certainty that he *would* be back. If the demons were to take him before he could reach the Door . . ."

Another deep breath, struggling to keep himself calm. "I know. Then it could be decades, even centuries, if ever. I know." Then, "*If* what we know about his resurrection is true. *If* Halba interpreted everything correctly."

I should have been the one with that knowledge! Me! I shouldn't have to trust . . .

Namenzida was speaking again, but Aradlugal couldn't hear him. His head throbbed; his mind burned with images he'd never seen, memories that were not his.

Wives, children, brothers he'd never had. Homes he'd never lived in, that had fallen millennia before he was born. Wars he'd never fought in. Blood he'd never shed.

Deaths he'd never suffered.

But nothing of the life beyond life. Nothing to offer Namenzida's grand plan.

Not like *she'd* gotten.

Aradlugal pressed the phone tight to his ear as though trying to drive it through his skull, and struggled to hear the words of his leader, his high priest, through the fractured, deafening memories of Gilad Anni-Padda.

EIGHT

". . . already on most of the accounts," Gilad said into the phone, speaking to Henry's voicemail. "I've added you as an authorized signer to the bank, the insurance, and the property. You can legally make any decisions that might be required.

"I've texted you the usernames and passwords to those accounts. Delete that once . . . uh, once you've memorized them."

Ridiculous thing to say. Henry's no fool. Gilad scowled at the device in his hand, lacking anything more satisfying to scowl at.

"I'm sorry I can't tell you more about what happened here tonight. I need to figure out what's going on. I'll try to check in on occasion, and as soon as I have something to share with you, I will."

Which wasn't entirely a lie, depending on how Gilad decided to define "something to share."

He might have had more to say, but his friend's voicemail cut him off at that point. Gilad grunted, then slipped the phone into the pocket of a dark-green duffel. The cell and the bag were two of a handful of items he'd retrieved on a mad dash back to the main house.

Now he leaned against the tailgate of his Nissan and gazed absently into the distance. Far behind him, the low clouds blinked red and blue, reflecting the lights of the many emergency vehicles that had converged on the Callahan Ranch.

"Hey!" The young woman who'd given her name as Halba leaned out of the passenger window of the Frontier. "We really don't need to be hanging around this close. The cops won't be thrilled that you didn't wait around to talk to them—again."

"My people weren't 'thrilled' with it either," he said as he climbed back into the cab. He sounded weird to his own ears, as if he still expected Jack's tone and speech patterns when he spoke. He tapped a knuckle on the steering wheel. "They still have no idea what happened tonight, or why."

"What were you going to tell them, the truth?"

Initially, he responded only with an irritable look. Then, "I feel like I'm abandoning them."

"You're not. The farther away you are, the safer they are."

"I know. That doesn't mean I'm happy about it . . ."

"Hey!" she barked again a moment later, snapping him out of a brief reverie. "If you want to nap, I'll drive, but we need to *go* already!"

"Mm." Gilad put the truck in gear and guided it back onto the highway. "Sorry. I'm still working through everything," he admitted. "Part of my . . . 'gift' . . . is the ability to function with the sheer quantity of memories I've built up, but them all coming back at once? After two years? That's a bit much even for me to process."

"Well, don't 'process' while you're behind the wheel, okay? You may come back after you drive us off an overpass or under a big rig, but I won't."

If she was expecting to garner a reaction by revealing she knew what he was, she was bound for disappointment. Gilad knew the Cult of Nergal—and the Cult of Nergal knew him.

Instead, he asked, "Do your people have the connections to find us if we show up on a traffic camera? Or if my license plates are recorded somewhere?"

"They're not my people anymore. And . . . maybe. I honestly don't know."

Not helpful. Still, until he could get the deluge of returning memories in order—and thus remember where to find the nearest of his many worldwide stashes of supplies and fake IDs—they didn't have many options.

Until then—and until he could come up with a plan to deal with this particular faction of his many enemies—all he could do was keep moving.

Some hours passed, Gilad driving and Halba dozing on and off. The roads were nearly empty, the truck and the sporadic other cars forming their own little islands in the emptiness.

One hand casually draped over the wheel, Gilad considered his passenger. He'd questioned her after the battle, of course, and again when considering his next steps. She'd confessed that she'd once been part of the same sect that had attacked him, until their vicious, nihilistic beliefs had soured for her. That she spent most of her time hiding, though she emerged now and again to make a nuisance of herself before going back on the run.

When he intimated that he needed to learn more of his enemy and their objectives, she'd agreed to travel with him for a time, to help him figure out his next steps, if it meant dealing a greater blow to her former compatriots.

And when he'd asked why she'd elected to help him, specifically, why she'd surfaced to interfere in this particular operation of theirs, she'd said only "Don't you remember?" and refused to elaborate.

No, he didn't, not with his memories still so chaotic, choppy as a raging sea. But with every hour, that sea grew calmer. He didn't remember, not yet; but he would.

As for the rest, if she'd wanted him to know more, she'd have told him more. Her reticence to share details was certainly understandable, for someone the Cult of Nergal now hunted as a traitor, but Gilad needed to know. He'd have to work for it, then.

"So," he said once she'd stirred enough to prove she was once again awake, "what's your real name?"

"I told you. Halba."

"Fine. Your birth name, then. You know mine, so it's only fair."

Her lip curled and she crossed her arms. "It's. Halba."

"No, it's not. Remember who you're talking to. That's Emeĝir."

Halba's brow furrowed.

"What you'd call Sumerian," he said. "Halba means 'frost.' I'm quite sure that's not the name your parents gave the doctors in the maternity ward. You took it on when you joined the cult."

He heard her teeth grinding. "Jada," she snapped before turning to face the window.

Don't push it. Not yet. "Good to meet you. If you prefer Halba, so be it."

It was her turn to grunt noncommittally.

Another mile marker slipped past, a lonely ghost in the gloom.

"Which sect?" he asked.

She took a moment to face him again. He wondered if the question hadn't registered. "Sorry, what?"

Her confused frown when he repeated his query was so raw, he couldn't doubt she genuinely had no idea what he was talking about. "They're followers of Nergal," she said. "You already know . . ."

She trailed off as he shook his head.

"Halba, the worship of Nergal has survived—and only barely, at times—in tiny underground pockets and scattered enclaves, for more than five thousand years. Do you really believe there's only one denomination, one sect?"

His passenger looked very much like a fish, the way her mouth hung open. Gilad forced himself not to laugh.

"No," Halba finally managed. "No, it's just . . ." She withered a touch at his pitying look, then straightened stubbornly in her seat. "Maybe there are others," she conceded, "but we're the real—"

"The *real* inheritors of Nergal, the *real* faithful. Yes. Guess what all the others believe as well?"

"I—"

"Your former compatriots, what did they call themselves?" Perhaps it was unfair to keep pelting her with questions while she was off-balance, still trying to process what he was saying. She had, after all, saved his friends with her intervention. Yet until he knew more, Gilad could not fully trust.

"*Melidarishe*," she whispered. Then, perhaps to prove herself less ignorant than he might believe, "It means 'the Voice of Forever.'"

Gilad already knew what it meant, of course, but nodded. "And your leader? Your priest?"

"Namenzida."

She seemed almost offended when Gilad laughed.

"It means 'True Lordship,'" he explained. That, apparently, she *hadn't* known.

"Such a name," he continued, "is the choice of a man who either wants to sound more significant than he is, or has delusions regarding his own importance. Do you know his real name?"

Either she did not and wouldn't admit it, or she did but was too irritated to tell him. He elected not to pursue it.

"I'm not familiar with the Melidarishe," he confessed. "It's not one of the sects I've dealt with, so far as I'm aware. Most of them, as you might guess, have no connection whatsoever to the original worship of the Inflicted Death. They're modern recreations meant to mold the disaffected and the gullible into puppets and tools for other, more sinister conspiracies.

"I cannot say whether the Melidarishe are among that number, or if they're one of the genuine minority who truly do trace their roots back to Sumer. What I *can* say is that you do not strike me as a woman who is particularly foolish or easily manipulable."

Again she gawped at him. Her anger, mounting at the constant challenge to what she had genuinely believed—even if she'd since tried to leave it behind—was now scattered by the unexpected compliment.

Gilad almost felt bad for deliberately keeping her off-balance like this. Almost.

"So I have to wonder whatever drew you to a cult like them."

Halba's eyes went colder than the frost from which she'd taken her name.

"The cultists I've known," he said slowly, deliberately, "were gulled into joining—and we've already established that's not you. Or else they sought power over others. I don't believe that's you, either, or you would not likely have left them.

"Which leaves the third sort. The ones who committed some act they considered unforgivable. Whose guilt would have torn them apart, so they escaped it in the only way they could: by deciding it didn't matter, that *nothing* matters. They committed ever-greater evils to prove to others, but mostly to themselves, that they truly didn't care. Who joined with the Cult of Nergal because it was the only place they could find that would welcome monsters such as they believed they'd become, who—"

"*Fuck you!*" Halba shook in her seat, and Gilad felt certain it took everything she had not to physically attack him. "You don't know a Goddamn thing about me! Fuck! If I knew you were this much of a fucking asshole, I'd have let them take you!"

No, you wouldn't. Of that, he was certain.

What he said, however, was, "My apologies. It seems my manners are one of the things I need to work on remembering. Anyway, as you say, I don't know you." He shrugged. "I've met very few who had the desire and the fortitude to leave the congregation of the Inflicted Death, so perhaps you are, indeed, an exception to the pattern."

She wasn't, of course. She'd never have reacted so strongly had his words not cut, and cut deep. Better to let it drop for now, to save further questioning for another time.

He still needed her help against her former brethren, the information and impressions she could provide. And Gilad didn't need his multiple millennia of memories to know that the oldest wounds were often the most difficult to heal.

NINE

Gilad was just wondering if he needed to kick the door louder this time, or whether he might have to drop his burden and go digging for his own key card, when Halba finally cracked it open.

Through the small gap allowed by the security chain, she looked him up and down, gaze lingering on the eight shopping bags that dangled from his arms and the additional sacks still sitting in the back of the truck.

"Did you leave anything at the store?" It was the longest sentence she'd spoken to him since their tense conversation in the car over twelve hours ago.

"Help me with this shit," he replied.

Between the two of them, they had everything inside soon enough. Gilad spread it all out—on the cheap and scuffed table, on the dresser beside the television, even across one of the two beds. His, of course; no need to be rude.

Halba locked the door, engaged the dead bolt, and even replaced the security chain. The chintzy little thing would buy them exactly zero extra time if someone stronger than the average Cub Scout tried to kick it in, but at least it made any sort of stealthy entrance a tiny bit harder.

Gilad had chosen a run-down nonchain motor court on the edge of a town barely twice Fabry's size—and he'd settled on a community even that large solely because he needed a variety of shops to get everything he required.

Now he started to sift through it all. From a particularly depressing Walmart that looked on the verge of closing and smelled like mop water and cheese, he'd picked up a dozen meals' worth of boxed or canned food and bottled drinks, extra shirts and jeans for the both of them, a shaving kit, heavy-duty rubber gloves, an array of hunting knives from their sports-and-camping department, and a few other odds and ends.

From a local shop called Hunt's Hardware, he'd bought what seemed to be nothing *but* odds and ends. Well, those and a number of metal pipes.

"Just how many buildings are you planning to blow up?" Halba asked, digging through the supplies with one hand while the other held a bag of chips she'd just torn into.

"I prefer to keep my options open. I—careful!"

The young woman leapt back from the pile she'd been about to dig into. "*What?*"

Gilad crossed the room and very deliberately removed a few identical boxes. "Neodymium magnets."

"Uh, what?"

"Magnets. Powerful ones. Get them too close together, they can crush a finger."

"And why do we need those, exactly?"

"Good way to attach bombs to targets."

"You don't like tape?"

"I've got that, too," he told her. "And some quick-drying epoxies. I like—"

"To keep your options open, yeah. I got that."

Gilad returned to the table. Even through his boots, he could feel how thin, how stiff, how gritty the carpet was.

Maybe we should've just camped somewhere. At least outside I know what the dirt's made of.

"Sorry if I startled you," he offered as he returned to his sorting.

"Hmm. You need any help?"

"If you could consolidate the food and drink into a few bags away from everything else . . ."

It was one step above busywork, but she got started.

With a speed and efficiency that would've been dangerously careless in anyone else, Gilad had four pipe bombs filled, sealed, and ready to go. It wasn't a mindless task, even for him; only a fool didn't pay attention when working with explosives, no matter how experienced. But it was familiar enough that he could allow a portion of his attention to wander among other topics.

To reassemble other memories.

"You never really told me why," he said.

Halba, who had moved on from the food and was removing tags and stickers from the new clothes, stopped and looked up. "Sorry?" Her shoulders visibly tensed. "If you're back on your 'unforgivable sin' bullshit—"

"No. Why you helped at the ranch. Why you're still coming along to help me now, when I haven't even decided precisely what I'm doing."

An array of conflicting emotions flickered across her features, almost like rapid channel changes. "You still don't know?"

"I . . . might have the beginnings of an idea. I'm recalling more—or rather, making sense of more that I recall. But it's not complete yet, and I certainly can't know *your* mind in any case. So please, if you would."

"Do you . . ." Her hands gestured nervously, almost but not

quite flailing. He was the one trying to put the memories of an entire life in order—and a life far longer than any other—yet she seemed by far the more distraught. When she finally spoke again, it was little more than a hoarse whisper. "Do you remember the ritual?"

"I remember . . . your people. Your former people, I mean. The Melidarishe. They had me imprisoned. A locked room somewhere. Manacles. A great deal of pain." His tone was flat, matter-of-fact. He'd been tortured many, many times in his years, and often by people—or things other than people—far more skilled at it than Namenzida's minions.

Halba, however, couldn't meet his gaze.

"And yes," he said finally. "I remember the ritual. A number of you surrounding me, a hooded man reciting from great stone tablets . . . He needed to learn something from me . . ." Gilad couldn't say what the Melidarishe wanted to know, but he felt sure it would come to him eventually. It was in there; he just had to put it back in its place. "And he knew I wouldn't break. He tried to get inside my head."

"Yes."

The young woman sounded on the verge of tears. And while Gilad still couldn't be certain why she was reacting so strongly to all this, he was beginning to suspect.

As when they'd butted heads in the car last night, pushing wouldn't get him the answers he needed. Instead, he stood up, grabbed the shaving kit he'd purchased, and dragged one of the room's smaller chairs into the bathroom.

Halba watched him, bewildered—and he could see her grow even more so when he stuck his head back out and asked, "Are you coming?"

He couldn't help but chuckle at the almost cartoonish blinking that followed.

"I prefer my hair shorter than 'Jack' did. If I chop it down myself, the results will be . . . Let's say 'ragged.' I'm not particularly vain, but I'd like to avoid anything that might attract even a small bit of extra attention."

"I . . . Are you asking me to help you *cut your hair*?"

"If you'd be so kind, yes."

She seemed vaguely mesmerized, almost zombielike, as she shambled over and squeezed into what little space the cramped bathroom allowed between the chair and the wall. Gilad sat, and for a long moment they watched one another's reflections in the old chipped mirror.

"I was a follower of Nergal," Halba said finally.

"So you've told me."

"You just met me."

"Yes, I know. I was there."

"You can't possibly trust me with scissors at your back!"

"Halba, leaving aside the fact that we both know I'd return eventually even if you did kill me, if you wanted me dead, you could simply have done nothing back at the ranch. Or shot me while I was shackled. There's no train of reasoning that runs from you stepping in to help me then and stabbing me with a cheap pair of scissors tonight."

"Don't be *so* sure," she grumbled. "I hadn't spent hours talking to you then."

Gilad offered a shallow grin but grew serious again quickly enough. "Besides, you may say that you're only traveling with me now to assist me in thwarting your former brethren, but we both know that's not the whole truth. After what happened, you need me as much as I do you."

"You think I need you to help me avoid the Melidarishe?"

He grunted an apparent affirmation.

"Well . . . maybe." She started snipping at his hair. "What

if it's not about trying to kill you, and I just suck at this so bad I stab you by accident?"

"We can always switch from scissors to your akinakes if you think you'll be more precise with those."

Halba's turn to grunt.

Scissors clipped. Hairs fell about the bathroom floor.

"It makes sense," Gilad said.

"What does?"

"That all this was the result of a mystic ritual. I thought it had to be, even before the memory of it returned to me."

"How's that?"

He watched carefully in the mirror as she cut, her own attention seemingly fixed on the back of his head. Watched for her reactions to what he was about to say. He'd alluded to this before, when they first set out on the road, but he'd never gone into detail.

"Immortality on its own would be a curse of utter madness," he said. "How much frustration do you experience because you can't remember this detail or that from a decade ago? A year ago? Even days? Then imagine that compounding itself more than two hundred times over. Part of my . . . 'gift' . . . is a mind as resilient as the rest of me."

"And humility to match," she joked, but this time Gilad didn't smile.

"I'm not boasting. I'm not claiming any greater intelligence. I'm saying only my mind protects itself. It stores everything I experience—*everything*—but it also allows me to compartmentalize it. File it away until I need it, or dull the emotional weight of a given memory until I want it to return.

"No physical trauma, no injury, could have accounted for my mental state over the past two years. Forgetting my truth, mistaking myself for one of my own false identities, even the difficulty I'm still having in putting everything in order now that it's returned to me? It *had* to have a supernatural cause."

There it was. A flash of comprehension, of understanding, on Halba's face. An answer to a conundrum she hadn't given voice.

Just as he'd come to believe for some time now.

"That's why it required so many of you," he told her. "And why the memories you absorbed are so prominent. They're as unnatural as the rest of me."

The woman literally dropped the scissors. She tried to step back, smacking into the wall with a soft gasp. "You . . . You knew? You remembered!"

"I suspected. The images are still scattered, but I recall enough to see a circle of you standing about me as your priest intoned his rites. I know your face from somewhere. And I recognized something familiar in the precision you fought with. You share some of my memories."

After a brief hesitation, she nodded.

"They're . . . well, as you said, scattered. I only got bits and pieces, and it's hard to make sense of most of them, but they . . ." She struggled, grasping for the words.

"They're stubborn. You can't put them aside."

"Not easily." She bent to retrieve the scissors.

"And the others who participated? I seem to recall most handled their share of my past far less well than you have." He kept any bitterness he felt at the violation buried deep. Anger wouldn't serve him here.

Halba said nothing of them, however. Instead, her tone rough, she said, "I expected fury at the world. Resentment at all the horrors and cruelty you've seen, at being trapped here for so long. Grief for everything you've lost."

"And I've no doubt you indeed felt a great deal of that." It wasn't as though his five thousand years had been much fun.

"I did, but . . . I also . . ." She touched her cheek, as if surprised to discover her own tears.

And he knew what she wasn't saying. His determination to do right for a world that did so much wrong. His love for the family he'd lost and the ones he'd made. His devotion to the people of this and every other era.

He knew, because every time he wanted to put down his weapons and walk away; every time the weight of humanity's horrors overwhelmed even his implacable will; every time he faced the trial of leaving behind an afterlife shared with those who'd meant the most to him, and of fighting his way through a valley of hell to pass through the Iron Door and return to this world of pain . . . it was those feelings, not anger or hate or exhaustion, that waged war in his heart.

He knew something else, as well, knew it as completely as if Halba had opened her mind and shared her own thoughts. It was his memories, his emotions, that had turned her against the Melidarishe. His own regard for what was right, for the people of this world, that had cracked the nihilism and hatred and disdain she'd built up to protect herself from her own past and her own pain. Walls the disciples of Nergal had done everything to reinforce.

What Gilad could not yet know, however, was how those clashing memories and those newly vulnerable psychic wounds would ultimately play out.

Halba resumed her inexpert efforts at trimming his hair, and the two of them—one an immortal, one barely more than a child, now forever linked by stolen memories—sat together once more in silence.

TEN

This dream is unlike the others.

He knows who he is now. Gilad Anni-Padda, not Jack Eren. He understands why he knows speech in languages not merely other than English but dead long before English existed. Why lands on the opposite side of the globe, in eras predating most modern religions, are as familiar to him as the Callahan Ranch.

Yet here, in this dream, he does not know where he is. The terrain shifts and changes, not between then and now, but from one place to another entirely different. Sand to stone to asphalt to steel. Cliffsides become trees, trees become walls, and the walls are wood, then plaster, then glass.

Around him, shapes move, shapes even more protean than his surroundings. Arms clasping swords become mighty, inhuman limbs of grasping and rending talons.

And beyond these shapes, fading into the distance no matter how hard he pushes through these intervening forms, no matter how fast he runs, is a young girl. A child, scarcely more than half Halba's age, whose body burns with power and whose eyes gleam with fear.

He cannot reach her. He calls her name . . .

"Hey. Gilad. Hey!"

Gilad had never entirely understood why he needed to sleep at all. One of the many benefits of his immortality was that he was nearly incapable of fatigue. Even the most strenuous of physical efforts, ongoing for hours on end, didn't wear him out.

Still, every few nights—far less often than normal folks, but perhaps a couple of times a week—he felt the need to doze. Perhaps it was a mental thing, but whatever the case, he'd long since given up trying to figure it out.

Normally he was an exceptionally light sleeper, alert for danger even in slumber, but the dream didn't want to let him go. It was, finally, not Halba's voice but the pillow she hurled at him that brought him fully to consciousness, bolting upright in the rumpled bed.

Another motel room, in different colors and different patterns of stains from the one in which he'd packed up his newly acquired supplies, but very much of the same cheap subspecies. He threw the blanket off him and glared at his companion.

"Don't ask me," she said. "You were the one tossing and turning and muttering for the past half hour."

"Hm. Brain still putting itself in order, I suppose."

"Suppose so. Who's Tama?"

Gilad's breath caught. "Where did you hear—?"

"From you. Just said you were muttering in your sleep, didn't I?"

"She's . . . nobody relevant. Not right now."

Yet he saw Halba grow contemplative. Before he could distract her, interrupt that train of thought . . .

"The Geomancer," she whispered.

Damn it!

One of the many obligations of Gilad's immortal life—perhaps even a partial cause of that immortality—was the line of Geomancers, sorcerers with a direct connection to the will of the Earth. His lot was to protect them from enemies both human and very much otherwise. Against the former, his track record was nearly spotless; against the latter, sadly less so.

Tama, the current Geomancer, remained hidden away from those enemies, removed not merely from their hostile gaze but even from her own proper time by some of the greatest magics Gilad had ever seen. He'd been watching over her, teaching her the ways of the modern era, prior to . . .

Prior to about two years ago, when he'd had to go deal with what turned out to be the Melidarishe.

That Halba knew of her, knew her name—probably from a fragment of his own memories!—didn't sit at all well. Gilad had no reason to think the young woman posed Tama any danger, but he'd lost too many Geomancers to ever grow lax.

As if casting about for the perfect question to make him even less comfortable, Halba asked, "Do you want us to go find her? You've been away from her a long time."

"No. No, I don't think so."

"You're not worried about her?"

He spread his hands in a partial shrug. "I left her in the care of people I trust, who are almost as capable of protecting her as I would be. Either she's fine, in which case a few more days or weeks of wondering whatever happened to me won't hurt her, or something's already happened to her, in which case I'm far too late to do anything about it.

"But I doubt it's the latter. Given the repercussions if the Geomancer falls, odds are I'd already be aware of it, scrambled memories or no."

"Some magical link?"

"Or just the right sort of disaster on the evening news."

That he also didn't want to risk leading the Melidarishe to Tama, if they'd somehow managed to track him and their former member from the ranch despite his best efforts, he left unspoken.

"Well, your call," Halba said. "But it's not like we have anywhere better to go."

Gilad wandered into the faintly mildew-smelling bathroom to brush the night's film from his teeth, pondering.

Halba wasn't wrong. In the long day's drive from the prior motel to this one, the prior town to this one, they'd come up with no workable plans to learn more of the Melidarishe's objectives, to find out what they wanted Gilad for or how best to thwart them. Halba knew of only a few gathering spots or safe houses beyond their main sanctum, and she'd no idea when anyone would be making use of those, or whether they'd have enough information to be worth a long stakeout.

They could keep running, keep on the move, and likely stay ahead of the cult's efforts, but that didn't hold much appeal. Gilad was more than willing to stage a retreat when called for, but only to gain time and better position. He was hunter, not hunted; an unending flight, during which the enemy could be scheming or accomplishing gods knew what else, was unacceptable.

Which left Gilad one option, an option he'd known he'd probably have to take since he and Halba left the Callahan Ranch, though he'd hoped to find a better one in the interim.

"In fact," he said, emerging from the bathroom, "we do have somewhere better to go: Namenzida's headquarters. Take me there."

Halba looked as if she were waiting for the punch line, then sighed when she realized none was forthcoming.

"I know I only got fragments of your memories, but I feel

like I should've been aware that you're completely fucking bugnuts."

"It's the only way to take control of the situation. Otherwise we spend our days running and accomplishing nothing until they finally catch us by surprise somewhere. We have no other choice."

"Sure, we do! We could choose to *live*. I know you're damn good, Gilad, and I'm no slouch, but coming at the Melidarishe straight on? At the heart of their power? It's suicidal."

"Yes, but only temporarily."

"Oh, he's got jokes now. You know what they'll do to you once you come back? And oh yeah, *some* of us aren't fucking Lazarus!"

"Calm yourself, Halba."

"You did not just tell me to—"

"I'm not a fool. We won't go in without a solid plan. And as it happens, I have the best source of intelligence on the sanctum and its defenses I could possibly ask for."

"And what, pray tell, is that?"

Gilad pushed past her, picked up the cheap pad and pen sitting beside the phone, and handed them over to her with a grin. "Let's start," he said, "with the layout."

"We," Halba told him firmly, "are going to die."

Gilad stood at the sink in the men's room of the twenty-four-hour diner—named, creatively, Mabel's 24-Hour Diner—and waited for the nausea to pass.

For three days, he and Halba had discussed and planned while driving the empty stretches of Montana, Wyoming, Utah. He'd already sprouted new thick stubble across his cheeks and chin, which he'd shaved clean right after his companion had assisted with his hair. He looked rough, unkempt, even disregarding the mild pallor that had now come over him.

It would fade soon enough, as would the stomach upset that caused it. For all his millennia of experience, there remained a few things even his body wasn't entirely accustomed to.

Indeed, he felt fine only a moment later. He straightened and pushed the door open, stepping back into the restaurant's main room.

He passed between scattered tables on one side, tight booths with worn and occasionally split vinyl padding on the other. The air was thick with conversation and grease. Gilad politely excused himself as he slipped past one harried waitress carrying a tray of eggs and bacon so glistening with some of that grease they could probably have lubed an axle, and finally reached the booth in the very back where Halba waited.

She watched him as he approached, looking up from the sketch of the sanctum they'd long been poring over. "You feeling okay?"

Gods, she could be observant, this one. Apparently, his cheeks hadn't *quite* regained their normal swarthiness.

"Fine."

"If you're still recovering from any of those injuries . . ."

"No, those are gone." Which was true. As badly as he'd been wounded in the attack on the ranch, it had been almost a week ago. That was more than long enough for his preternatural resilience to heal from almost anything that hadn't cost him whole limbs or killed him outright.

"I guess I'm still struggling with putting some of my last few memories in order," he continued. Which was also true. With every passing day, he'd completed more of the puzzle that was the abrupt influx of all his life's experiences, but there remained a few fragments he hadn't properly fitted into place.

That his *implication* was *not* true, that neither lingering wound nor mental effort was the reason for his brief bout of nausea, he left unsaid. Some of his preparations needed to remain secret even from Halba.

"We're close?" he asked as he took his seat.

"Yeah. Few more hours."

In fact, they'd taken the drive somewhat slowly. They could have reached their destination yesterday, but they'd agreed to take the extra time to plan.

They hadn't yet agreed on the plan itself.

"Gilad . . ."

"Yes, I'm still sure." He took a long drink of lukewarm coffee. "Don't ask me again."

She so clearly wanted to argue, but they'd already been through every objection she could raise. He now remembered much of the sanctum—the cell in which he'd been held, the great chamber where he'd been strapped to a heavy table while the Melidarishe tortured him or wove their violating ritual—and Halba's sketch and descriptions had filled him in on the rest.

But she couldn't speak to how their security procedures might have changed since her betrayal. She couldn't tell him how many of Nergal's cultists might be on-site at any given time. Couldn't assure him Namenzida would even be present. Couldn't provide any sort of ingress the defenders wouldn't know about, wouldn't be watching.

Thus far, the only "plan" he'd shared with her involved creeping as close as possible, learning more about precisely those details—their numbers, their activities—and improvising from there.

She'd told him, in a wide variety of colorful terms, how idiotic that was. How disappointed she was, given everything she'd heard about his tactical acumen. He'd only smiled, assured her that he'd pulled off far more difficult and more dangerous efforts with less, and once more challenged her to provide a better idea.

So Halba took a gulp of her own beverage, angrily shoveled a forkful of waffle into her face, and glared but did not protest as Gilad once more resumed studying her map.

ELEVEN

Night had fallen, dark and somewhat clouded, very much as it had been during the attack on the Callahan Ranch.

Poetic, that.

Gilad and Halba sat in the Nissan, engine and lights off. He'd pulled off the highway into a small protruding copse of the larger forest, twenty-some-odd miles outside of Cedar City. He watched through a pair of binoculars, studying the structure they'd come so far to find.

It was a massive church, all bright brick and gleaming glass, a monument to everything the religion it represented claimed to despise. The sort of place where a priest or reverend or elder would pontificate about the sins and suffering of the world from a beautiful podium worth more than anyone below the poverty line would see in a year.

This church, however, was closed to the public. Scaffolding hung against much of its western wall, pallets of bricks stacked beside it. Heaps of dirt rose from multiple spots along that side of the property, and both an excavator and a cherry picker were parked in the lot.

Renovations, most would think as they drove on by, and never give it a second thought.

Facade, Gilad knew—would have known with merely a glance, even if he didn't remember those same signs of construction from two years prior.

This church absolutely *was* in use. Just not for any purpose or devoted to any god most people of the world would ever envision.

For nearly an hour they sat, Gilad constantly shifting between the church and Halba's sketch, confirming that this angle lined up with that, *that* window in the wall corresponded with *this* room on the map.

"Only a couple of cars in the lot," he said. "What does that mean as far as a Melidarishe presence?"

Halba chewed at her lip. "Probably no service tonight. They don't hold ceremonies—or meetings—on any regular schedule. Since most of the brethren keep their true allegiances secret, hide behind normal lives, the order doesn't want any of them falling into patterns someone could anticipate and track."

Gilad nodded.

"But there are more than a few who live on-site," she continued. "And some of the ones who visit pull off the road at a distance and come on foot through the woods. So the number of cars here doesn't prove anything."

"Makes sense. Wouldn't look abandoned if the lot was regularly used."

Her turn to nod.

"Then I think," Gilad said, "it's time for a closer look. Keep an eye on the place for a moment."

Without waiting for a response, he slipped from the truck and around to the tailgate. There he quickly laid out the hunting knives he'd purchased, sheathing one at his waist, one at his back, one in a boot. The pipe bombs all went into a single backpack.

And he carefully slid one particular satchel into the thick underbrush around a nearby tree. A backup plan, just in case.

After that, he tapped on Halba's window.

"You ready?"

"I still think you should've brought a gun," she said. "Or twelve."

"Would've taken too long to get hold of any pistols, and long guns would just get in the way. Besides, this either happens through stealth, or it doesn't happen."

"So you've said." He could hear the nerves, the doubt, in her tone.

"Keep at least six paces behind me." He shifted the backpack so it hung comfortably from his shoulders, and set off at a running crouch through the woods.

The growth this near the road wasn't especially thick, but still more than sufficient. Gilad vanished into the flora and the shadows; after the first few steps, not even the wavering of branch or leaf marked his passing. Had he and Halba not preplanned their direct route to the church, he'd have worried about losing her entirely.

Yet the forest could provide cover only so far. The church property itself, parking lot and sidewalks and patches of lawn, boasted no trees at all other than a single narrow oak, barely more than a sapling.

Gilad lurked for several long minutes, kneeling at the edge of the woodland. He watched the patterns of traffic, of headlights, on the nearby road. He watched the slow drift of the clouds, hiding and revealing the face of the moon. Only when the night was darkest did he move again.

The piles of dirt, the vehicles and construction equipment in the lot—all provided barriers to hide behind. He stopped at each, waiting again for the optimal time. Once the moon slipped from behind the overcast faster than he'd anticipated, with no cover to be had, and still he all but vanished, dropping to his stomach and seeming to blend in with the asphalt.

He'd been doing this for a *very* long time.

Now he neared the front entrance, a wooden double door, deliberately old-fashioned, atop a stoop of three stone steps. He wasn't planning to enter that way, but he wanted a look as he passed it by, to determine how well it might serve as a running exit if things went south . . .

An array of floodlights sprang to life atop the church with a series of resounding snaps, brightening the parking lot like high noon. Melidarishe soldiers streamed from around the far corner of the building, as well as through those front doors, which suddenly swung open. Even one of the vehicles in the lot, a small sedan, disgorged a trio of Nergal's worshippers. Some were clad in the same night camouflage as those who had raided his home, others in tactical body armor, still others in civilian clothes, but all bore weapons they now aimed at Gilad. Some held crossbows, but many brandished pistols or carbines. Whatever precept or tradition had kept them from using guns at the Callahan Ranch apparently didn't apply here.

From behind him, he heard the racking of a pistol slide. Or more specifically, the slide of a Beretta M9.

"Keep your hands well the fuck away from those knives, Gilad," Halba commanded. "And your backpack."

"Do I look to be making a move for any of them?" he asked mildly.

She stepped around to his side, keeping well out of reach, lips twisted in a faint smirk. "I can't believe you made this so easy. After all the horror stories I'd heard about you? You're supposed to be the damn boogeyman. You really didn't see this coming? You're not nearly as clever or as observant as they told me."

"I imagine it looks that way." He smiled. "You can tell your backup units to come out of hiding, by the way."

"Our . . . what?"

"The backup units. The group behind the dirt pile at your nine o'clock . . ." He pointed, being careful not to move his hands in any threatening manner. "And the snipers hiding behind the curtains in the second window from the right on the second floor."

The smirk dropped from Halba's face. Gilad practically expected to see it rolling across the lot. Before she could say anything, however, two more figures emerged through the open doorway.

One, wearing slacks and a sweater all in black and an Eastern saber at his waist, was a younger man, about Halba's age. His features and straw-blond hair suggested British ancestry to Gilad. Of the other man, he could tell little, save that he was much older. Also clad in black, he wore a full face mask resembling a hangman's hood, and a priestly cassock with loose, draping sleeves. Embroidered in gold at the ends of those sleeves was the lion-headed mace of Nergal.

"Well, well." Even through the mask, the hooded priest's gloating grin was obvious. It tainted every word, an oily residue. "I welcome you, Gilad Anni-Padda. It's been far too long since you last graced us with your presence. I hope you find our hospitality just as pleasant as the last time you were—"

"Can we speed this up, Namenzida? Even as an immortal, I really don't have the time for this level of blathering nonsense."

Whatever Namenzida might have said in response to that was lost as the younger man at his side exploded in fury. "*How does he know that name?!*" he demanded of Halba, his shout carrying well beyond the lot and vanishing into the trees. "*How much did you tell him?*"

"I told him enough to maintain my cover!" she spat back. "Nothing he could actually use against us!"

"Oh, know that for a fact, do you? We're supposed to trust your judgment, when there was no need for you to step in at all? The operation was *working*! You were our fallback! But you—!"

"Aradlugal! Halba! That's enough!" Namenzida advanced a step, raising a hand for silence. "It's rude to fight in front of our guest."

Aradlugal. Servant of the King.

Turning to the rest of his flock, the priest continued, "Please escort Gilad inside. As he's clearly in a hurry, I'd like to resume our work as soon as possible."

"It's not going to go as well for you as it did last time, Namenzida," Gilad told him as the Melidarishe assembled around him.

"Bring him." Namenzida turned, cassock flaring dramatically, and disappeared back through the door.

Halba shoved Gilad by the shoulder. "Move!" Then, as they began walking, "You really believed a handful of your memories and emotions would change who I am?"

Again he offered her that same small smile. "You really believe they haven't?"

Without the slightest hint of struggle, he allowed his captors to strip his knives and tools and explosives from him before leading him inside, leaving Halba behind to stare after him in growing apprehension.

TWELVE

Had there been any gaps or missing connections remaining in his memories, the sight of the sanctum's central chamber filled them instantly. He remembered it all, now.

Two years ago, almost to the month.

Time and again he is brought to that cavernous space, what had been intended by the church's architects as the sanctuary and the nave. He is dragged from the tiny room that is his cell, half marched and half carried, bound by manacles at hands and ankles. He knows how to escape those bonds, but he is injured and unarmed. Until he comes up with a plan that can win him through the ranks of Nergal's cultists, that can get him beyond the walls of the church, showing his captors he can free himself is foolish. For now, all he can do is ready himself, bracing for what's to come.

At the base of the dais on which the altar was meant to stand, a heavy wooden table awaits. Metal bands reinforce it and serve as anchor points for an array of chains. The grain, permanently stained and darkened, reeks with the stench of sweat and blood and worse. A grate-covered drain has been added to the floor beneath it.

It was already soiled when he arrived nearly a week ago. He's far from its first occupant. The most recent additions to those stains and stenches, however, are his.

Again, half a dozen cultists hold him down while his manacles are swapped out for the table's restraints. Again, they then retreat as two new men approach.

One is their leader, the masked priest whose name Gilad hasn't yet heard.

The other is much older, slightly stooped, painfully gaunt, and shaved completely bald from the top of his head to the knuckles of his toes. Gilad knows this because the old man is always naked. Considering his role, Gilad has no doubts as to why.

Far easier, this way, to wash off the blood and other fluids when he's done.

As has been the pattern for days, the old man wheels over a cart to stand beside the wooden table. Atop that cart are the tools of his trade: small blades of a dozen different designs, a few handheld power tools, small glass vials of chemicals, a blowtorch, and scissors and shears of varied make.

Gilad's breath scarcely even quickens. He cannot claim to be *wholly* free of fear; for all that he's learned to endure it, he's no more immune to pain than anyone else. Yet he also knows that nothing done to him here will last and that the old man—however much pride he might take in his craft—is nowhere near so skilled or so sadistic a torturer as some Gilad has endured. Literal demons of the underworld have tried to break him and failed. What, ultimately, can this man do?

So, yes, while Gilad scarcely looks forward to the coming torment, he can swallow any sliver of fear that might wind through him. The enemy will never see a hint of it.

For perhaps an hour and a half, the old man works gleefully, as if his amusement is the true purpose here. Skin splits, tissue tears, blood spills. Pained grunts? The occasional flinch? Those he manages to elicit. But no scream. No cries. And no words, certainly no pleas.

When those ninety minutes or so have elapsed, and the wood beneath Gilad has grown hot and slick with his own juices, the priest steps forward to ask his questions.

"Tell me of the Faraway. Describe it to me."

"Tell me how you got there. How *I* might get there."

"Tell me of the Timeless Word!"

This bastard, this priest of Nergal, should have known nothing of these. His reach and his resources must be extensive indeed for him to have learned of them. Knowing of them and being able to do anything with them, however, are two very different things.

These are the same questions he asked yesterday, and the day before, back to last week when Gilad's ordeal began. And as every day before, Gilad says nothing.

Today, in fact, he laughs.

The torturer looks incensed, reaching angrily for his tools. The priest, however . . . Well, the man's mask hides his features, but his body language, his eyes, show no such fury. No impatience.

He knows. He already knows he cannot break me this way.

So why do it? Taking delight in the pain of an enemy is certainly not out of character for Nergal's faithful, but that can't be the only reason for the daily torture. Perhaps . . .

Perhaps they want him weakened, spent, for something else. The priest expects no answers; the torture is meant only to soften him up.

Gilad clenches a fist and vows to show them, whatever they have in store for him, that he doesn't *do* "soft."

For all his effort and all his will, however, he cannot pretend his condition is less than awful.

What the Melidarishe drag back to his cell that night is little better than a glistening slab of raw and bleeding meat. When he awakens the next morning, the worst of his injuries have already healed, but he knows he won't be given the time to recover from the rest. Even Gilad Anni-Padda needs more than one night's rest to mend from that degree of damage, and each day the torture continues sets him back just that much more.

For the first time since this all began, however, his immediate future holds no such tortures.

When the guards once more drag his manacled form into the central chamber, the thick wooden table is gone. In its place sits a slab of granite, its base covered in Sumerian iconography, symbols dating back to the time of Gilad's own youth.

Even more peculiar, an array of massive stone tablets leans against the nearby walls. He spots over half a dozen of them, each nearly as tall as him. It must have taken enormous effort to move them all in here.

He recognizes these tablets. He's seen them before, in a dark underground chamber lit by the flares of soldiers who should never have been there. Eighteen years ago, beneath the streets of Nasiriyah.

"I see," he says to the hooded priest, who stands halfway between the slab and the first of the great tablets. His voice is rough and ragged from his recent ordeals. "Major Wheeler was one of yours."

"A tool, not a follower. But a good one, at least until he was court-martialed for the 'unauthorized excursion' you ruined. It took us years to finally get hold of the tablets after that."

"I am so deeply remorseful to have inconvenienced you."

The fact that Wheeler and the soldiers would have been

slaughtered to a man if the elders who knew of those ruins hadn't caught wind of the corrupt major's endeavor, hadn't contacted Gilad so he might protect the tablets and keep the supernatural guardians from escaping—and thus the Melidarishe still would not have had their prize—he does not bother to explain.

Gilad also cannot help but notice that some of the writings on the tablets, ancient carvings etched into the stone five millennia past, have been altered. Notes and modifications, made with both chalk and chisel, show white against the otherwise darkened surfaces.

From the far end of the nave, ten more of Nergal's faithful filter in and approach the pulpit. Every member of the procession is dressed in mask and robe similar to, though less ornate than, those of the priest himself. All of them carry censers that emit a sickly yellow, almost sulfurous fume.

"So, tell me, Gilad," their leader asks as the prisoner's guards begin fastening him to the granite slab with an array of thick leather straps that run across its surface. "Do you know what this ritual is? What is about to happen, since you won't tell me what I need to know?"

Gilad says nothing. He won't offer this man even that much satisfaction. Nor will he explain that this cannot work, that no mortal mind can possibly absorb . . .

Then he looks again at the ten cultists taking up positions in a circle around the slab. He understands the changes made to the potent spell inscribed across those massive tablets, what they are intended to do.

Whether they will work or not, he has no way of knowing—but they could. He cannot quite prevent his jaw from twitching as his teeth clench.

"Begin," the priest orders, then strides from the chamber. Apparently, he is equally uncertain if this modified rite will function as intended and doesn't care to be present if it does not. Doubtless he'll be watching on some monitor elsewhere in the building.

Half the robed figures hand their billowing censers to their compatriots, who begin to chant well-practiced readings from the tablets. Gilad recognizes most of the sounds as Sumerian in origin, but they are not Emeğir, nor are they any other of the many regional dialects he heard in his youth. They sound older, more primal.

The five Melidarishe whose hands are now free file past the rolling cart normally used by the torturer, collecting narrow brushes and a few glass jars before gathering around the stone to which Gilad lies strapped. All he can do is brace himself.

For perhaps fifteen minutes, they carefully paint ancient symbols across his flesh with the caustic, lye-based jelly within the containers. His skin burns, peels, blisters as they work, covering his limbs and torso with mystic writings. Finally, they step back, slipping into place between their fellows and reclaiming their censers.

Now all ten chant in unison. The sounds thrum not only in Gilad's ears but within his ribs, in his chest. The sickening fumes burn at his eyes, his nostrils, his lungs, and their touch aggravates the burns and welts on his skin.

All of that he can endure. The tendrils of magic intruding into his mind, his thoughts, are something else.

He feels them, a cold and inhuman touch trying to sift through his very memories. Sluggish at first, almost lethargic, they coil around this one, examine that, leaving a trail of psychic slime in their wake.

Swiftly the incursion accelerates, those mental digits now speeding through the seemingly endless moments of Gilad's long life, yanking each to the surface long enough to glance at it, then casting it aside like a finicky child at a toy box. His heart races as the memories of each day, each event, each breath crash against him in a fearsome sandstorm of sensation.

He strains to force it back, this potent magic, drawing upon a will of iron forged by scores of lifetimes of hardship and struggle. For the span of several heartbeats, he succeeds, but he knows it to be only the briefest of reprieves. Strong and steadfast as he is, he lacks the might to resist the ritual for long.

Maybe, if he were at his best, if he weren't drained from constant agony . . . But that's why they tortured him for days on end.

Just because he cannot resist directly, however, doesn't mean he cannot fight. Five thousand years have taught Gilad nothing if not to adapt.

He deliberately falls back into his memories, drawing upon his impossibly perfect recall. Images of pain: the wounds of battle, the illnesses of his youth before he was rendered immune to such maladies. Of love and contentment: his brothers, the wives and children of his many years, and the homes and meals and joys they shared. Of grief, terrible stomach-piercing and soul-rending grief: the loss of almost everyone who'd ever brought him a moment's happiness.

These memories and more, and all they mean to him, and the feelings that burn around them in a blazing fire as hot and bright as the day they were kindled, he hurls into the ravening maw of the occult invocation assaulting him.

In the chamber around him, the first of Nergal's acolytes starts to scream.

This terrible spell, developed by sorcerers of the ancient world to violate the memories of one subject and force them open to another, was intended for mortals. No normal mind, however strong, could possibly survive the sheer span of sensations, emotions, recollections that make up the life of Gilad Anni-Padda.

So the Melidarishe had modified the invocation, intending to split the burden among ten of their number. Strong and willful men and women, no doubt, zealous and well trained.

He would crush those minds beneath the weight of all he was.

The first collapses to his knees, clawing at his mask, ripping it from his face and leaving jagged, bloody furrows across his skin. Aqueous humor drips down one cheek as his desperate scrabbling opens an eye.

A second simply topples, catatonic.

With each that falls, the weight on the others grows all the heavier. Chaos erupts in the Melidarishe sanctum.

One drops to sit on the floor, rocking in place and babbling like an infant. Three, swept up in the horror of ten thousand battles, hurl themselves at each other, beating and pummeling, ripping and tearing. Blood flows across the tile.

A masked woman flees the chamber, shrieking and pulling tufts of hair from her head. One man beats his own face bloody against the nearest wall, cackling hysterically at each impact.

Only two seem to retain any semblance of sanity, of self. Both fall to hands and knees, crying out, but they do not run, do not fight, do not gibber. They yank their masks free, revealing features startlingly young, a Black woman and a pale white man; they clasp hands and stare at one another, drawing strength from whatever bond and whatever experiences they share.

Yet they will be no more of an obstacle than the others, for maintaining a grasp on their own minds takes everything they have.

Gilad thrashes, pulling against the straps. He feels his own thoughts fracturing, tumbling from him in a way he's never felt before. His recall has always been perfect, his control over his memories close to absolute, but this is a magic he's never experienced. His own efforts at drowning the participants in the ritual with specific memories has forged a link that's now collapsing as the spell does, and he cannot quite yank himself free of it. Not in time.

His skin gives way before the leather does, but that's fine. One loose hand, even injured, is enough to open the rest of the fastenings. A bloody mess, nearly deafened by the whirlwind in his own head, Gilad topples from the stone and staggers for the nearest window.

Gilad's memories slip away from him with each step, one by one. The notion of *forgetting* fills him with a terror the likes of which he never felt when it was merely his body, his blood, his pain, his life on the line.

He has to get clear. To lie low, give himself time to recover. He has to . . .

He needs resources. Funds. One of his many emergency caches is only a few days from here. He needs to reach it while he still knows where it is. It ought to be enough to keep him going for some time, until he's able to put his mind back together.

Money. Supplies. A false identity behind which he can hide for a long while. Which identity is . . . ?

Right. Eren. Jack Eren.

Already halfway to forgetting who he is, what has brought him so low, Gilad crashes through the window and disappears into the forest, leaving utter bedlam behind him.

THIRTEEN

On the second floor of the church, near the entrance to the steeple, was a particular room.

Its interior was simple enough. A table with a handful of chairs. A desk with a computer. A large plasma screen on the opposite wall. Two different doors, one opening out into the main hall, the other into a suite forbidden even to most of the Inflicted Death's faithful. One of the Melidarishe's most skilled and most zealous guards stood post in the hall at all times, ready and eager to shed blood at the flimsiest provocation.

This was the personal office and meeting chamber of Namenzida, high priest of Nergal, master of the Melidarishe. Here, and only here, he could relax his guard, shed the mask and hood that hid his face—a face that must never be linked to his sect and his true faith, that far too many outside his ranks would recognize. Even his closest aides and servants entered these chambers only at his explicit invitation.

At the moment, his two most recently invited followers

were screaming at each other like infuriated children.

". . . what I thought I had to do!" Halba shouted, clearly sick of repeating herself.

"Had to do?!" Aradlugal demanded. "*Had* to? He was beaten! We had him! Your plan was a fallback, only if the attack had failed! It didn't!"

"It was about to! You want to talk about screwing up, blame Uri, not me!"

"Uri's dead." Aradlugal leaned over the table on the knuckles of clenched fists. "As is the rest of his team, several of them at your own hands!"

Halba leaned back in her chair, visibly calming herself, though her left hand still trembled beneath the table. "Uri was an idiot. Ordering Anni-Padda's friends executed while he watched? You've studied the man, you should know his chains wouldn't have stopped him if that happened. He was about to either break free or get himself killed."

"He'd have come back if we killed him."

"Probably. But after how long? Our orders were to keep him alive if at all—"

"You murdered our brothers!"

"The team knew they were likely dead as soon as they volunteered for the raid. They died for Nergal. We can ask no better end—"

"Don't you fucking spout doctrine at *me*, Halba!"

"Stop interrupting me!"

Namenzida took a long drink from the glass of red wine sitting before him.

Aradlugal sat back, but his own scowl hadn't softened in the least. "And what precisely did you two talk about on your little road trip? You gave him Namenzida's name."

"His chosen name, not his birth name. It makes no—"

"What *else* did you give him? You certainly took your time getting him here!"

"I had to wait until *he* suggested it! If I'd brought it up, he might have been suspicious! He—"

"Bullshit! What are you—"

Now it was her turn to bolt upright, sending her chair skidding back. She looked ready to leap the table. "I said don't fucking interrupt me!"

Aradlugal seemed ready to rise again as well when Namenzida spoke. "That's quite enough, both of you. Halba, sit."

Without hesitation or even thought, she obeyed. Yet she could not stop the next question from escaping her lips, anger mixed with a wounded hurt. "After everything we've been through together," she asked Aradlugal, "how can you doubt me now?"

"I said," Namenzida repeated before his younger servant could respond, "that's enough. Aradlugal, you are out of line."

Aradlugal's glower darkened still, but he bowed his head.

"Halba," the priest continued, "he's not wrong that some of your choices here have been . . . questionable. I believe you did what you thought best, and it has worked out in our favor, but we'll be having a talk later about your decisions. And your behavior."

She, too, nodded deeply.

"For now, I need to know what he might have revealed to you about his memories of the Faraway or the Timeless Word."

"Nothing," Halba replied. "We talked a lot about memory in general, since he was trying to make sense of everything that'd come back to him. But he didn't say anything about them specifically, and it wasn't really the kind of thing I could bring up." She paused, studying her leader's changing expression. "But you can't really have expected him to."

"No, but I'd hoped . . ." Namenzida scratched at his chin.

"What he said, when we brought him in. That this wouldn't go as well for us as it did the first time. I don't like that."

"Empty posturing," Aradlugal said with a dismissive wave.

"I'm not so sure. Anni-Padda is a defiant bastard, certainly, but not given to empty boasts."

Halba stood and began to pace. "We did talk about how his mind works." She repeated what he'd told her about his memory, his complete and perfect recall (mystical interference notwithstanding), and his ability not only to separate himself emotionally from those recollections but to put them entirely aside, filing them away from his conscious mind until he needed them.

"He could have been lying," Aradlugal suggested, but he clearly didn't really believe it himself.

"No," Halba said. "He had no reason to. Besides . . ." She winced as her own portion of Gilad's stolen memories echoed within. Her head began to throb as she forced them back down. "I think . . . I think I *know* it's true."

Almost unwillingly, Aradlugal nodded his agreement. "Yeah. I do, too." The mask of barely repressed rage swiftly returned. "But it doesn't matter! The Thief of Yesterdays can still pull it from him! It'll just take a little more effort."

"Wait, seriously?" Halba turned incredulously from her old companion to her priest. "We're going to try the ritual again, even after what happened?"

"Why did you *think* we wanted him back?" Aradlugal asked her. "We know better how to prepare this time! More participants, more safeguards. And I can absolutely take more of his memories myself—I'm *more* than ready!"

Halba felt a chill. He didn't sound "ready." He sounded *desperate*. She'd struggled for two years with how to carry the weight of the thoughts that were not hers, a constant effort that left her bewildered, pained, uncertain sometimes of who she was anymore. Only now did she begin to wonder if Aradlugal's own experiences might differ wildly from her own.

Again Namenzida stepped in before the discussion—or brewing argument—could progress. "For now, our guest will simply resume his . . . physical therapy sessions. I don't think he'll break, but you never know. Now that he remembers his previous visit, maybe he'll prefer to avoid a repeat of last time. In the interim, yes, we'll prepare for the Thief of Yesterdays, but not for a while."

"Namenzida . . ." Aradlugal began.

"Not for a while. I want to continue researching the new modifications and precautions. *I* don't want a repeat of last time, either."

"We've 'researched' for two years! We're as ready as we're going to—!"

"Did I sound like I was asking a question, Aradlugal?"

The younger man swallowed his words, and nearly his tongue along with them. "No, Namenzida, you did not. Apologies."

"Mm." The priest stood. "Our plans *cannot* progress until we know how to access the Faraway, how to find the Timeless Word. The ritual *has* to work this time, so we don't perform it until I'm sure it will."

"Of course."

"Then, if there's nothing more . . ."

Halba half raised a hand. "Actually . . ."

Namenzida motioned her to continue.

"I'm . . . concerned. About Gilad."

"What of him?"

After Aradlugal's shouting about her jumping the gun on her backup plan to deceive their mark and lure him here, she cringed at the thought of admitting any doubts. She'd already spoken up, though—too late to change her mind.

"I'm not sure this was any kind of surprise to him. His behavior, some of what he said . . . I don't know, I just . . ." She had to brace herself to say it. "I think he knew this was a trap."

Aradlugal's breath exploded in some unintelligible combination of a sigh and a scoff.

She refused to let him interrupt again. "Or suspected, at least."

"Yet he still walked into it," Namenzida reminded her.

"Yeah. And that's the part that really worries me."

"Understandable. I'll warn the guards to be extra wary, not that they don't already know how dangerous he is. But otherwise, all we can do is proceed."

"And if there *is* a problem," Aradlugal added over his shoulder at her as he followed their priest from the meeting chamber, "let's remember whose fault that'll be."

Halba's glare was sharper than her akinakes, but her gaze rapidly fell from the young man's back to her left hand hanging at her side.

She wished she knew why it wouldn't stop shaking.

FOURTEEN

Cassandra Reyes gazed down over the railing of the Hyatt Regency's seventeenth floor, listening to the echoing din of a hundred different conversations throughout the atrium below, and wished desperately for someone to administer her a good, solid drink.

Or even a good, solid club.

The first day of the Insurance Providers of America 49th Annual Conference had concluded its official programming about an hour and a half ago, which meant Cassandra would now be expected to mingle *without* the barrier of schedules and tables and microphones to protect her from . . . well, from the sorts of people who would voluntarily attend the Insurance Providers of America 49th Annual Conference. As soon as she'd concluded her final presentation, she'd excused herself back to her room, ostensibly to change.

Since said change involved swapping a charcoal-gray suit with pants for a chocolate-brown suit with a skirt, and her Volvo-sized handbag for a tiny purse, it had only required a few minutes. The rest of the hour and a half had been spent either dreading the coming evening while ensconced in her room or dreading the coming evening while staring down from the walkway.

"I don't think it counts as mingling from almost two hundred feet up, Cas."

"I'm not thinking of mingling," she answered. "I'm thinking of jumping."

She turned at the soft chuckle. Behind her stood Peter Garrison, wearing one of those "no, this *is* my casual wear" sports coats. Between that and the glasses, he looked the sort of not-quite-nerd that Clark Kent only pretended to be.

Cassandra liked him well enough, in part because he was one of the few guys at Coswell Security Consultants who'd never made a crack about her height. She wouldn't quite have called him a friend—they'd never spent much time together outside of work functions—but certainly an amicable associate. They'd even run a few cases together.

If she had to be trapped in the layer of hell that was this conference, there were worse people to be imprisoned with.

"Look on the bright side," he said with a grin. "Only two and a half more days of this."

She replied with a fake sob. "I can't believe Val did this to me. I'm going to mail her a box of spiders."

"You think you can find spiders willing to bite Valerie Coswell?"

"I still have friends overseas. They'll find me spiders who haven't heard of her."

Again Peter chuckled. "Come on, Cas. The sooner we get down there, the sooner we can get some alcohol to soften the blow."

Cassandra allowed herself to be coaxed with that argument, and a few moments later the pair stepped out of the elevator—she had, almost reluctantly, decided that was a better choice than the express route over the railing—and onto the floor of the wide-open lobby.

Through the ever-shifting tides of cotton- or wool-covered flesh and banal conversation, the investigators made their rounds. Standing in this cluster, hovering around that table, from bar to dining room and back through the atrium they wandered. Chatting, smiling, until Cassandra was sure her jaw would petrify and her teeth shatter.

Despite her earlier comments and her desperate wish otherwise, she was nursing only her second drink a couple of hours later. Getting blitzed and making some hideous faux pas—such as, for example, telling even one of these people what she truly thought of them—would do irreparable damage not only to her career but to CSC. She'd risk neither.

"There they are! Hey, detectives!"

Oh, God . . .

Cassandra plastered her smile back on and turned. The particular suit waving her down was Samuel Gorman, VP of Something-or-Other at American Fidelity. He stood amid a gaggle of others who were probably also VPs of Something-or-Other.

"Fantastic presentation," he said, pumping first Peter's hand, then Cassandra's. "Just fantastic. These are the two I was telling you about," he told the others. "Ran the panel on Employee-Planted Ransomware."

You mean the one where you spent the entire forty-five minutes checking your texts? Cassandra wanted to ask.

"Thank you," she said instead. "You're very kind."

"You should hear this," Gorman continued. "Right in your wheelhouse. Marge was telling me . . ." He gestured at the woman standing beside him. "You've met Marge Horowitz, right?"

"I don't believe I've had the—"

"Marge was telling me the craziest story, and I thought, well, hell, that's the kind of thing you want an investigator for, right? Love to get your take on it. Craziest story. Tell her, Marge."

The problem with carrying the small purse is that it's not heavy enough to beat this guy to death with.

"Uh . . . yes, well." Marge Horowitz took a sip of her drink and cast what might have been an apologetic glance at the two newcomers. "I was just telling Sam that we got the strangest claim a few days ago. So, we underwrite the coverage for this small cattle ranch, out in the middle of Nowhere, Montana."

Cassandra already felt her brain trying to pull up the blankets around itself.

"This claim comes in, and the damage itself isn't that weird, right? Equipment shed burned down, with a whole bunch of tools and supplies still inside. It happens. But the *circumstances* . . ."

Clearly Horowitz wasn't telling the story fast enough for Gorman, who'd already heard it. "They say the ranch was *attacked*! Like, twenty guys or something! Burned down the shed trying to kill the owner!"

Cassandra's wandering attention immediately snapped back into focus, and she could practically hear the *click* as Peter's did the same. Wherever she'd thought the story was going, that was *not* it.

"Ah, yes," Horowitz said. "That was the listed reason. Obviously, that's not the sort of thing you take at face value, but our agent immediately checked with the police, and it was *absolutely true*."

"Gang violence?" Peter asked, rapt.

"Craziest gang I ever heard of, if it was," Gorman interjected. "Whole lot of them were dressed in, I don't know, like ninja pajamas. Right out of the movies! And all of them dead, killed by the owner and his people!"

"*And*," Horowitz continued quickly, unwilling to have *all* her thunder stolen, "the owner? Not even the first time *that week* it happened! He was in some convenience store days earlier when some guys tried to rob it, or something. Killed one of them, almost killed the other."

"Maybe the guys who came to the ranch were friends of the robbers?" one of the other mingling executives suggested.

Now sucked in despite herself, Cassandra couldn't help but ask, "What'd the owner have to say about it?"

"The police can't find him," Horowitz said. "He took off right after."

"Not suspicious at all," Peter muttered.

"Right? I mean, he's obviously hiding *something*, even if it really was self-defense."

"Wait," Cassandra said. "Then who filed the claim?"

"Guy's chief ranch hand. He's on all the policies along with his boss, so . . ."

"So you're the investigators—what would you do?" Gorman asked, somewhere between curious and challenging.

Cassandra and Peter exchanged a shrug. "I mean," Peter said, "if the police really have confirmed the report, that'd probably be the end of it. Weird as the whole thing is, the cost of an equipment shed and its contents doesn't really seem worth pushing any further."

"Yeah, but if you were going to?"

"I suppose, if the owner committed a crime or otherwise did something to bring this kind of violence down on himself, there might be a case to be made against paying out. I'd probably start by looking into him. His activities, his history."

"Right," Cassandra said dryly. "Because nobody welcomes people poking into their business like Montana ranchers."

"Police are already doing that, in fact," Gorman said,

producing a ridiculously large smartphone and stabbing it with a finger. "See?"

Cassandra politely allowed him to shove the phone in her face. He'd pulled up a local news report on his browser and was rapidly scrolling through it. She couldn't possibly read at the speed he was going, and she only half paid attention to the various pictures—

"Wait! Back up!"

Gorman stopped, blinking at her. "Sorry, what? Uh, how far do you—?"

He could only blink more as she pulled his phone from his hand, now scrolling as frantically as he had, but with far more purpose.

There.

Gorman, Horowitz, and Peter were talking, asking questions of one another, of her, but none of it penetrated. In that moment, nothing existed but the picture of the ranch owner. "Jack Eren."

The hair was different. The beard was new.

Even without those changes, it was a face she'd seen only once, so long ago. Seen only for a minute or two, through the worst pain of her life, on the worst *day* of her life. A face she'd never thought to see again and, on restless nights when she doubted herself the most, wondered if she'd ever really seen at all.

But it was *this* face.

Her left arm began to itch.

Still without a word, ignoring the protests and concerns called after her, she thrust Gorman's phone back into his hands and walked—almost marched—from the atrium.

"If this is a joke, I can't even begin to tell you how funny it's not."

Even through the tiny screen that was the Zoom app on Cassandra's own phone, Valerie Coswell looked as displeased as Cassandra had ever seen her.

"Not a joke, Val. I'm dead serious."

"I'm real close to firing you for even *asking*!" the boss snapped. "I can't believe you would try to pull something like this! I know you didn't want to go, but I thought we'd dealt with—"

Cassandra kept her own temper in check with a deep breath and a fist, out of sight of the phone's camera, clenched so tightly it ached.

"This is *me*. I'm not some middle school girl trying to get out of class here. When I say something's come up, I mean it."

"Then tell me what!"

"I *can't*!" She turned away. Forced another breath, and another. "It's a personal matter, and I'm honestly sorry about the timing. But I *have* to go."

"Are you willing to lose your job over it?"

"Valerie, I'm one of the best investigators you have."

That brought a silent glare.

"When was the last time I took more than an hour's personal time that wasn't scheduled in advance?"

More silence.

"Jesus Christ, I've only ever taken sick leave twice!" That was true; once had been a week's recovery after her car was T-boned by a Domino's delivery driver, the other a ten-day quarantine after coming down with COVID.

"If you really think I'd make up a personal emergency, after all that, just to get out of this damn conference . . . then, yeah, I guess you should fire me."

Still Valerie said nothing, but Cassandra recognized the change in expression. The boss was pissed that she couldn't argue with anything she'd just heard, but she desperately didn't want to admit it.

Finally, her jaw unclenched. "All right, Reyes. You can take your personal time. But you get to tell Peter he's on his own for the rest of the conference. And we're going to have a long talk when you get back."

Cassandra had already expected that much, especially given the switch to last names. "Thanks, boss. Seriously."

Valerie ended the chat without replying.

The fuck are you doing, Cas? She sat at the desk in her hotel room, absently flipping the phone in her hand. What was she even going to say to the man? Why did she think he'd answer any of the five thousand questions she was burning to ask? How likely was he to appreciate a stranger digging him up?

If he was in some sort of trouble—and she knew damn well he could take care of himself, no matter what the attack on his ranch or his subsequent disappearance might mean—what in God's name made her think she could be any sort of help to a man like that?

But she owed him. It was a debt he probably didn't even remember, but that didn't make it any less real. She owed him, and she owed herself the chance for answers to questions that had plagued her since her whole world had changed twenty years before.

Cassandra woke her phone back up, opened the browser, and started checking airfare to Bozeman, Montana.

FIFTEEN

He should be heaving corpses atop the nearest pyre. His garments are stained already with the fluids and viscera of a dozen dead men, his blade bent and caked with gore. The stench of blood and bile and bowels, baking under the heavy sun, will give way soon enough to the miasma of rot.

Most of Ur, not only the warriors who fended off the attack but the young and the old and the unwell, work now at burning the dead lest they attract plague-bearing demons of the air to add to the city's woes.

He should be helping. Instead, Gilad Anni-Padda rolls in the dirt, his shouts bordering on inappropriate laughter, as his older brothers try their hardest to wrestle him into submission. Aram, the middle brother, is far stronger than him; Ivar, the eldest, more intelligent.

Still it takes both even to pose a challenge, for Gilad has grown to live for the fight. Swift, cunning, and burning with an anger that, even in his calmest moments, boils and bubbles within.

This has already been a day of battle, of carnage. Was this the third time the hordes of Nergal have flooded the streets of

Ur? The fourth? Gilad doesn't recall. The city's defenders, aided by Ivar's fearsome inventions—this time a mixture of substances that ignited into an unquenchable spray of flame—repelled them, as they always have.

Now the three Anni-Padda brothers wrestle and punch not in fury but in relief, a release of tensions taut enough to bend iron, a jubilance even in the face of so much death, in defiance of the grief that must follow. Gilad has already forgotten what started the tussle, and doesn't much care. Let the corpses of the enemy—and yes, even those of friends and neighbors—sit an extra few moments. This, the voices of three brothers raised together as they struggle, this is life. The dead can wait.

A cry like an arrow pierces the brothers' joy. Gilad recognizes that voice: Cuth, a woman of impossible age and servant of one older still. A woman the young warrior knows to be without fear, now calling out in terror.

Gilad is up and running, clutching his battle-battered axe, his alacrity leaving his slower brothers far behind. Through narrow streets of cramped homes, then the broad courtyard of Ur's heart. Beyond him rises the great ziggurat of the city's gods and the palace of the near-decrepit king.

Neither mean a damn to Gilad, not compared to the one who needs him.

Cuth's mistress. The Speaker of the Earth. The witch. The Matriarch of Clan Anni-Padda itself.

Breath huffing, Gilad dashes up the stone steps, bursting through the curtains into the foliage-bedecked quarters of the ageless Anni. He does not know the *thing* he sees.

A humanoid horror more fearsome than any warrior of the horde. A figure of desiccated age, its flesh pulled tight to its bones, its beard a wiry and brittle tuft, its eyes burning with a fanatical hatred that must surely exceed that of Nergal himself.

Its bony fingers wrapped about the Matriarch's neck.

The terrible thing rants at him of endings, of victories, but Gilad can make no sense of the words through the pulse pounding in his ears. With a scream he brings his axe down upon its vile skull.

It makes no move to stop him. The blow, whether through the strength of Gilad's rage or some foul softness of an inner decay, splits the creature fully in two. The odor spilling into the room along with the gore is a sickening fume, turning even Gilad's stomach. The leaves of the nearest plants begin to brown and curl.

Gilad has already turned away, kneeling with tear-streaked face beside the woman who has been the heart of his home and culture since before his grandmother's grandmother was born. Words, or what should be words, crack and crumble as she tries to force them through a broken throat.

"Shh . . . Please . . . Don't speak." Gilad is not certain he's ever begged before in his life. He begs now, and though he speaks to Anni, it is not truly to her his pleas are aimed. He lifts her, oh-so gently, placing her in her bed. "You need to rest . . ."

She swallows once, a near-superhuman act, and this time her words, though soft and wavering, emerge intact.

"No . . . *You* have what is needed, Gilad . . . The fire . . ."

She reaches up with blood-covered fingers, leaving streaks across his cheek.

"Forgive me . . ."

She does not speak again. Neither can Gilad, even as his brothers and the servant Cuth finally burst in through the curtains behind him.

He can only stare up at them, his own tears mixing with Anni's blood, painting even more trails down his face.

It will be some time before Gilad understands that the

Speaker of the Earth—she who would come to be remembered as the first Geomancer—chose him in this, her dying moment.

And longer still before he can truly comprehend what he was chosen for.

Gilad sat in near darkness, back pressed against the cold brick wall, allowing the pain of his most recent injuries to subside.

Some was the result of the tortures, three days now of cruel brutality. Cuts and punctures, bruises and burns, twisting and bending where biology had never intended. That he'd suffered far worse, that he healed swiftly and knew he had no need to fear permanent maiming, made the experience no less grueling.

A portion of that pain was, instead, the chafing and pressure of the manacles that weighed him down, rubbing wrists and ankles raw.

And some still lingered from the extra beating he'd taken last night. As they dragged him back to his cell, Gilad had abruptly stomped the foot of the nearest guard, shattering bones. An elbow had broken the jaw of another, followed by a blow to the skull with the manacle chains, one from which the Nergal worshipper would never rise again.

Even as the remaining guards had swarmed him, bearing him down by sheer weight of numbers and bludgeoning him with fists and dagger pommels and pistols, he'd laughed at them until his burst lips and broken teeth sprayed blood across every face.

"How many of you?" he'd taunted them. "How many of you will Namenzida feed to me? How many of your limbs and lives will he let me take while you're forbidden from finishing me off?"

It accomplished nothing more than to aggravate them further still, make his beating far, far worse. Yet that was fine. He'd *expected* to accomplish nothing more, had known that injuring or killing a handful of the Melidarishe brought him no closer to escape.

They'd have expected him to try something, out of defiance and spite and pride if not strategy. So he'd obliged. Let them think he'd done whatever he meant to do, at least for the moment.

Now it was time to actually get the hell out of here.

It was an objective far more easily said than done; the room in which they kept him, converted into a cell in the heart of the sanctum, was nigh escape-proof.

All four walls were brick, heavy, and thickly mortared. The room had no window, and the single vent allowing a modicum of air circulation was barely broad enough for a cat to pass through, let alone a man.

The room was bare. No mattress, no furniture. He had only a flimsy tin bucket, far too soft to make an effective weapon, for use as a toilet. The stench of his own slowly marinating waste suffused every surface.

Gilad's only clothes were the jeans he'd worn on his arrival, and he was otherwise dressed in nothing but his own sweat and blood.

The door was hardwood, too tough even for Gilad to break through—or at least, to break through with any speed. Even if he were to manage, it would require prolonged and very loud effort, more than enough time for the entire cult to assemble in the hall to intercept him. Its hinges were on the outside, and it had no lock to be picked or attacked. Instead it was fastened with a thick metal sliding bolt, heavily screwed into the wood and docking with a hollow in the brick. The only light in the chamber was what tiny bit leaked through the narrow gap at the bottom of the door.

For all that, however, Gilad had one advantage Namenzida and his zealots had not considered when they locked him in here:

The fact that he'd been locked in here once before.

This time, once his memories had returned clearly enough for him to be sure of what he needed, Gilad had prepared.

He had not waited, enduring three full days of excruciating torture, for fun. Nor had it even been an effort to lull his captors into complacency.

No, he'd waited because that's how long it had taken for him to access the tool of his escape.

Digging through the bucket was not a pleasant experience, but for a man who'd been born thousands of years before the concept of indoor plumbing, it was nothing new.

Finally, he had it: a finger cut off one of the rubber gloves he'd purchased, then tied shut. It had been swallowing this little tube—and the all-important object within—that had made him briefly ill in the restroom of the diner where he and Halba had stopped.

Between the discomfort of his injuries, the weight of the manacles, and the poor lighting, untying the rubber proved frustrating. For long minutes he worked at it, cursing under his breath and freezing when his chains clanked a bit too loudly for his comfort. Still, it was only a matter of time before it was done, and a small metal disk dropped into his palm.

Gilad moved over to the door, placed the neodymium magnet against the wood, and carefully slid it upward until he felt resistance as it grabbed the metal of the bolt on the other side.

There he left it while he dealt with the manacles.

Not even he was strong enough to bend the steel, hardened and thick as it was—but he was strong enough, by bracing a heel against the chains before straightening with every muscle in his back, to yank both hands and one foot free in a single, agonizing instant.

Skin and flesh tore away, and several bones cracked, but he

was loose. Gilad choked back a scream of pain and leaned hard against the wall, sweating, bleeding, heart pounding. For hours he waited, letting the supernatural resilience of his body do its work.

He couldn't fully heal that degree of savaged tissue or fracturing in the time he had, but his wrists and ankles had at least recovered enough that he could use them. It would hurt like hell, but pain was an old compatriot; he'd probably do himself further damage, but that, too, would heal in a few days.

When the agony had finally faded to a point that would no longer slow him, Gilad lay down and placed his ear to the wood, near as he could to the tiny gap. He couldn't hear much from the hallway beyond, but every now and again he caught the faintest hint of half a word here, a low chuckle there. Enough to know the guards who were always stationed a dozen paces down the hall were deep in conversation.

Only then did he take hold once more of the neodymium magnet and slowly, carefully, a fraction of an inch at a time, drag it across the wood—sliding the steel bolt along with it.

He knew, by the change in the muffled scraping sound and the sudden extra tug on the magnet, when the bolt would go no farther. The door was unlatched.

One more brief pause to step back and collect the bucket of waste, the one his captors were certain posed no danger. Container in one hand, he pressed the other flat against the wood. Tensed . . .

And charged.

The door slammed open against the brick, shocking as a gunshot. Completely unprepared for the surprise assault from a cell they'd thought entirely secure, the guards were still scrambling for weapon or for radio when Gilad had nearly closed the distance.

Only two paces from them, he hurled his distasteful burden.

The bucket might indeed have made for an ineffective weapon, but the enemy farthest from him got a face full of its contents. Repugnant sludge trailed down his cheeks, made him gag, burned his eyes with ammonia. Choking, he clawed frantically at his face, all else forgotten behind primal revulsion.

The other cultist had gotten one hand on the blade hanging from his waist when his knee shattered beneath the impact of Gilad's foot. He collapsed, writhing and screaming on the floor.

Another pace, and the one who'd been drenched in filth went silent and limp, his skull cracked between a vicious elbow strike and the brick wall. Even as the corpse slumped against the wall, Gilad stepped back, stomping the back of the other man's exposed neck.

That simply, that swiftly, the "prisoner" was the only one left alive in the hallway.

Had escape been his only goal, he could probably have made a clean break for the exit then and there. Doubtless he'd have to fight through more of the Melidarishe, but so long as he was quick about it, reached them before the dead were discovered, they wouldn't be prepared for an attack from within. He'd be out and long gone before the enemy could mount any sort of organized effort.

Gilad, however, hadn't knowingly walked into a potential trap just so he could fight his way back out again. Thus far, while he'd gained a better sense of the cult's numbers, he knew little more about their leadership or their plans than he'd remembered or pieced together from his first captivity: that their high priest knew more than he should about Utnapishtim—the realm called the Faraway—and the Timeless Word, and that he sought to break Gilad in order to learn far more.

It wasn't enough information. So he couldn't leave yet.

Few of the Melidarishe other than Namenzida bothered

wearing their masks within the church, so stealing a uniform from one of the bodies would prove no benefit. Gilad did, however, strip them of multiple blades, a single pistol he'd use only in desperate straits, and a radio. He then dragged them both into the cell, tore a length off one of their shirts, and gave the site of their skirmish a quick wipe-down. Anyone who spent more than a moment here would probably spot a stain or two, and would *certainly* smell the residue of the bucket's contents, but at least a quick glance from passersby wouldn't detect anything amiss. Finally, Gilad retrieved the magnet—no sense alerting them to *how* he'd escaped, in case the trick might come in handy again later—then relocked the cell door behind him and moved, ghost-silent, further into the sanctum.

First one hall, then another, proved unoccupied. That made sense; as best Gilad could tell, it was early morning, still an hour or two before dawn. The Melidarishe had deliberately avoided any regular schedule with him, shifting the time of his tortures to keep him off-balance, so he couldn't say precisely, but his internal clock was better than most. If the bulk of the cultists were asleep, that would make things easier to—

He heard a door open around the corner, followed by low conversation. Three of them, to judge by the voices, probably two men and a woman, voices kept down for the early hours. They grew gradually louder, coming his way. Gilad drew blades, a serrated combat knife and a dagger, gave the trio a few more steps . . .

Then he spun around the corner, drawing the first weapon across a throat and putting the second through the front of a skull in a single move. The man on the left and the woman on the right dropped, already dead or silently dying, while the gore-soaked blades kissed the sides of the central man's neck like deadly scissors.

"Namenzida's chambers!" Gilad demanded.

Give the zealot even a moment to think, and if he was truly devoted to Nergal's teachings, he would welcome death before answering. Gilad hoped, however, that the lightning-swift strike, the loss of the man's companions literally between one word and the next, would shock an answer from him before his brain caught up.

"S-second floor! By the . . ." The cultist trailed off as he realized what he was saying, his expression shifting toward defiance.

Well, it was a start. Gilad's stolen blades met one another through yielding flesh, and a third body joined the other two.

The second floor. At least that narrowed it down. As before, Gilad dragged the bodies out of the hall, this time into the room from which they'd just emerged, and headed for the nearest stairs.

Again Namenzida and Aradlugal sat in the high priest's suite, along with three of the most trusted Melidarishe. Namenzida's mask lay in a crumpled heap beside him on the table, a luxury he allowed himself only in the presence of his closest servants. The man so revealed was perhaps in his sixties, clean-shaven, with hair only now beginning to gray and a touch of a tan hiding what was otherwise a slightly unhealthy pallor. That and the faint bags under his eyes suggested a growing fatigue, despite the intensity of a will determined to push through it.

Halba was conspicuously absent. Indeed, Namenzida and Aradlugal had chosen to meet at such an ungodly hour in part to ensure the young woman caught no wind of the gathering.

". . . understand your obligations," Aradlugal was saying to his leader. "But to leave *now*?"

"We do what we have to," Namenzida replied. "You know the demands on my time."

"But—"

"I should only be away for a few days." He waited until Aradlugal's reluctant nod. "Until I'm back, keep at him. Bleed him, break him, whatever you can do to keep him weak. But you *do not* kill him, and you *do nothing* mystical without me."

"Namenzida . . ."

"*Nothing!* Is that clear?"

This time all four chorused their understanding.

When the priest spoke again, he made a point of addressing each of his servants in turn. "And while I'm being clear . . . you are each to enforce this. Including on each other, if necessary."

He hadn't singled out Aradlugal, but the angry young man scowled all the same. "Don't you think it's time—with all respect—that you told us *why* we're doing this? We still have no idea what's supposed to happen once we have the information you're after!"

"I've told you, *when* it's time, you'll be the first to know."

"We need to know now."

The others shuffled in their seats, trading furtive looks. Even for Aradlugal, this bordered on insubordinate.

Apparently, he realized so as well. Before Namenzida could respond, he continued in a far more measured tone, "In case Anni-Padda breaks while you're away."

"He won't. We already know torture isn't enough."

"It hasn't been, no. But even he's got his limits. If he does break—"

"He won't, Aradlugal. Don't ask me again."

Aradlugal began to speak—and then, in a single blurred motion, rose from his chair, swept a Glock from the holster at his back, and fired.

Bullets punched through the wood of the door at the room's other end. Namenzida and the others fell back, shouting, scrabbling in confusion for their own weapons.

From beyond, a hiss of breath that might have been a curse, and the sound of retreating footsteps.

Shaking from the impact, the door slowly drifted open, loose on its hinges—yet it had been latched when the meeting began! Not only had someone been listening in, but they had cracked the door open in near-perfect silence.

Near, thank Nergal. Only the faintest clink of metal and the whisper of wood brushing the carpet—warning signs that Aradlugal would never have caught before his own collection of stolen memories had taught him new tricks—had tipped him off.

"Well," he told the stunned Namenzida, "you're right. He's not going to break." Aradlugal hadn't seen the eavesdropper, but he had no doubt—nobody had any doubt—who it must be.

"He's seen me!" None of them had ever heard their high priest sound quite so horrified. So *frightened*. "Find him!"

Aradlugal was already striding out into the hall, kneeling beside one of the murdered guards he was not remotely startled to find, and reaching for the man's radio.

"Find him!" Even as Aradlugal pressed the button to speak, sounding the alert for the entire church, Namenzida's desperate shouts echoed from the chamber beyond.

"*Find him!*"

SIXTEEN

She giggles, the world a delight, her life a flood of joy and exultation.

Even the roar of the engine is music, the lead singer and lead guitarist of the band. Playing backup: the rush of the wind through open windows, the occasional staccato calls of distant traffic on these late-night roads, and the laughter of her best friend in the passenger seat beside her.

Jada Lowry—she is not yet Halba, has not yet even heard the word—turns to grin at Benjamin Boyd, who looks back and only snickers harder, which spikes her own laughter in turn.

This is the good shit, some of the best they've ever gotten hold of. They were supposed to share it with the others, but nah. Not this quality. Keep it all for themselves. Should last weeks.

"Hey," Ben asks her, "how're we gonna get your car back?"

"Wait, this isn't my car?"

More shared laughter. Her foot sinks down on the accelerator. The Challenger growls, leaping forward, an orange hound ecstatic to be let off its leash.

"Don't you fucking worry," she says. "We'll have it back before Marcus knows it's gone."

"You think he hasn't noticed already? Marcus loves this car. I think Marcus may be fucking this car."

"Man, Marcus ain't noticed shit. That fucker is *high*."

Another burst of hysterics, lessened only slightly by the knowledge that she will, indeed, have to get the Challenger back before much longer.

Going from this back to her twenty-year-old Honda will be a bigger comedown than the, well, comedown, but just as inevitable.

For tonight, though, for now, everything is excellent.

Everything except . . .

"Hey!" Her gaze flickers in jagged, frantic bursts between Ben and the road ahead. "Hey!"

A moment of incomprehension, then he feels at his face, nearly slapping himself. Her laughter threatens to bubble up yet again.

"Oh, God damn it." He wipes a hand under his nose, an effort that only smears the blood rather than cleaning it.

"You bleed on anything in here and Marcus's gonna kill us," she whines. It's the first thing either of them has said in long minutes that isn't funny.

Ben tugs his shirt up, stretching the fabric and shoving the hem up under his nostrils.

"Thought we were only taking this shit together," she says, accusing. "How much you been doing?"

Muffled by the wadded-up shirt, "What're you talking about?"

"*I'm* not getting nosebleeds!"

"Whatcha want from me? Maybe you've got thicker sinuses, I don't fucking know. Fuck, that's a lot of blood!"

"Hang on." She cranes around, looking over her shoulder. "Thought I saw a box of tissues in the back—"

"Jada!"

Twisting halfway back. Two figures, larger and smaller, barely visible at the far edge of the nearest streetlight, hustling across. A desperate hauling on the wheel, stomping on the brake.

A shudder that shakes the car. A shattering headlight, slightly crumpled bumper.

The scream of tires as the Challenger skids to a halt.

Then everything is slow. The shared horror. The *clunk* of the doors opening as Jada and Ben pile out to stare behind them.

One shape sprawled out on the street, unmoving. The smaller shape kneeling beside it, pushing and tugging at a limp, flopping arm.

"Mama? Mama?"

"Oh, God." Is she speaking? Just thinking? Is *he* speaking? "Oh, God, oh, God, oh, God . . ."

They're drunk. They're high. They're driving someone else's car, someone else who didn't exactly give them permission to take it.

She remembers the panic. She remembers the conversation that follows, though many of the details are gone.

She does not remember who made the obvious observation.

She does not remember who made the suggestion.

Jada and Ben clamber back into the Challenger, that much she is sure of. But whether the knowledge lies buried behind the drugs or the trauma or her simple unwillingness to remember, she can never recall from that day forward who sits behind the wheel, her or Ben . . .

As the car starts up.

Reverses.

Turns around.

And lunges, thousands of pounds of fear and fury, toward the surviving witness.

We have to. It's them or us. They're probably better off this way, without their mom, anyway.

Then the child beyond the windshield, near glowing in the headlights, is not who they were. This is a boy, younger, far darker of skin, wearing nothing but a simple wrap of cloth around his waist.

The street is dirt, not asphalt. The surrounding structures are tiny, mud and clay.

And Jada is not Jada.

The sun rises, falls, rises, falls, days and weeks and months and years, all one.

His (her) wife. His (her) children. His (her) brothers.

Clay becomes wood. Wood becomes stone. Stone becomes brick. Brick becomes glass.

One family becomes another, and another. Not replacements. Not substitutes. Just different. Later.

Living. Then dead, then nobody, then a family once more.

Walking becomes running. Running becomes battle. Blood spatters. Bones break. Flesh splits.

Yet it is not the faces of the enemy that matter, though she remembers so very many. Not the faces before him (her), but those beside. Those behind.

For the thousands he (she) has killed, so many more have been saved.

Behind their ranks, the Geomancers, an unbroken line ending in the girl she recognizes as Tama. So many saved. So many more lost. But all those saved who have also gone on to save so many others . . . An endless spreading web, life begetting life.

They are gone. All is black. A single dark-complexioned girl stands before her, gazing up at her.

A sister. Her sister? Or his? Jada weeps, horrified at the realization that she can't remember, can't tell the difference.

Then the girl is once more the child in the street, who screams before she vanishes beneath the Challenger . . .

Another scream joins her, and another face. The old man in a San Diego alley, her first *deliberate* kill. The Korean woman who barely spoke English at the check-cashing service. The off-duty cop in Vegas. The rabbi in Buffalo, her first mission for Namenzida. Dozens upon dozens more.

And she is screaming along with them, and something else screams as well . . .

The scream of the alarm filled the church, every hall, every corner.

Probably intended by the manufacturers as a fire alarm, though it served a very different purpose for the Melidarishe.

Gilad could scarcely hear it over the sounds of the men dying around him.

In a swift tangle of arms, wrists and elbows catching, he stopped the incoming blade inches from his chest, reversed it, and drove it deep into the throat of the cultist who'd tried to stab him.

He twisted, dragging the corpse with him, sidestepping a second foe who charged with a pair of hatchets, letting the enemy sweep past. Gilad then hefted the limp body over his head with shockingly little effort and hurled it. Two more of the Melidarishe, farther down the hall, were bowled over by the impact.

Gilad spun to meet the hatchet wielder coming up again behind him, breaking ribs and stopping the man in his tracks with a brutal thrust kick. One swift grab and the axe was now

Gilad's, and a follow-up punch drove already shattered bones into the lungs behind them.

Another turn, an overhand toss. One of the pair who'd been knocked sprawling by the corpse-missile had just regained his feet when he dropped yet again, this time for good, hatchet buried in his skull.

That left only one survivor of this group. Gilad let the man draw close, then grabbed the extended arm and drove his opponent headfirst through the nearest door.

Unlike the cell in which he'd been kept, these rooms had no reinforcement. The door was thin, flimsy; the impact would disorient but almost certainly not severely injure, let alone kill.

Gilad's axe kick, however, driving the man's body down and dragging his throat across the jagged, broken wood, was another story.

He bent over the nearest corpse, replacing the dagger he'd lost in a previous skirmish with a Marine Ka-Bar knife. None of this group carried magazines that would fit the pistol he'd first collected, so instead he dropped it in favor of a salvaged Glock 17 and broke into a light jog, a compromise between stealth and speed.

Three times now. He'd been intercepted three times since he'd nearly been shot outside Namenzida's chambers, and not once had he been under any real threat of recapture. Perhaps if any of the enemy had spotted him at a distance, they might have gunned him down. The many corners of the church halls, however, combined with the chaos of his unanticipated escape, ensured that every encounter happened in tight quarters, where neither their guns nor their numbers had any chance of evening the odds.

Now he was almost out, one more hallway between him and the nearest fire exit. He still hadn't learned as much as he'd hoped when he let himself be taken, but with all the Melidarishe mobilized against him—or at least all who were present in the sanctum—escape was the only viable option. And he had, at least, caught a glimpse of Namenzida's face, as well as confirmed that the hotheaded Aradlugal had grown impatient with the high priest's secrets and decisions. Gilad didn't yet know how to use either of those discoveries, but he was certain they'd prove valuable.

A quick glance around the next corner, a T-intersection, and there it was: a metal door at the end of an empty hall. A heavy chain connected the push bar to the doorframe; the Melidarishe, perhaps unsurprisingly, made the security of their sanctum a higher priority than fire codes.

He wasn't worried. The chain might stop most, but from him, a few solid kicks should break a weak link, if there was one, or else rip the fastener from the frame. He started down the hall, building up speed, ready to hit the obstacle with a running start . . .

"Stop!"

Gilad halted, turned. She stood some distance down the hallway, past the junction; she must have come from a side room. She held her Beretta on him, but the barrel quivered.

"Halba," he greeted her.

"Make it stop."

Whatever he'd expected her to say, that wasn't it. Gilad cocked his head. "What?"

"*Tell me how to make it stop!*" The sounds she shrieked at him—they could only in the most general sense be called words—were high, tearing. He almost expected to see blood, they were so raw. Her chest heaved with ragged breaths.

He knew now what she was talking about. "I don't know. You're the one who stole them. You'll have to live with them."

"Get them out of my head!" She took her gun off him for an instant, smacking herself hard with the grip before aiming once more. A stream of red trickled from just above her temple where she'd struck.

"It wouldn't help. What you're feeling is more than just my emotions."

"No! No, it's not! I don't care! None of it mattered, until you! For the past two years it's gotten . . ." She sucked desperately at the air, tears rolling down her face. "Everything you've seen . . . everything you've done . . . How can *you* still care?"

He didn't have time for this. More of her brethren could appear at any moment.

Yet he couldn't walk away. "How can you?"

"I didn't . . . I *don't*!"

"You do and you did. The memories you stole just made it harder to stop pretending."

"*You don't know!* You . . . How could you know?"

She reminded him so much, in that moment, of Dayo. They scarcely resembled one another beyond gender and complexion. Halba was nearly four times Dayo's age, hard and cold and violent where Dayo had bubbled with laughter and joy.

But that tone: plaintive, pleading, begging to understand . . . That had been Dayo's, three thousand years ago, before the sickness claimed her.

He didn't have time for this. He couldn't walk away.

"Henry. Jessica. Mateo."

She stood, uncomprehending.

"At the ranch. You saved them."

"I didn't want to give you more reason to resist us!"

Gilad smiled at her—not the smirk of an enemy or even the grin of a comrade, but the gentle smile of a friend. Perhaps even a father.

"You could just as easily have swept in and injured *me*, Halba. Taken out a leg, or put a bullet in my stomach. Nothing that would kill me, but enough to ensure I couldn't fight, especially as scrambled as my head was. Besides, I saw how quickly you hit them. You were moving before he gave the order to kill my friends. Because even before you *knew* they'd be hurt, you wouldn't risk it."

Halba's arm dropped, her pistol pointing at the floor. Her entire body shook with rasping sobs.

"Come with me." Gilad extended a hand as if he could reach her, though she remained many paces away. "This place. Nergal. They're not for you."

"They are! You . . . you don't know. What I . . . What Benjam—Aradlugal and I, what we did . . ."

"Is done, whatever it was. But you needn't remain the sort of person who would do it."

Halba physically jolted, that thought landing like a punch.

Gilad kept talking, taking a step closer. "I don't honestly know how much of this is my memories, my influence, and how much is you. Old you or new. And it doesn't matter. You wanted those memories. They're yours now, as much as they are mine. You have to decide how you want to live with them. Let me help you."

Another step toward her, and another . . .

Shouts echoed from back the way Gilad had come. They'd discovered the latest cultists he'd slain. They were almost certainly calling it in over their radios, and in moments they would appear from around that bend. He was out of time.

"Come with me!"

But Halba only stared, whether at him or through him or past him, he could not tell.

And he could not wait.

With a curse on his lips and a pang in his gut that felt almost like guilt, Gilad sprinted for the door, turning his shoulder into it and bursting through the chain and the latch with a single explosive impact.

He was gone into the predawn darkness beyond before the echo of the crash had faded.

SEVENTEEN

From an almost overwhelmingly clear blue sky, the sun beat down on Cassandra's rented Audi, forcing the AC to work to excess.

An oddly perverse urge to turn that AC off entirely, to let the car become a toaster oven on wheels, kept flitting through her mind as she drove along the open highway. Given who she was tracking, where they'd met, it *should* be hot. Nothing else would have felt appropriate.

She didn't go quite so far as to actually do it, but she couldn't shake the thought.

After half an hour of silence, of hills and plains, fenced-in cattle and distant mountains, and only sporadic vehicles passing in the opposite direction, the maps app on her phone finally spoke again. "In a quarter mile, turn left."

No street name. She was close.

Indeed, it wasn't any sort of street at all, just a dirt road that ran between two brick stanchions supporting a wrought iron arch whose design spelled out the name of the property.

Callahan Ranch.

The gate between those stanchions was shut but not locked or latched. Cassandra popped out of the car long enough to haul it open and continued along the winding path.

As she approached the main house, which was her destination, she couldn't help but note a spot to the left, far enough from the road that it was almost hidden. Scorched grass and a few tiny outcroppings of charred wood marked the grave of the equipment shed she'd heard—and then read—about.

She stopped the car and got out again, making a show of stretching her back, and then wandered over to make a circuit of the miniature ruin. She knelt, pretending to poke at the ash, and took a few pictures with her phone.

It might all be for nothing, a charade without an audience. If anyone *was* watching from the house or out in the fields, though, it ought to lend a touch of extra credence.

Back in the car once more, and then she stopped a third time in front of the house—and yes, someone had been watching. She knew because the door opened less than two seconds after she rang the bell, revealing a man several inches shorter than her in battered work clothes and scuffed glasses.

"Help you?"

Amazing how much that sounds like "Fuck off."

"Good morning!" she said in her brightest customer-service voice. "I'm looking for Mr. Jack Eren?"

"He's not here."

"I see. Can you tell me when you expect him back?"

"No."

The breeze blew. A hawk circled high overhead.

"I . . . see," she said again. "Well, maybe you can help me, Mr. . . . ?"

"We're not talking to any more reporters. No podcasters, no true-crime writers, no—"

"My name," she interrupted, "is Cassandra Reyes. I represent Coswell Security Consultants."

"Never heard of it."

"Among other things, we conduct insurance investigations for, ah, unusual claims."

Which was absolutely not a lie, even if she wasn't actually claiming what she hoped he'd infer.

She had more than enough skill at reading people to spot the signs of his shoulders slumping and his eyes rolling, even if he managed to head both reactions off at the pass.

"Another one? Jesus." Then, his manners edging out his frustration, if only just, "Luckenbill. Henry."

Figured as much.

"Well, Mr. Luckenbill . . . do you mind if I come in?"

"I . . . No. Come on."

Which also *sounds an awful lot like "Fuck off."*

He walked a few steps ahead, leading her into a living room with mismatched chairs and vaguely ethnic carpeting before turning again to face her. He did not ask her to sit.

"Ms. Reyes," he said, "we've had cops. We've had inspectors. We've had insurance adjusters. I don't know what it is you're looking for, and I don't know what you're expecting to hear. We've done nothing but tell the truth, we've showed everyone everything they could possibly want to see, and honestly, it's getting real old."

"I understand that, Mr. Luckenbill. I do. And look, everything that's been examined supports the validity of the claim you filed."

"So what's—?"

"You have to admit it's a funky story," she told him, following up with a grin she hoped wasn't too plastic. "Especially with the owner taking off right afterward."

"He needed time to process what happened."

"Of course. But you must understand why we need to speak with him."

Henry looked to be chewing on something that didn't exist. "That doesn't change the fact that he's not here."

"Can you at least give me his number?"

"I'm handling all the—"

"Mr. Luckenbill, I know you're handling all the official correspondence. I'm asking for Mr. Eren's personal cell." Then, when he continued to hesitate, "Surely that's not a problem if nobody's hiding anything."

"It won't help you. He hasn't been answering calls."

Cassandra didn't have to be a detective to pick up the discordant note there. Luckenbill wasn't just irritated at her questions; he was genuinely worried about his boss.

"Then that'll be my problem, won't it?"

In the end he gave her the number, as she'd known he would—if only because he had no good reason not to. He'd almost certainly gotten the same request from other investigators, police and insurance both.

They, on the other hand, were limited by minor impediments like "laws" and "warrants" and the delay of "due process."

As the Audi bumped and rattled over the dirt road, Cassandra shut down her own cell phone and pulled a second one—a cheap burner, taken from a sizable lot purchased in cash by CSC—from the glove compartment. She punched in a number she'd memorized earlier in the day, then set the phone on speaker and laid it down in the center console.

"Felix? Hey, it's Cassandra Reyes. Yeah, I know, been a while. Fine, thanks. So, listen, I'm going to need you to pull a string or three for me . . ."

Gilad lurked in the shade of the forest, watching the church through cheap binoculars, and berated himself for what was proving to be a severe miscalculation.

Following his escape from the Melidarishe, he'd retrieved the satchel he'd hidden in the underbrush prior to the abortive infiltration, then skulked through the trees for miles. Only then, using cash taken from those emergency supplies—which also included clothes, a couple of blades, and a few other necessities of life—had he ensconced himself in yet another cheap, no-questions-asked motel.

He'd given himself two full days in that run-down rathole, time to fully heal and recover from almost a week of . . . Well, he wouldn't call it hell. He *knew* hell, and nothing Nergal's faithful had done to him came close. But bad enough.

It was a risk, giving the enemy that long to fortify against his return, but it was worth it. For the first time since he lost himself to the flawed invocation of the Thief of Yesterdays rite, to the identity of Jack Eren, he was truly himself. His mind in order, his body healed and hale.

Let the Melidarishe prepare as they liked. Against Gilad Anni-Padda at his peak, it would make no difference.

Except he'd discovered, when he once more crept up on the church outside Cedar City, that they hadn't "prepared."

They'd *departed*.

From the outside, the stone-and-brick structure appeared no different, but he'd sensed its emptiness in the flavor of its silence, in a hundred different unconscious cues.

In the faintest whiff of charred wood and melted plastic and lightly roasted meats that hung in the air even a hundred yards distant.

The exterior may have remained intact, almost pristine, but within . . .

The Melidarishe had fled, swiftly but all too efficiently. Every computer, every phone, and every file had been dumped into heaps in several of the rooms, doused in lighter fluid, and ignited. The walls, the carpets, and the furniture had been treated the same, scorched by what Gilad recognized as the kiss of makeshift flamethrowers. They hadn't even bothered to collect the bodies he'd left behind in his escape, electing instead to bathe them in a brief torrent of flame as well.

With mounting frustration he'd scoured every chamber, every hall, every closet, and found nothing to offer the slightest insight into where they'd gone, or any further details of Namenzida's plan. All he *had* found were a few booby traps he'd easily disarmed, crude IEDs Nergal's followers had left behind for him.

It was the one possibility he'd genuinely failed to consider. This had been the sanctum of the Melidarishe, their altar and their home, for *years*. When he slipped from their grasp the first time, two years prior, they'd had no reason to suspect that he'd lost himself, that he wouldn't be launching a counterattack at any moment, yet they'd stayed put. So far as he knew, from his conversations with Halba and the taunts of Namenzida, they'd never given so much as a thought to leaving back then.

So why now? What had changed?

And what the hell was he going to do about it?

Another day had passed in contemplation and observation. Gilad planted himself in the woods, keeping careful watch over the church. One of the faithful might yet show up; somebody might have to retrieve something they'd forgotten, or one of the Melidarishe who wasn't here at the time might have missed the message that they'd abandoned the place. It was, he knew, unlikely—but until he came up with something better, it would have to do.

With hours of nothing to do but watch and think, he found

himself with a theory. One thing *was* different between this escape, this period of captivity, and the last.

He'd seen Namenzida's face.

It seemed a small detail, but he couldn't think of any other. And if that was indeed the reason for the Melidarishe to abandon their home, if a single glimpse of him was enough to make Namenzida panic, then he had to be someone who thought of himself as recognizable. Famous, or at least a public figure.

Unfortunate, then, that whoever he was, however well-known he might think himself, Gilad had never seen him before.

Evening fell. Set back from the lights of the highway, the church grew dark, the forest darker still. Gilad felt his fist clenching of its own accord, and he wanted to scream his fury to the heavens. If he'd taken all this time, put himself through all this suffering, only to wind up losing track of the foe entirely, he—

From one of the sporadic clumps of traffic on the nearby road, a single car pulled off onto the shoulder, dousing its lights. It was nearer to Gilad's own hiding spot than it was to the church, which meant either someone knew precisely where he was—all but impossible—or someone had the same thought he had.

The vehicle sat for long moments, the occupant hidden in darkness, probably watching the church just as Gilad had been. Eventually a figure exited, features and details curtained off by the night, and advanced. Its approach to the building was slow, careful. Keeping to cover or concealment, methodically checking corners and blind spots.

Trained.

Probably not one of the Melidarishe, based on behavior, but Gilad wasn't prepared to rely on "probably"—nor to assume this newcomer wasn't hostile even if they weren't one of Namenzida's minions.

Silent as snow falling on running water, he followed.

Creeping at first, then at a light-footed jog to close the distance once the figure had vanished through the front doorway. Flashlight in one hand, though not turned on, hunting knife in the other, he stepped over the threshold . . .

"Hands!"

She stood against the wall to the left of the doorway, face partly concealed by a pair of night vision goggles. Her SIG Sauer P226 pistol, held in a perfect two-handed stance, didn't waver.

Gilad knew he'd made no sound on his approach to alert her. She must have been covering the door just in case anyone had spotted her and followed her in. Smart.

Equally smart, her chosen position gave her the drop on anyone coming in after her, forcing them to turn before they could fire on her. It would have been an almost insurmountable advantage against almost any opponent.

Gilad was not any opponent.

He began to raise his arms as though complying with her shouted command—then, with a flick of the wrist, sent his flashlight speeding through the space between them like a spear. The impact wasn't hard enough to deal real damage, but it knocked her goggles aside, yanking her head around and blinding her for a fraction of a second.

In that time he closed the distance, knocking her pistol away with one hand, placing the flat of his blade against her neck with the other.

Then, feeling he'd made his point clearly enough, Gilad stepped back, crouching to once more collect the flashlight and thumbing it on.

He saw clearly now that the woman had come prepared. Dressed in black turtleneck and jeans, she also wore a small backpack, and a Ka-Bar knife at her waist.

Slowly she reached up and removed the goggles, revealing

sharp features and a vaguely shocked expression that slowly turned into a nervous grin.

"I'd . . . forgotten how fast you are. And I'm sorry. I hadn't realized it was you coming in."

"I . . . Have we met?" For a moment, Gilad felt as if it were two weeks ago, as if his brain were still scrambled. Without mystical interference, he never forgot—*could* not forget—anyone he'd ever met. He didn't know this woman, yet she seemed familiar.

"Briefly," she replied. "You saved my life."

"At the risk of sounding boastful, you've no idea how little that narrows it down."

"Twenty years ago. Just outside Nasiriyah."

Just as the answer dawned on him, she spoke again and confirmed it.

"I was, ah, presenting a little differently." Slowly she pulled back the sleeve on her left arm, revealing an old burn scar that even multiple surgeries had never been able to remove.

Now Gilad nodded. "Private Beltran."

She seemed surprised he remembered. "It's Reyes, now. Cassandra Reyes."

"All right, Cassandra Reyes. What's your connection with the Melidarishe?"

"The what?" The bewilderment in her expression convinced him, more than anything she might have said, that her response was genuine.

Still, he pushed. "The Cult of Nergal. Or one of them, anyway."

"I don't have the foggiest idea what . . . Nergal? The Sumerian god, *that* Nergal?"

"Well, he was just chieftain to a band of bloodthirsty and savage marauders when *I* knew him. Bunch of fools declared him a god afterward, and it stuck."

Gilad swore he could practically *hear* her jaw fall slack.

"So if you're not looking for them," he continued, though he felt he already knew, "why *are* you here?"

"I was looking for you."

Yeah, that's what I thought.

Again he knelt briefly, collecting her SIG Sauer and sticking it in the back of his belt for the time being. Cassandra seemed ready to protest, then thought better of it.

"Why?" Gilad asked. "And how?"

"I saw your picture in a news story about the ranch. Though, uh, I'm going to take a wild guess that Jack Eren isn't your real name?"

"You wildly guess correctly."

"That was enough to get me to your people. I was hoping to trace you through your cell phone, but . . ."

Gilad scowled. "I took the battery out, except to check in with Henry or look up information online. I didn't want anyone doing what you tried to do. I normally don't carry one at all; that was 'Jack's.'"

"Okay. But I'm an investigator. I wasn't about to let that stop me. I figured, a dozen people attacking you? That had to involve some coordination. I had someone check for any other signals pinging off the local tower around the time of the attack. You lived out in the middle of nowhere, so I figured anyone else making a call out there in the middle of the night was probably involved. Couldn't identify them—burner phones on both ends—but I was able to track the phone. It's here, or at least it was for a good while before it went dead."

"More than dead," Gilad muttered. "Now it's *literally* a burner."

"What?"

"Nothing." Then, "What you did can't possibly be legal."

Cassandra shrugged. "Nope. But my profession's made me a lot of contacts. Had to call in more than a few favors and cough up enough cash to cover more than three months of my mortgage and property taxes, but . . . here we are."

"Yes, here we are. Why?"

She met his gaze, something most people were, consciously or not, far too afraid to do. "Because twenty years isn't *nearly* long enough for me to forget the seventy thousand questions I've had since that day. I never thought I'd have the opportunity to find you, and I wasn't about to let it slip by."

Gilad had no patience for this. He had no *time* for this. And yet . . .

He also had no idea how to find the Melidarishe. No notion of where to go from here.

If fortune or fate or the gods had provided them, maybe a trained investigator and her contacts were exactly what he required.

"Perhaps," he told her, "we can provide some answers for each other."

EIGHTEEN

Gilad would very literally die before he would admit this to anyone, let alone to his brothers, but he is afraid.

Not of death, no. He has known almost since he could walk, since before he even had the words to articulate it, that his love of battle must someday lead him to his end.

Nor is he scared of failure. He hopes and prays and works toward success for his own glory and for the good of his people, but this is a task bestowed upon the three sons of Anni-Padda by a bent and scheming king whom none of them love. Shameful as it would be, disappointing his sovereign is far from the worst fate Gilad can envision.

Rather, it is the utter strangeness of their journey, and even more so of their destination, that inspires the youngest traveler's fear—for if he cannot even *understand* the world around him, how can he know if his skills and prowess will be enough to protect his brothers from its dangers?

Almost two months have passed since the king summoned Ivar, Aram, and Gilad to his side. Since he led them deep into the chambers beneath his stone palace and showed them a most peculiar corpse: a creature with the torso of a man but a scorpion-like lower body, made as much of unknown metals and interlocking cogs as of flesh.

A creature that, before it finally perished under the blades of the king's torturers, had revealed to them its home, and how to reach it.

Utnapishtim, a mythic land of which priests and storytellers sometimes speak. A separate world, called also the Garden of the Sun; the Faraway. A land that purportedly holds the secrets of life, the cure to plague and famine and all the ills that beset the mortal realm.

It was a quest none of the Anni-Padda brothers could possibly have declined, though each had motives more personal and more self-centered than the sake of Ur and its citizens.

Long and deadly the journey has proved. Amid the thick boughs of the Cedar Forest, brave Gilad led his siblings to victory against hordes of inhuman bandits, shaggy beasts that mimicked the shape of men.

In the burning desert of Humbaba, the mighty and charming Aram sufficiently entertained the nomads so that they did not attempt to slaughter the brothers in tribute to their anthropophagous gods.

And through the ever-dark caverns and vales of the Mountain of Mashu, where they had to travel over a dozen leagues without the slightest hint of sun, ingenious Ivar constructed lanterns that glowed, however faintly, not with open flame but with every movement and every pace of him who wore it.

Now, finally, they have passed through a strange cerulean glow, the final step in the man-scorpion's directions, to find themselves in a land of impossible beauty, on the banks of a breathtaking lake.

The green of the leaves and the crimson of the berries, the

glimmer of the waters, are bright and sharp, almost painful to the eye. And indeed, the slightest touch proves painful to the skin as well, for the leaves are thinnest razor-edged jade; the berries carnelian; the water quicksilver.

It appears an artist's rendering, a precious simulacrum of a world. Yet the dirt beneath their feet is proper soil, the tall grasses genuine foliage. A place, then, of nature and artifice both, with only the haziest of lines separating one from the other.

Gilad is the first to observe, as they make their way through this alien landscape, that "Garden of the Sun" is an ironic misnomer at best for Utnapishtim, for whatever the burning ember above them may be, it is no sun at all. The light is wrong—too stark, too white. Of greater import still, after the brothers have walked and camped and walked some more, for many hours, it has moved not one single degree across the sky.

With a rustling in the tall grass and a fearsome cry, the trio discovers the Faraway has its own hazards to throw at them. A bizarre creature nearly the height of a man, boasting the feathers and talons and posture of a raptor but the teeth and limbs of a monstrous lizard, seeks to make one of them its next meal. It is Aram, with his mythic strength, who crushes the life from the thing, and Gilad who suggests they build a fire and not waste its meat. Invigorated after their meal, they press on, no longer entirely certain of their next steps now that they have passed beyond the limits of their instructions.

As if in answer to their unspoken need, the peak of a high ziggurat appears between hills on the horizon. The stones of which it is built, the countless steps and sweeping arches, reflect a dull yellow, almost gold, against the white and cloudless sky. Discounting a few decorative flourishes in the stonework around the archways, it appears identical in construction to the greatest architectural works of Ur.

Why the structures in this mystical realm should so closely resemble those of their homeland becomes but another mystery stacked on the edifice of questions the three brothers dare not even give voice.

A long climb brings them to the archways and, through them, into a massive stone chamber, draped in vines. At its center stands . . .

Something.

It seems a monolith of some smooth substance not quite stone or metal, perhaps a quarter again the height of a tall man. Perfectly etched lines draw simple patterns across the base. Near the top it holds a crystalline sphere, swirling with patterns of blue and white.

Although Gilad may not have the faintest notion of what it is, what it does, he can sense the sheer power within. Energy. Magic.

Fate.

"No mortal man has gone this way before."

The brothers spin, startled, at the sound of the voice. The speaker is one of five figures, cloaked and hooded in robes of white and mantles of red.

The chamber has no niches to provide concealment, no pillars to hide behind. No place these strangers could have come from.

Yet they are here.

Gilad tightens his grip on his axe, but it is Ivar who responds. "What is this place?"

"It is where you are."

"And who are you?"

"To whom you speak."

Already Gilad's confusion turns to fury at the unhelpful nonanswers. "We did not come here looking for riddles!"

"Can one ever truly expect what he will find in a place he has never been?"

He has more to say, but Gilad scarcely hears it, struggling to keep his irritation in check. For all his temper and his love of battle, he has rarely shed blood for minor slights, but right now it is all he can do to keep his axe hand still.

Whether because he senses the need to intervene or out of his own impatience with these robed figures, Aram interjects. "Sages, we have not had a proper drink since we entered the gate at the Mountain of Mashu. Have you any water to spare?"

"We do not. Neither we Keepers of the Timeless Word nor any of the lost creatures who have been found here require food or drink. Rather, it is our Boon"—here, despite the hood concealing half his features, the man's attention clearly flits toward the peculiar monolith—"which sustains all living things in the Faraway."

"You need not fear thirst, then?" Ivar demands.

"No."

"Nor starvation?"

"Never."

"What of death itself?"

"Where there is no time, there can be no ending."

It is everything the brothers sought, everything they traveled so far to find. What surprise, then, that they immediately elect to claim the device, the monolith, for the people of Ur?

Bending at an angle, mighty Aram takes the great slab upon his back. Had it been true stone, normal stone, even he might have found it an impossible burden; as it is, he bows beneath its weight but does not yield. At a slow but steady pace, he carries it toward the arches and the steps leading down, his brothers falling in behind.

The robed strangers, the so-called Keepers of the Timeless Word, follow as well, at least so far as the top of the steps. Though they continue speaking, each in turn, they make no effort to stop this theft.

"When the gods created man they allotted to him death," the first intones, "but life they retained in their own keeping."

Ivar pauses briefly to argue with them, to declare the Anni-Paddas' right to claim this cure for their people's ills, but Gilad can scarce be bothered to listen. His gaze flits across the horizon, then down the steps, watching for any threat. Surely this prize cannot simply be theirs for the taking without challenge!

Indeed, it is not, though said challenge presents itself only once the trio has reached the base of the ziggurat. They emerge from the surrounding trees of mineral and jade: more of the half-metal man-scorpions, riding astride hunched and feathered lizards many times larger than the one Aram killed.

"Go," Gilad orders the middle brother. "We will catch up once we've eliminated any pursuit." And then, Gilad and Ivar shout in conjunction when Aram tries to argue, "*Go!*"

A few arrows from Ivar's bow, a fearsome shout and a strike with Gilad's axe, and the great beasts give chase, ignoring the heavily burdened Aram creeping away. Either the arachnid-like riders fail to recognize the diversion for what it is, or whatever control they exercise over their mounts cannot overcome the beasts' anger at the sting of their wounds.

Gilad and Ivar dash through the tall grasses and into the forest, Gilad suggesting tactics and choke points as they run. Yet it is clever Ivar who takes note of the strange nature of the trees around them.

Like the jade leaves and carnelian berries, the towering foliage here is nothing like wood, but rather a reflective, glittering crystal. He reaches for the tools he carries with his arrows, wondering if he can create a sound at the proper pitch and volume to shatter them, to rain razor-edged shards down upon those who follow.

Yet even if his idea is feasible—and his younger brother can hardly say if it is—he'll need time.

Without hesitation or reluctance but only the predatory grin of battle lust, Gilad turns and hurls himself at the oncoming foe . . .

"That's the last I remember of our journey to Utnapishtim," Gilad said, turned so he could halfway lean against the cool glass of the window. "They tell me I bought Ivar the time he needed to rig up . . . something."

"But you . . ." The disbelief in Cassandra's voice seemed directed not at his tale, outlandish as it was, but at her own willingness to accept it. "But you died."

"Yes. For the first time."

They sat ensconced in Cassandra's rented Audi, allowing them to find a bit more comfort than the church's ravaged interior while still keeping watch over the building. At this point, Gilad was all but certain nobody was coming back, but he wasn't *quite* ready to give up on the idea.

In the back seat was an open satchel, containing a couple of telephoto-lensed cameras and a parabolic mic, and beside it a paper bag full of jerky and bottled water. She'd been prepared for a prolonged stakeout herself until she'd realized the church lay abandoned.

"So how . . . ?" She seemed to grope even for the words of the question.

"Ivar . . . didn't take my loss well." Gilad's vision went slightly unfocused as he called further upon old and unpleasant memories. "He declared that if our prize, this 'Boon,' really did contain the cure to all humanity's ills, that must include death itself. He determined to find a way to use it to bring me back."

"I guess it worked."

Gilad chuckled. "My brother is brilliant, but some things even he can't entirely grasp." He saw Cassandra's confusion at his use of the present tense but didn't stop to explain. "He *thought* he'd figured it out, but . . . we still don't know for sure how the damn thing was meant to function in the Faraway. Whether it was entirely safe, or whether the Keepers of the Timeless Word had some means of mitigating or controlling its effects. Maybe they used it to cull Utnapishtim's population. I mean, no realm, however plentiful, can support an ever-expanding population if none of them die . . ."

He allowed himself a moment to drift in his memories. "When Ivar activated the Boon," he finally continued, "it poured a torrent of energy—of life—into him. Into Aram, who stood at his side. And into me. And it took that life from every other living thing in Ur, and for miles around. A literal ripple of instant and inescapable death."

Cassandra's gasp was almost more of a choke.

"It was more than a generation before crops and livestock would grow there again, before anyone repopulated Ur. For those years, it was a graveyard, known far and wide as a cursed land. Once it was reoccupied, tales of its prior extinction were forbidden to be told, let alone written down, for fear of attracting the attention of whatever caused it. But for my brothers, the Boon granted immortality."

"And for you, obviously."

"In part, perhaps. I had been . . . anointed by a holy woman a couple of years before. Chosen by the first Geomancer. Whether I would have been immortal even without the Boon, or whether her power and the Boon somehow interacted and made me different, or whether her touch made me fated to find the Boon, or . . . I don't know. I know only that I didn't return that first time until the Boon was activated, but that my eternal nature differs from theirs. That it has an innate purpose theirs lack."

Silence. An almost unblinking stare. Until, "Are you telling me that not only did the three of you all *happen* to have gained immortality, but it didn't even all come from the same *source*?"

Again Gilad chuckled. "When you put it *that* way, it almost sounds improbable."

"Psht. Yeah, almost."

"You were the one who wanted answers, Cassandra."

"Mm." She leaned back, though she continued absently tapping a finger on the wheel. "I shouldn't believe a word of this," she said. "But I guess once you've been rescued from some invisible Persian demon, a lot of things get easier to accept."

"It wasn't Persian. Not technically a demon either, though I suppose it's as good a description as any without getting into the underlying—"

"Not Persian?"

"No."

"Sumerian? Babylonian?"

"Caral."

"I don't think I've heard of—"

"They were a pre-Nazca civilization," he explained.

"Nazca! As in the Nazca Lines?" Then, at his nod, "The thing that almost killed me in southern Iraq was from *Peru*?"

"Well, the Andes. Current national borders don't quite—"

"What the *fuck*!"

"I just finished telling you a tale of travel through an eldritch portal to a realm outside our own," Gilad said with a faint smile. "The world of the mystical—what you'd call the supernatural—is more complex than your maps. Or concepts like distance, for that matter. Someone called for beings to guard those tablets, or whatever other artifacts might be found there. These were what answered."

"But this . . . this cult, the Mal . . ."

"Melidarishe." He'd explained to her the most recent chapter of his story, or at least its broad strokes, before they'd moved from church to car.

"Right. The Melidarishe got those tablets anyway."

"Unfortunately."

"Is that why you were in Nasiriyah that day?"

"It is. A community of scholars and keepers of pre-Persian lore live in the region. They're not formal enough to be called an order; it's really just a line of tradition, a smattering of experts among the populace. I've dealt with a few of them in the past. They learned one of the cults of Nergal—we didn't know they called themselves Melidarishe at the time—were seeking something nearby, and they called for me. I hoped to arrive in time to help them, but . . ." For an instant his expression turned flinty.

"The old men." Cassandra looked down at her hands. "I'm really sorry. We were told—"

"I know." He offered a dismissive wave and his scowl relaxed. "Not your fault. I just wish I'd known for certain what they were after, or why. Perhaps I could've done more than just slow them down by a few years."

"Is that what you do with your immortality? Oppose some cultists who think they're Indiana Jones villains?"

"Cults of Nergal. Ancient conspiracies. Necromancers and demonologists. Literal monsters. Anyone who threatens the Earth or the Geomancers who guide it, and any other evils I happen to meet along the way. You know, the usual."

"Why?"

"Because I was chosen to do it. And because nobody else can."

"It . . . doesn't sound like much of a life."

"I have time for what I need. Even a few families, over the centuries." *But none of them were immortal.* He didn't say it, but he felt she heard it all the same.

He could have told her the rest. That he still saw them, visited with them, on the occasions he died. That each time it was harder to leave them, to return to the mortal world and his everlasting duty—let alone to face the literal army of demons he had to battle in order to make the journey back.

As it was, he'd already been far more open with Cassandra than was his wont. Other than a few specific details, he didn't consider his life story much of a secret, but neither did he particularly revel in telling the tale.

Had he been forced to say, he'd have claimed that telling her now was simply because he intended to ask for her help, her skills. Clearly, she felt she owed him and would probably agree to assist even if he hadn't opened up, but better an ally of choice than of obligation.

And it was far more practical to save that debt until a day when he might need a favor she'd be more hesitant to provide.

While all that was true, however, it was not his only motivation. As confident as he was that he'd focused through the disorientation of his returning memories, talking about his past was a way of testing himself. Of being certain it all made sense even when it wasn't just locked in his head.

Now he *knew*.

But his wife, his children, those all-too-fleeting hours or days of peace between death and resurrection . . . Those he would keep all his own.

Cassandra obviously read his reticence to pursue the topic, even if she couldn't know why, and changed the subject. "So what do the Melidarishe want? You said they asked about the, uh, the Faraway?"

"And the Keepers of the Timeless Word. And the Boon. But I can't say why. I gave them no answers, so they never drilled down to more specific questions."

"Okay, but they can't be the first ones to ever wonder . . ."

"No, but there are many possibilities, none of them good. They might hope to recreate the curative powers of the Boon, though Nergal's teachings would celebrate plagues more than cures. They could be hoping for a way to kill me for good. They might be looking for the secrets of immortality; it's happened before."

"Yeah, I'll bet," Cassandra muttered.

"Don't be envious. It's not fun." Gilad pondered, though he'd given this substantial thought already and didn't expect to come up with anything new tonight. "There might be something they want in Utnapishtim—or even just access to the portals themselves."

"Portals? Plural?"

"Mm. The path my brothers and I took through the gate in the Mountain of Mashu is only one of many throughout the world. Some are permanent, some only open at certain times. All of them lead not only to Utnapishtim but to the same general region of Utnapishtim. They're closer together on that side than on this. So, a small force of raiders with the right knowledge of when and where to find the portals . . ."

". . . could potentially strike even defended targets or move between combat arenas instantly. Yeah, that'd be a pretty big deal."

"So whatever they're doing, I have to find out what it is and stop it."

"Which means finding them."

Gilad nodded.

"Which you have no idea how to do."

Another nod.

"It's almost like you need a detective."

"Almost, yes."

"Your hotel room or mine?" Cassandra's lip quirked. "Don't read into that. You haven't even bought me flowers."

"Are you particularly fond of cockroaches and mildewed bath tile?" he asked.

"I've been in the army *and* college, so I've had my fill of both, thanks."

"Yours, then."

Cassandra started the ignition.

NINETEEN

On the eighteenth hole of the Independence Hills Golf Course, the grass shone almost emerald, a gentle breeze took the edge off the sun in the clear sky, and the gabbing and chortling of wealthy men politely quieted as Congressman Raymond Pfinster lined up his stroke.

Carefully . . . carefully . . .

Iron hit ball with what any halfway-skilled player would recognize as way too much of a *thwack* when its position on the green, really not that far from the hole, required more of a *tap*.

When the ball sailed over the hole and rolled to a stop nearly as far on the opposite side as it had been on this one, Pfinster couldn't muster up the slightest bit of surprise to go with his muttered "Well, shit."

"Come on, Ray." Bill Maguire, CEO of Ewing Air, thumped the congressman on the shoulder. "The hell were you thinking?"

"Oh, I don't know, Bill. Maybe that your next campaign contribution's going to be a whole lot smaller if I beat you in front of everyone."

Maguire leaned in and said in a stage whisper, "But you've got to at least *look* like you're trying!"

Pfinster and the rest of the assembly all offered tribute of an appropriately polite level, enough of a chuckle to indicate appreciation, not so much as to feel like sucking up.

It was *all* sucking up, of course, politician to lobbyist to CEO and back to politician, everyone present to everyone else. But there were still formalities to be observed.

As it happened, neither Pfinster nor Maguire won the round or the game, thanks to pharmaceutical lobbyist Chuck Gelder coming in two under par on the final hole. Congratulations and compliments were duly exchanged, and the small flock of pasty flesh and overpriced clothes drifted toward the clubhouse. Their course took them around a decorative fountain that burbled in their wake, across the circular drive, and finally through glass doors into an excessively air-conditioned lobby.

There, in one of the many overstuffed chairs scattered about for members and their guests, waited a young man with a drink in his hand and a disturbingly intense gleam in his eyes.

For all his years of practiced deceit, Pfinster's jaw twitched.

He spent a couple minutes more exchanging empty pleasantries and glad-handing his fellow golfers, then strode across the hall and into one of the establishment's private meeting rooms. Windowless, its walls adorned with inoffensive landscapes, it smelled of citrusy cleanser and the fumes of old cigars and cigarettes whose holders gave not the slightest care for the relevant nonsmoking statutes.

When the young man entered a moment later, carefully shutting the door behind him, the congressman was red and practically shaking with rage.

"Namenzida." The newcomer greeted him with a shallow bow.

"You don't ever approach me in public, damn you!"

Pfinster—Namenzida—snarled in a spray of angry spittle. "Not *ever*!"

"You haven't responded to calls or messages in days," Aradlugal said. "Not since you had us abandon our home."

Unnecessarily. Foolishly. Cowardly. He didn't use the words, not this time. He'd been pretty free with them when Namenzida first gave the order, though.

The priest still hadn't decided whether to forgive that or not.

"Is this your first week with us, Aradlugal? Have Anni-Padda's memories scrambled your own? I make contact when *I* choose, and you will keep your thoughts on my silence, and your curiosity about my activities, to yourself! As always!"

"With my deepest respect, Namenzida, I'm not sure that works anymore."

Slowly, deliberately, the older cultist advanced, knuckles brushing against the edge of the conference table, until they stood less than an arm's length apart. His fury spread, transforming from fire into ice.

Yet beneath it, perhaps hidden even from himself, shone the first glimmer of fear.

"And what, pray tell, do you *think* has changed?" he hissed through bared teeth.

"Again with respect . . . you have."

Namenzida nearly choked on the insolence. Yes, Aradlugal had been a bit off since the ritual two years ago. Angrier, fiercer, a step removed from the slavishly devoted disciple he'd been prior. In the past few weeks, however, since Anni-Padda had resurfaced on that blasted ranch and the Melidarishe had moved once more against him, the young cultist's attitude had grown harsher still. More fanatical, more wrathful.

More defiant. *I should have taken more drastic steps before now.*

Aradlugal continued speaking even as the priest's mind

raced. "You panicked, Namenzida. Anni-Padda saw you unmasked, as if that makes any difference, and you panicked. You ordered us to run, not for the sake of the congregation but your own, and then you left us without direction."

"How *dare*—"

"I don't think it's unreasonable for us to insist on knowing what comes next."

In his life as a politician, as Raymond Pfinster, he was accustomed to disrespect, to argument. As Namenzida, priest of Nergal, the questioning and doubt left him stunned. Mostly to provide himself more time to think, he demanded, "Just what is it *you* believe we should be doing, Aradlugal?" He put an almost spitting emphasis on the name, a reminder of who the younger man was. *Servant of the King.*

"We should have lain in wait for him. He would have come after us, one way or another."

"You have no idea who Anni-Padda is! No idea how stupidly lucky we were to capture him the first time! Weakened and injured, he still escaped us twice! You've never faced him at his peak!"

"*I* don't know who he is? How many of his memories do *you* have boiling in your head?" Aradlugal turned, paced to the far wall and back. "We could have taken him. We'd have lost a lot of people and probably had to kill him, but he'd have come back eventually."

"Yes, *eventually*. But after how long?"

"Sooner than we'll have him now!"

As swiftly as Aradlugal's rage had erupted, Namenzida watched it fade. "But that's done," the younger man continued. "What we should be doing now is preparing the Thief of Yesterdays for *me*. Or for Halba."

It was, to say the least, an unexpected turn.

"I'm sorry, what?" Namenzida asked.

Aradlugal gestured toward the chairs at the conference table, but the priest ignored the suggestion.

"Anni-Padda has perfect recall," Aradlugal said. "Perfect mastery of his own memories. Including the ability to shunt them aside, to bury them, and to draw them out again. My mind . . ." He scowled around words that apparently tasted bitter. "I don't have that capacity. Halba doesn't. It's possible that she or I has the information we've been searching for, buried somewhere we can't access it. If so, we don't need Anni-Padda back at all."

"And what does Halba think of this notion?"

"Who the fuck cares what she thinks?" The rage returned, so intense Aradlugal seized the back of the nearest chair, which creaked and strained in his grip. "We can't trust her anymore," he insisted, all but prying his fingers from the wood. "Whatever notions or feelings she got from him, she's too weak to handle. They've . . . tainted her."

"You've made that accusation before, but you still haven't proved—"

"She let him go, Namenzida!"

"She says he was already gone when she reached the hall."

"Lies."

The priest shook his head. "Perhaps, but—"

"She's gotten soft. Weak. But still useful."

"You're awfully eager to condemn the woman who was your closest friend. You've been with her far longer than with us."

"I do as Nergal teaches. As he demands. Anyone who does less deserves no mercy."

Namenzida had preached that precise doctrine time and again. Coming from Aradlugal, however, it brought a faint shiver to his spine.

"Regardless," he said, "you and Halba both received only a

fraction of Anni-Padda's memories. The chances that either of you have what we need without knowing it are . . . slim."

"Still, we should—"

"And even if you did," Namenzida continued, refusing to be interrupted, "the ritual doesn't do what you suggest. It only copies memories from one to another. It won't open your subconscious mind to you, and anyone who got your own suppressed memories would find them just as inaccessible."

"We've modified it once already! And if *we* can't alter it to do what we need, I'm sure there are those who can. You've told me about the old men who kept the tablets. I doubt they were the only ones. We just have to know how to . . . 'ask.'"

"And then what?" the priest said. "If you did succeed in altering the ritual, whether to dig the knowledge from your own mind or Halba's, or to make it work on Anni-Padda better than it did last time, what would you do with it?"

"Well, that's what we're discussing, isn't it? What's this all meant to accomplish? What are we doing all this for?"

Namenzida very much wanted to tell him he would find out when they got there, that he had no right to demand knowledge his betters hadn't seen fit to provide. Just as he always had.

If Aradlugal was questioning, however, no doubt others were as well. Namenzida *had* shown weakness; he *had* panicked. He couldn't afford to lose his followers' faith and devotion, not now.

So, though it galled him to acquiesce to any such demand, to grant his minions even that much power, he decided he would best be served by answering.

"All right, Aradlugal, though I'm surprised you haven't already guessed."

His disciple waited, expression turning eager. He was, briefly, once again the zealous young believer, hanging on his priest's every word.

As he should be.

"I seek nothing less than to recreate Gilad Anni-Padda's immortality!" His proclamation of what was the most obvious possible answer was intense, even grandiose, as if delivering some great revelation from the heavens themselves.

Aradlugal said nothing. His face froze, as still as any mask.

Perhaps he simply hasn't processed all the implications.

"Think on it, Aradlugal! The Melidarishe would have an unshakable grasp on power throughout the so-called civilized world. Yes, we'd be literally unstoppable, able to destroy whoever we chose, but it goes so far beyond that! Every world leader, every oligarch, every CEO would come *crawling* to us! They'll dance to our strings for just the promise of what we can share. We can set whole industries, whole nations, to destroying *each other*. An endless cycle of blood and devastation, all in Nergal's name and for Nergal's glory, with the leadership of the Melidarishe at the top of it all! Forever!"

For a few more silent breaths, the younger man gazed at him, emotionless, impassive.

Then, like a striking mamba, Aradlugal knuckle-punched his high priest in the throat.

Namenzida collapsed to the carpet, slumping against the table on his way down. He clutched at his throat, struggling to suck ragged gulps of air through a swelling windpipe he had to hope was merely bruised. Panic spilled behind his face, pooling and turning his skin red.

A shadow loomed over him, and it was all he could do to flop halfway over, to see.

This isn't happening this can't *be happening . . .*

"You pathetic, *blasphemous* old coward!" Aradlugal hissed, bending low over the fallen priest. "Eternal life? You're after literal otherworldly magics for *eternal fucking life*?! And you have the balls to claim you act in the name of the God of Inflicted Death?"

A wordless wheeze was all Namenzida could manage.

"'The reason for the beginning is the end.' That sound at all familiar? *You* taught us that! You brought us to the revelation of Nergal! For what? To abandon it? Our calling is to lay civilization low, burn it to ash, and salt the earth! Not to vaguely reshape the world just so we can be on top!"

"You d-don't . . ." The syllables were gravel and sandpaper. "Don't . . . understand." Every breath was flame. "We des-destroy but . . . not *everything.* Not so mu-much we cannot . . . prosper. No-nobody . . . wants *that.* Ev-even Ner-Nergal . . . gathered riches . . . when he . . . he was a . . . mortal raider." He reached out an imploring hand.

Aradlugal slapped it away, nearly breaking his elder's wrist on the table leg.

"Nergal rose above his mortal limitations in his apotheosis! We were meant to do the same! You," he accused, "were never worthy to lead us. It's so clear now. You're selfish. Weak. You have no faith. You have no fealty."

"C-can't . . . destroy . . . *everything* . . ."

"And you have no imagination or will. You could never do what needs to be done."

Aradlugal leaned closer still until his breath was a hot gust on Namenzida's ear. "I should have done this years ago."

He stood. He lifted the nearest chair, holding a leg squarely over his *former* priest's face.

Namenzida's dying terror couldn't even find voice in a final scream.

TWENTY

Cassandra's suite at the downtown Radisson was indeed far nicer than Gilad's fleabag motel room, and not merely because it lacked mildew and roaches. The pullout sofa was cozier than many beds he'd known, the room service and delivery options were plentiful, and this was the first time he'd had a really *good* shower in weeks.

Gilad had never particularly prioritized comfort. Growing up in a time when the closest thing to a mattress was a scattering of reeds with an animal pelt thrown over it, he could sleep on more or less anything. Still, he couldn't deny that the past few days here had been more pleasant than most.

He'd have traded it all in a heartbeat, though, would have gladly agreed to sleep on a bed of needles and fire ants, if he just had something to *do*.

After they moved to her suite, Cassandra had set about grilling him with all manner of questions, trying to draw out any and every detail that might aid her in her hunt. Unfortunately, while Gilad could, of course, recall every sight, every experience, every moment, precious little of it offered any clue.

Namenzida's face did him no good, at least not yet. Not without some notion who he might be, where to look for him. He'd made a detailed sketch for Cassandra's reference, but even if such a drawing would prove sufficient for most modern facial-recognition systems—and it wouldn't—those were beyond what even his present partner could access from her laptop.

Cassandra had spent hours digging into the ownership of the church that had been the Melidarishe sanctum, but after multiple layers her search had dead-ended at an on-paper-only shell company with the creative and informative name of Diversified Services Inc. So far as she—and a few less-than-legal contacts she tried calling on—could tell, it kept its records only in hard copy. No online search and no hacker would produce anything more.

Eventually, tricky as it would be, they'd elected to make use of the only real names they had.

Jada. Even with a detailed description of the young woman, it was far too common a name to search on its own. But Gilad had more.

She'd called Aradlugal "Benjamin," or at least she'd started to. A more common name even than Jada, but just maybe the two of them together might produce something.

"Their accents," Gilad had told Cassandra, "suggest north-eastern Midwest. Probably Ohio."

"I'm not even going to pretend to be surprised you can identify that sort of thing."

"What, you can't?" He could tell she didn't know whether he was kidding, and he wasn't about to clarify.

"Check criminal records," he'd suggested. "Including juvenile, if any of your connections can get into them." Even if they hadn't ever been officially connected with whatever "unforgivable" act had set Jada and Benjamin on their path to becoming

Halba and Aradlugal, Gilad had no doubt they'd gotten into trouble on plenty of other occasions. Probably before, and most certainly afterward. One didn't go from a lone atrocity to a loyal foot soldier of Nergal in a single step.

Then he'd had little to do but wait while Cassandra did all the work, and it was driving him as close to madness as his inhumanly resilient mind could ever get.

He knew Cassandra was frustrated, too. Normally she'd have had assistants helping with the basic searches, access to additional databases, connections available to Coswell Security Consultants that she couldn't call on personally. But knowing that didn't help him. No way she was *as* frustrated; at least she was doing something.

Gilad went out, picked up a cheap used laptop and a burner phone with cash, and tried to contribute to the search. Of his many skills and talents, however, deep-dive computer searches weren't among them, and he quickly gave up. Nothing he could pull off Google or DuckDuckGo would provide any leads that Cassandra's legal and journalistic reach couldn't.

He spent hours in front of the television, distracting himself with various antiquing shows, testing his own knowledge and instincts by trying to figure out which items were genuinely old and which were worthless. (He was right more than 95 percent of the time and was fairly certain even the hosts were wrong at least twice.)

He briefly called Henry, just making sure the ranch and, more importantly, the ranch hands were okay. Gilad might not have been Jack Eren, but the bonds he'd developed during that period were real enough. Even if Henry ended that conversation angry that "Jack" wouldn't tell him much of anything, Gilad was happy he'd checked in.

He even went out late one night, wandering the darkened

downtown streets and back alleys until someone made the mistake of trying to mug him. Gilad came back with blood on his fists but not really any more satisfaction in his heart.

Then, *finally*, on the following afternoon, as he was certain this whole thing had been an utter waste and he was feeling every week of his five-thousand-plus years . . .

"I've got them," Cassandra announced, throwing open the door between rooms. She wore a loose T-shirt and sweatpants, and her hair was slightly flattened on one side, but her grin was gratified, even smug, despite her obvious fatigue.

Gilad instantly straightened on the sofa. She turned the laptop so he could see the screen.

The mug shots were unmistakable. The hairstyles were a half decade or more out of date, and Halba's face still clung to the last vestiges of a childhood roundness, but otherwise they'd changed little between their late teens and today.

"Definitely them," Gilad confirmed.

Cassandra turned the laptop back around. "Jada Lowry," she read aloud, "and Benjamin Boyd. Multiple arrests for both, though this is the only time they were pinched together."

"Pinched? Really?"

"I read a lot of mystery novels. Shut up." Then, going back to the screen, "Between the pair of them, we've got assault, larceny, B and E, vandalism . . . even an attempted-murder charge that didn't stick. Charmers, these two. Then, after about five years ago, nothing."

"Probably when they joined the cult," Gilad mused. "They'd have had more focus to their violence. Allies. Connections. Easier not to get caught."

"Right, but the problem is, it's not just the arrests. There's *nothing* in their names. No rent, no bills. And even the last few times they were arrested they had no known address."

"Damn. So we're not any closer to finding them, then."

Cassandra tapped a nail on the laptop. "It's not impossible. May take some time."

Gilad must have made an expression he hadn't meant to. "I take it you're in a hurry," she said.

"I don't know what they're up to. I don't know what memories Halba and Aradlugal have of mine, consciously or otherwise, or what additional sorceries they might use to access them. The sooner I can stop the Melidarishe from doing whatever it is they're doing, the better."

"Gilad . . ." She stopped, started to say more, stopped again, then put the laptop down on the desk and half sat beside it. "When you talk about 'stopping' them, you mean . . ."

The unspoken question hung between them.

"I don't exactly have the infrastructure to take prisoners," he told her. "You were a soldier. You understand war. That's what this is. What it's always been."

"I get it. I do. I just . . . I'd thought I was done with all that when I mustered out."

Gilad certainly sympathized—for all his love of battle, it was a wish he sometimes shared, especially in those moments with his wife and children—so it took him a moment to recognize the implication in Cassandra's words.

"You *are* done with it!" he said then. "This isn't your fight. I'll accept any help you can offer in finding them, and I'm grateful for it, but that's the end of your involvement with—"

"Like hell! I didn't track you down looking to get involved in something like this—fuck, I'd never even *imagined* anything like this!—but no chance I'm walking away. And don't," she continued as he opened his mouth to retort, "try to pull any 'I work on my own' or 'I don't need your help' bullshit! What if they capture you again? You think you can escape a third time?"

"Yes, I do!"

"*Before* they use their . . . their magic to get what they want from you? You think they haven't learned from their failures?"

Unable to refute that, Gilad settled for a grim scowl. "I won't let them take me again."

"And of course you're sure you can manage that. You know for a fact there's no chance they'll just get sick of it all and have an entire squad gun you down so they can lock up your corpse and wait for you to pop back?"

Again he couldn't answer. They hadn't been willing to take that step so far, not without any way of knowing how long he'd be gone, but they had to be growing as tired of the back-and-forth stalemate as he was.

Still, he also couldn't let it go. "You don't owe me anything. I didn't save your life just so you could risk it for me later."

"You didn't just *save* my life!" Her voice shook. "You *gave it* to me!"

Silence. Gilad's brow furrowed in confusion.

Cassandra took a long, steadying breath. "I . . . It took me years to admit who I was to myself. I struggled with coming out for a long time. With the idea of transitioning. And then I thought about that day in Iraq, and I realized . . . if those kinds of . . . of *monsters* existed, and someone—you—knew about them and had the courage to fight them anyway . . . then I could damn well find the courage to be who I really am."

She crossed the room until they stood face-to-face. "So if you want to physically stop me—kill me or cripple me so I *can't* keep up—do it now. Because that's the only way I'm not seeing this through with you, no matter what it is."

"I have no doubt," Gilad said softly, "that you would absolutely have become who you are without me." Then, with a firm nod, "All right. We do this together." He could always leave her behind later if she proved a liability—though that possibility felt less likely to him now than it had.

He pretended not to see the smile Cassandra pretended not to have as he turned away.

"So," he continued, "tell me how we find them."

For the better part of an hour, they discussed possibilities and options, methods by which they might track down Jada Lowry/Halba and Benjamin Boyd/Aradlugal, and through them Namenzida and the Melidarishe. They would have discussed it for longer, had Cassandra's phone not abruptly sounded a notification, in the form of the wheezing groan of Doctor Who's TARDIS, from the bedroom.

Cassandra popped into the neighboring room for a second, reemerged with the phone in hand—and then tossed it over to the desk while scrabbling for the TV remote.

Gilad read the text at a glance, a message from someone listed in the contacts as "Val," before the phone went dark. *Dont know what ur in the middle of but you need to turn on the news*

It took about a minute for her to find MSNBC on the hotel's service, and about half that long again for her jaw to drop as they both realized what the talking heads behind the desk were discussing:

The murder of a United States congressman.

Gilad didn't recognize the name Raymond Pfinster, nor was he a man who maintained, as some people did, that "there's no such thing as coincidence." Of course there was. They happened all the time. He'd seen thousands upon thousands of them in his millennia of life.

What he did not believe in was *assuming* coincidence. The violent death of a politician now, with one of Nergal's cults neck-deep in some scheme or other? Even without any obvious reason to connect them, he found himself deeply suspicious.

Then the newscast played some old footage of Pfinster, and Gilad's suspicions now had their "obvious reason." At least it explained how the Melidarishe could access the resources and connections they did.

"Son of a bitch . . ."

TWENTY-ONE

They pulled up in a decade-old Ford sedan, stopping in front of a house slightly but noticeably more well kept than the other cheap, and in some cases run-down, homes that made up the neighborhood. Most of the lawns were overgrown and often strewn with children's toys or nonrunning cars; most of the porches sagged and the window frames peeled. Most, but not this one.

Sura and Miri, two of the most zealous Melidarishe soldiers, accounted for half the car's occupants—the former driving, the latter directly behind. Also in the back were Halba and Aradlugal. The passenger seat beside Sura remained open, awaiting the one they'd come in hopes of collecting.

The sect ought to be in absolute chaos at the loss of the man who'd been their leader and high priest from before most of them had so much as heard of the Melidarishe. They ought to be scrambling for answers, for purpose, ongoing operations forgotten or at least put temporarily aside.

That they were not, that the overwhelming bulk of them had fallen in behind Aradlugal readily, even eagerly—and that their new leader now seemed poised to continue their prior mission without interruption or hesitation—made Halba deeply uneasy.

Nor had she failed to note, during the long drive to get here, that Aradlugal had seated her constantly in the middle, with himself and Miri always to either side, even though they had no reason to remain so cramped until their fifth passenger joined them. It only increased her unease.

Was her concern legitimate? Was she reading too much into coincidence? She couldn't tell. Couldn't think. Nothing had been clear since her encounter with Gilad in the church hallway. Her mind felt swamped, suffocated, pinned beneath a rockfall of thoughts and doubts and memories, only some of which were her own.

"Halba, Miri, with me," Aradlugal commanded, opening the door and stepping out onto the curb. "Sura, stay with the car." He exchanged a prolonged, knowing look—a signal—with the driver.

Or perhaps he didn't. Perhaps Halba was just losing it.

I've trusted Aradlugal with my life for years. Since before he was *Aradlugal. Why am I thinking this now?*

The question itself was a lie, of course. She knew damn well.

Aradlugal led them across the block's most well-manicured lawn. To any curious neighbors peeking through worn curtains, they should just seem a group of friends, perhaps come for a visit. Their new leader had ordered civilian clothes and no obvious weaponry—which didn't stop every one of them from carrying hidden blades and even a pistol or two.

He was, after a short delay, just raising his fist to knock for a second time when a shadow passed behind the age-stained peephole. The door opened so far as the security chain—one far thicker and heavier than the norm—would allow. Through the gap peered a man in his mid-fifties or early sixties, his hard features only starting to soften, his gray hair cropped in an almost military cut. He kept one hand conspicuously behind his back, and Halba didn't need to be remotely at her best to anticipate the large handgun it almost certainly held.

"Yeah? What?"

"Hello, Major Wheeler," Aradlugal said.

"Haven't been 'Major' anything in a long time, son," Wheeler replied, scowling. "And I don't know you."

"No, but you did some work for my . . . boss. Raymond Pfinster."

Had Wheeler known him as Pfinster? Halba blinked hard, trying to remember what she'd learned about those days, long before her time with the Melidarishe. Yeah . . . yeah, he had. Wheeler had played mercenary for a politician who dabbled in weird occult shit, not for Namenzida, priest of some cult of wackos.

Wheeler's posture didn't relax, precisely, so much as it shifted to a different sort of wariness. "And look how well that went for me. Haven't talked to Pfinster in years. And I watch the news. He's . . ." The man's shoulders tensed. "You here for me?"

"Not the way you mean it," Aradlugal assured him. "The congressman was murdered by Gilad Anni-Padda—the same man who interfered with your operation in Dhi Qar."

It was the same story he'd told the Melidarishe in their grief and despair, the day they'd heard of Namenzida's death. That their escaped enemy had come for their priest in vengeance, that Aradlugal had been unable to stop him.

Halba kept her expression as still now as she had the first time she'd heard it, and could only hope the man who knew her better than anyone else in the world couldn't read her as well as he used to.

"No," Aradlugal continued, "I'm here to hire you."

The old man's skepticism was an almost visible emanation.

Halba stifled an inappropriate and slightly hysterical giggle, thinking suddenly of the stench lines around Pigpen, the *Peanuts* character.

"If you're looking for military connections, I don't—"

Aradlugal interrupted, a flicker of his usual impatience breaking through his polite facade. "I'm not. We've got that covered. But I need your knowledge. Your expertise. Your personal experience."

"Look, son—"

"And you'll be well paid. Unless of course you're content doing"—his gaze flickered to encompass the house, the neighborhood; not precisely signs of recent wealth—"whatever it is you're doing."

Wheeler studied him, turned his focus to Miri, then Halba, finally back to Aradlugal. Then he disengaged the security chain and stepped back from the door.

"Let's talk numbers," he said, waving them inside. "And you can tell me exactly what you want from me, and where we're going."

Lying prone on a neighbor's roof, all but invisible on this cloudy night, a gray-clad Gilad peered through a night vision scope at the home of the late and unlamented Congressman Raymond Pfinster.

It was a three-story monstrosity overlooking a yard far larger than it warranted and an excessively long circular drive. Not a mansion by any formal definition, but it certainly wanted to be.

Precisely the sort of house one would expect of a politician who wished to boast about how rich and successful he was, while still pretending he wasn't *entirely* corrupt.

A front? A role Namenzida played to the hilt, hiding his devotion to a nihilistic god behind an expertly configured facade? Or did Pfinster represent more of the truth than he would have wanted to admit, with Namenzida and the Melidarishe serving more as tools than showing genuine belief?

Gilad couldn't say. He'd met both sorts in his millennia of fighting the servants of Nergal, and he had no doubt he would encounter both sorts again.

What he did know was that, even if Namenzida had indeed been a true believer, he'd been careful about it. Patient, methodical, concerned with consequences.

But Aradlugal? Not just a fanatic, but an angry one. He'd recognized the young man from a sketch shown on the news: according to witnesses, the last man who'd spoken with Pfinster. Normally dissent within enemy ranks would be a good thing, but if the former lieutenant was now in charge—if the "Servant of the King" was now king himself—things could get very ugly.

Aradlugal's stewardship wouldn't have the sort of longevity Namenzida's had, but the carnage he could leave in his wake . . . Well, Gilad had seen whole cities fall before Nergal's most maddened and most violent of raiders. He'd lived in several of them.

It wasn't anything he meant to let happen again.

Nobody had lived here since Pfinster's death; the man had no wife, no children, no live-in servants. Yet the house and the grounds were not unoccupied. Through the tiny circle of green light, Gilad watched at least half a dozen men in suits with deceptively loose jackets wander the property.

Congress members didn't have Secret Service protection, and even if they had, it certainly wouldn't have extended to their homes postmortem. If these were cultists, though, they'd continue their assigned tasks until their new leader commanded otherwise; and if they were private security, a reputable firm would keep them on the job until the end of their current contract.

If Gilad had to guess, he'd say these were the latter, not the former. As careful as Namenzida had become about keeping his private and political identities separate, it seemed unlikely he'd assign his religious followers to so public a position. And if they were just uninvolved professionals doing a job, Gilad very much preferred not to hurt them.

So he watched, unmoving, late into the night, though it would have been simplicity itself to take them all down. They stood no specific posts, walked no particular patrol routes; the property wasn't *that* big. Still, by the time midnight had receded, Gilad had a strong sense of their patterns, however unconscious or accidental they might have been.

He slid the scope into the pack that lay behind him, slung it over his shoulder, and crept to the roof's sloped edge. From there he dropped to the lawn beside the driveway, the two-story plunge no obstacle at all to his unique combination of expertise and resilience. Even his landing was silent and left no trace but a pair of shallow imprints in the grass that would spring back by morning.

Crouched beneath the nearest window, just in case any of this house's occupants happened to wake, he watched again until he was sure nothing unanticipated had happened to change the guards' routines. Then he was across the street in an inhumanly quick dash.

A fearsome leap had him vaulting over the wrought iron fence without so much as putting a hand to metal. He dropped and rolled beneath a nearby hedge.

One man stepped out on the front porch, lit faintly orange by the glow of a cigarette. Another planted himself on the living room sofa, where he could idly gaze out the window into the dark of night, sipping from a can of Fresca. Neither so much as glanced toward the foliage where the intruder had hidden himself.

In his time, Gilad had crept past Egyptian temple guards, Persian "Immortals," the handpicked sentries of Genghis Khan. He'd penetrated the trenches and tunnels of the Viet Cong, drug cartels, and half a dozen factions of the First World War. He'd freed a captive—one the US government denied to this day it had ever held—from Area 51 without any alarm being raised; and once he'd even infiltrated a band of ninja *while they sneaked into the villa of a rival clan.*

Where these rented soldiers were concerned, he might as well be less than air. The only real risk of giving himself away would be if he couldn't suppress the urge to laugh at them.

Don't get cocky, Gilad. It wouldn't be the first time his own arrogance got him caught, and while he liked to think those days were behind him, it wouldn't do to prove himself wrong.

The two men finished their breaks, the one outside dropping his cigarette butt to the porch and grinding it under a heel. Pfinster probably wouldn't have been happy about that if he weren't well past caring. Then he headed back inside, while the other disappeared from the window.

Still Gilad waited. Two minutes. Four.

One of the other members of the security team wandered idly through the yard, close enough for Gilad to see the precise fit and hang of his jacket even in the gloom.

Whatever he was packing was longer than a pistol. Something akin to a Škorpion, perhaps, or a MAC-10 with a suppressor. Definite overcompensation for a job like this. Gilad's already mediocre assessment of these guards dropped lower.

Another minute once the guy had passed, just to be sure, and then Gilad moved.

Across the yard, into the bushes. Down the side; paused on

his belly next to the roses until he was sure the other smoker of the team wasn't catching a few puffs of cancer on the deck out back. Then around and into the shadows under that self-same deck.

Paused. Listened to the footfalls. Over and around to the back door. Listened again, made sure nobody's hanging out in the mudroom for some reason.

Now came the first test of Gilad's conclusions. With security wandering both the house and the yard, regularly stepping in and out, it was almost a sure thing that the house's alarm system wasn't currently armed.

Almost. It was *just* possible they were taking the time to turn it off every time one of them opened a door and back on again after it was shut. Unlikely in the extreme, but possible.

Kneeling, Gilad removed a few stiff wires from inside his pack. He reached up, picked the lock almost without effort, and nudged the back door open less than an inch.

Had any alarm blared, he would've been across the side yard and over the neighbor's fence well before anyone could spot him. The guards would find the door hanging slightly ajar, with nothing else disturbed. They'd poke around a bit, then argue over which of them had left the damn thing unlatched so it could drift open, and Gilad would have to return hours later, or perhaps the following night.

No alarm. No sound at all, save a soft cough and some receding footsteps in the house, several rooms away.

Now that he knew for sure the system wasn't armed, he pulled the door shut and carefully relocked it. This had been a test only; he wasn't about to make entry by so obvious a path as the door.

Gilad moved to the side of the door and jumped, pushing off the deck's railing to catch the roof with his fingertips. Once he hauled himself up, he padded over the shingles, peeking through what tiny gaps various curtains allowed until he found what looked like the primary bedroom, dark and untouched since its previous tenant had his skull crushed on the floor of a golf course clubhouse.

Another moment with a wire to slip the latch, and Gilad was inside.

He'd never really warmed to night vision technology, but this operation had no room for flashlights. The house wasn't large enough for him to be sure nobody would see the extra illumination from underneath a door. So, with an exhalation that was almost a sigh, he slipped on the goggles he'd borrowed from Cassandra. At least, unlike the scope he'd used earlier in the evening, it kept his hands free.

Nothing in the drawers but socks, underwear, some casual clothes, and—in the nightstand—a .357 Smith & Wesson. In the closet, various suits, coats, shoes, watches, ties, a rifle safe—everything one might expect to find and nothing one wouldn't. Nothing on the bed but pillows and blankets.

Ah, well. Convenient as it would've been for the bedroom to prove the alpha and omega of Gilad's break-in, he certainly hadn't expected it to be.

Ears to doors. Quick steps down halls. Checking the rest of the upper floors was easy enough; the sentries spent little time up here, so avoiding them required little effort. Unfortunately, these rooms also provided nothing useful.

The study, of course, was downstairs, because why should this be simple?

From the top of the staircase, Gilad listened until the hall below was clear. He vaulted the banister, dangling for a split second and then dropping. He vanished into a coat closet, waited some more as wandering guards came and went, and then dashed down the hallway and slipped through the door to the study.

Or what he thought was the door to the study. He found himself in a small dinette. A few soft curses, *more* waiting and listening, and then he tried again, this time correctly.

It was a large room, designed for comfort and privacy. Plush carpet, bookcases, a heavy desk. Gilad started with the last.

Only one of the drawers was locked, and it took barely a moment to unlock, but it contained nothing more important than a bottle of very old bourbon and another pistol. The contents of the rest were even less interesting. Atop the desk were plugs for connecting a laptop to a power cord and external speakers, but no computer.

Hmm. Neither the news nor Cassandra's contacts in law enforcement had said anything about Pfinster being found with a laptop. Didn't prove anything, but hopefully it meant the device was here.

Somewhere.

First Gilad checked behind the room's only painting—an "amber waves of grain" landscape—in case Pfinster had seen too many movies. Lifting the frame, however, revealed nothing but wall.

Next came the bookcases, and that proved more productive. Moving aside a number of the books revealed a safe in the wall behind them. It was a modern model with an electronic keypad, but like most such safes, it also had a small keyhole as a backup in case the power died.

Gilad's lockpicks weren't designed for this sort of mechanism, but a small flathead screwdriver and sheer muscle power did the trick well enough. It wouldn't take much examination to reveal the lock was now broken beyond repair, but he was pretty sure nobody would be conducting a close study of the safe for a while. The cops would get here eventually, once all the red tape required to get a warrant for a congressman's private records finally cleared, and the broken lock would doubtless raise a whole lot of new questions, but by then it'd be too late to matter.

Inside was yet *another* pistol, a few stacks of paper, a few thicker stacks of cash, and the elusive laptop. Gilad shoved all of it but the gun into his backpack and made his way from the house as stealthily—and as easily—as he'd entered.

—

It would be inaccurate to say that Gilad's infiltration of Pfinster's home had been the easier of the two assignments, but it *was* the faster and more straightforward of them. As such, he returned to Cedar City, and the hotel suite he currently shared with Cassandra, a few days before she did.

He spent that time once again driving himself to distraction with impatience.

He fumed. He paced. He wandered the city. He tried breaking into the laptop himself, but hacking wasn't any larger a part of his skill set than computer searches, and the levels of security—not top of the line, but certainly stronger than a simple Windows password—thwarted his efforts.

He even returned to the abandoned church for a few hours, intending to search it yet again, even though he knew he hadn't missed anything. The structure, however, was now taped off, with several police vehicles still in the lot. Apparently, someone had finally discovered the fire damage and the scorched corpses inside.

Gilad was on the verge of going out to try to get himself mugged again, just for the exercise and the brief diversion, when the electronic door lock chimed and Cassandra entered, dragging a wheeled suitcase behind her.

Manners overcame impatience, if only just, and Gilad allowed her time to settle in, to shower the day's travel off and get changed, before hitting her with the inevitable "How did it go?"

"Slow," she said, feet up on the sofa and a steaming cup of way-too-pricey microwave noodles in her hands. "Frustrating. It's been five years, and these sorts of places don't exactly keep comprehensive records at the best of times."

"So it was all a waste?"

"I didn't say that." She slurped a mouthful of noodle. "It took throwing around some cash and talking to enough people to populate a small nation, but I finally found a few neighborhood regulars who recognized the photos."

She turned, putting the cup down on the end table and removing her smartphone from the side pocket of her suitcase. With the press of a few buttons, she brought up her notes app.

"Like we figured," she told him, "Lowry and Boyd spent their time bouncing between cheap motels and homeless shelters before they hooked up with the Melidarishe. I'm sure this isn't a complete list, but here are some of the ones they frequented."

She slid the phone across the table, and Gilad picked it up. None of the names meant anything to him. "You're the investigator," he said. "How does this help us?"

"Every piece of information helps. We put it all together, we keep adding to it, and eventually something falls into place. You never know which puzzle piece is going to fit where when you . . ." She halted beneath the weight of his stare.

"In other words," he said, "you have no idea."

"I have no idea *yet*."

"Uh-huh. Why don't you take a look at this computer?"

"Why don't I do that, then?"

The next hours passed with Cassandra huddled over Pfinster's laptop on one side of the suite's work desk, her own on the other, from which she held a long-running Zoom conversation with Armand Idrissi, cybersecurity expert and another of her many professional contacts. Between the two of them, they finally had Pfinster's extra security cracked just after midnight.

"Here." She handed the congressman's laptop back toward Gilad as soon as she'd closed her conversation with Idrissi. "I'm seeing double."

As she rubbed at her eyelids, Gilad sat down with the computer and scanned through the first layer of files and folders.

"Anything?" Cassandra asked.

"I've been looking for approximately forty-seven seconds. Were you expecting a directory labeled 'Cult of Nergal Stuff' to be sitting on the desktop?"

"I mean, it would've been nice . . ."

"I told you, he kept a thick wall between 'Pfinster' and 'Namenzida.' We're not going to find anything obviously linked to the Melidarishe on here. We're hunting much more subtle connections. Some of those puzzle pieces you mentioned."

"No, *you're* hunting. *I'm* done for the night. Even my tired is tired."

Cassandra wandered off to bed, while Gilad leaned closer over the laptop and dove deep into what was liable to prove a tedious, brain-numbing search.

TWENTY-TWO

When Cassandra blearily emerged from the bedroom again around nine-ish the next morning, he was still at it.

"I think I've found something," Gilad told her without looking up.

"No, you haven't."

"No?"

She shambled over to the suite's coffee maker, brewed herself a cup, poured in enough sugar to give a rhinoceros a severe case of the zoomies, and chugged most of it down without taking a breath.

"*Now* you might have something."

"You know, I don't even remember what that kind of fatigue feels like."

"You know what else? Fuck you." One last swallow finished off the cup. "What have you got?"

"Charitable contributions." He turned the computer so she could see a screenful of PDFs and Excel spreadsheets.

"I need more coffee. Possibly with alcohol."

"He makes—made—a lot of them. Some hefty checks to some

pretty big organizations, but the bulk of his efforts went toward smaller entities in any number of cities. Food banks. Clinics."

"I still don't see how—"

"Homeless shelters."

Just like that, she was beside the sofa, leaning over to see more clearly. "Don't tell me . . ."

He pointed to an alphabetically clustered set of files in the subfolder. "Safe Harbors Housing."

Gilad knew he didn't need to remind her the same shelter was on the list of Halba's and Aradlugal's former residences.

"Well, whaddaya know?" She straightened, stretching until her lower back gave a deep pop. "You think it's a recruiting ground for him?"

"Almost certainly."

"This *could* all be a coincidence," she warned. "Might be no link at all, just a random charitable pick. Not damn likely, but—"

"But definitely possible, yes. Which is why I didn't stop there."

"All right," she said, perching on the arm of the sofa opposite where Gilad sat. "Thrill me."

"I'm no expert, but even I know how to look up a web page and follow a chain of links. I dug into everything I could find online about Safe Harbors. Lots of social programs and testimonials, all the necessary nonprofit paperwork—at least the publicly available stuff—but not much about them on a business level. They're owned by a company called Charitable Endeavors."

"My, how . . . generic." Cassandra thought for a moment. "The Melidarishe church is owned by one called Diversified Services. It's a shell company, incorporated in the—"

"Cayman Islands?" Gilad asked.

"Uh, yes. It's common enough that it borders on a real-life cliché, but that didn't sound like you were guessing."

"I wasn't. That's where Charitable Endeavors is registered, too."

Cassandra started to chew on a lock of hair, then brushed it away, looking vaguely disgusted at herself. "I wasn't able to find out anything more about Diversified. There was nothing else available online."

"I had similar luck with mine last night. These shell corporations seem to be where the electronic trail ends."

"Damn it. Then the only way would be . . ." She stopped. "You already know what comes next."

"I do. I checked, and Charitable Endeavors has a physical mailing address. We just have to go look through their records."

"In person," Cassandra said.

"Yes."

"Records that are in a drawer somewhere in the Caymans."

"Yes."

"Records that we have *zero* legal right to even request, let alone demand."

"Three for three," Gilad said. "You truly are an investigator."

"Hey, remember fuck you, from before?"

Gilad chuckled but went right back to serious like a flipping switch. "You're going to need a passport. Unless you're willing to revisit the notion of being done with this. You've already done more than—"

"I have my passport," she interrupted just a bit irritably. "Never travel without it."

"Even domestically? That's a bit unusual."

"Most of my travel is work related, and you never know where an investigation might take you."

"Fair enough." He cast a glare at the computer.

"Problem?" Cassandra asked.

"I don't like the notion of traveling commercial for this. Leaving aside that we're at the mercy of schedules and delays, we still have no idea how far the Melidarishe's connections go. They might have people in major airports or at the big airlines. And I have no way of knowing if any of my cover identities might be compromised. Halba or Aradlugal might remember any one of them, or several, or none."

"Hmm. Coswell Security Consultants has worked with a couple different charter companies. But I can't use CSC funds on a private venture, and chartering a private plane is a little, uh, let's say 'outside the reach' of my bank account. I . . . What's the grin for?"

"Just out of curiosity, what sort of number does 'outside your reach' mean? As a ballpark?"

Little more than twelve hours later, Gilad and Cassandra watched the ground and the occasional wisp of cloud roll away beneath them from the thickly padded seats and ludicrously spacious cabin of a Dassault Falcon 2000LXS.

"I never tire of this," Gilad said. "Of everything people have accomplished since my youth, I still find this among the most astonishing. Even if most modern companies have done their best to ruin it. How often do you—"

"Shh!" Even with Cassandra facing away from him, the hiss bounced its way to him clearly. "Can't talk. Decadence." She raised a glass of Scotch to her lips.

"I thought your company dealt with charters."

"Doesn't mean I usually get to *ride* in them!" She took another sip, sighed, and finally turned from the window. "Why didn't you ever tell me you were loaded as hell?"

"I'm not, really."

Cassandra made an absolute production of rolling her eyes.

"Oh, excuse me. Not *you*. Just a whole bunch of your false identities!"

"Shout louder. The pilots may not have heard you." Then, after she repeated her disdainful expression, he said, "It was never relevant. But how did you *think* I managed for thousands of years? None of my identities are going to appear in Forbes, but yes, many of them have more-than-comfortable long-term investments. Hopefully that'll still matter in a few weeks. Though this"—he gestured at the cabin, the screens, the liquor cabinet, the bed—"is going to eat into a few of them. We didn't have to go *this* luxurious. Anything private that would fly far enough would've done."

"Sorry, I'll tell Val to start developing connections with *cheaper* charter companies so . . ." She stopped as Gilad's earlier comment finally registered. "What do you mean you hope those investments will still matter?"

"The Melidarishe. We still don't know what they're after."

"Yeah, but it's one small group who just lost their leader, and his replacement is a punk. I know they're looking for something magical and otherworldly, but it's not like they can do anything *too* destructive, right?"

"Probably not."

"Probably?"

Silence. Cassandra's expression, somewhere between a smile and a scoff, started to slip.

"*Probably?!*"

Gilad turned to look once more out the window.

In a squat, stone-walled hallway that baked in the desert sun, Halba slumped against the wall with her hands pressed to her ears, nails digging into the skin under her hair, coated in a sheen of sweat that had little to do with the heat.

The door to the room at the end of the hall was shut tight, but it didn't matter. The wood couldn't block out the screams or the sobs any more than her hands could.

It shouldn't bother her. It wouldn't have bothered her before . . . before *him*. Before that fucking ritual. It *didn't* bother her; it was just the lingering phantom of Gilad Anni-fucking-Padda that made her *think* she was suffering along with the poor saps in the room, that her stomach was tied in knots, that some of the wetness on her cheeks was tears and not sweat. All him, all artificial, just something she had to work through, like an illness. No, like a drug. It'd be out of her system soon enough.

It would.

She wasn't bothered. She *wasn't.*

Another scream, this one wet, choking. It seemed to go on forever. Someone whimpered softly along with it, an atrocious harmony of pain, and she realized the whimpering was her own.

I can't let this happen.

She'd taken two strides down the hall before she recognized the thought, and a third before she wondered if it was *her* thought, or *his*. She halted, leaning once more against the wall, slamming the back of her head into it over and over, fighting for control over her own emotions and instincts.

But why had she stopped?

Because these were still her people? Because while she might not care for everything Aradlugal was doing, he was still the person she'd known longest, cared for the most, through every kind of hell. Her closest friend and compatriot in the world, whom she ought to trust—*had* trusted—as readily as breathing.

Or was it tactical? No way she could take on everyone in

there. Yes, she'd killed four in the attack on the Callahan Ranch, but they'd been distracted by an active threat and she'd been at the top of her game. Here she'd be facing a lot more than four, including Aradlugal himself, and she was nowhere near her best.

She wanted to fall on her knees, put her arms around Aradlugal's waist, and beg his understanding, to slip back into the fold of Nergal where she belonged. To act without compunction, to live without this feeling. This *pain*.

She wanted to burst into the room and put a bullet in the head or an akinakes in the heart of every Melidarishe present. To punish them for what they had done, to put an end to what they were doing. To murder every bit of her own culpability with all of it.

The four of her brethren she'd murdered that night on the ranch . . . Had she truly believed she was gifting them a meaningful, sacred death in the service of Nergal as she'd claimed? Had she known it was the righteous thing to do for the sake of the innocents caught up in their violence as Gilad had suggested?

Halba didn't know. She couldn't begin to recall what she'd felt, truly felt, in that moment, and she *certainly* couldn't quiet her screaming, thrashing thoughts enough to figure out what she felt now. She knew only that, without absolute conviction, without coming down wholeheartedly on one option or the other, she wasn't sure she could even bring herself to shed Melidarishe blood.

They were evil. They were family.

She straightened almost violently as the door briefly opened, allowing out a louder scream and a single glimpse of huddled, horrified figures. Wheeler stepped out into the hall, sweat-stained and grease-tinted face twisted in a scowl, then pulled the door shut behind him.

"You mind?" he asked, holding up a cigarette.

"You care?" Halba replied.

"Not much."

"Same."

Wheeler grunted something and lit up.

She watched him, watched the ember draw closer as he burned quickly through the cigarette. Watched the sporadic sideways glances he directed at the room he'd come from, the stiffness in his posture he couldn't hide.

"Not taken with what we're doing in there?" She tried to make the question sound casual, maybe even a bit snide.

"No. No, I'm not."

Well, now. Halba hadn't thought much of Wheeler, either from what Namenzida had told her of him in the past or from what she'd seen for herself in recent days. But just maybe, if the man had more of a soul than she'd expected, she might find herself an unexpected ally in the midst of this—

"It's a fucking waste of time!" Wheeler continued, clearly giving free rein to a rant he'd been suppressing for some while. "Your boss says he wants me for my 'expertise,' and then he turns around and grabs up a bunch of strays! These nobodies don't know shit! All he's gonna do is turn the neighborhood against us. I told him who he should be—"

"And I listened." The door was once again ajar, and Aradlugal stood in the frame, wiping blood from his hands with an oil-stained rag. Halba felt hot coals around her mind as she wondered how the hell she'd missed seeing it open.

"Did you?" Wheeler asked. "Sure as shit doesn't look like it."

Aradlugal made a condescending *tsk-tsk* sound. Wheeler's face scrunched up like he was about to swallow the butt of the cigarette.

"You were here twenty years ago, Wheeler. You met three of these men. You saw how willing they are to die for what they believe."

"Yeah, so?"

"So what we're asking, they consider part of a sacred charge, and they're not going to reveal any of it easily. We could be days, even weeks, questioning them, and that's assuming they don't die before they break."

"And getting your rocks off torturing a bunch of random civilians is gonna make that go *faster*?"

"No. Torturing a bunch of their neighbors, friends, perhaps cousins in front of them—after they've already suffered, already learned that we do not bluff and do not relent, when they *know* to fear us—will make it go faster. It's easy to endure pain for what you believe, at least for a time. Harder to endure the pain of others. Well. Harder for some people, anyway."

He tossed the bloody rag to Halba, who snagged it out of the air mostly by reflex. It left a wet warmth on her fingers. Her skin crawled at the sensation, as if it were a web covered in spiders.

Long after Aradlugal had returned to the room, Wheeler following in his wake, she stared down at the cloth in her hand. And though she was not remotely aware of it, though her thoughts still crashed and shattered against one another like icebergs, a portion of her mind grew calm and still.

Halba did not know it yet, but Aradlugal had done her one last favor.

With his help, she was starting to decide, after two years of questioning and several weeks of crisis, who she was.

TWENTY-THREE

A weak storm had blown in off the Caribbean and was now in the process of spreading a slow but steady deluge across most of George Town, and indeed nearly half the island of Grand Cayman.

It was nothing at all compared to the other storm that had just come aground via the Dassault Falcon, passed impatiently through customs, and then hailed a taxi.

Near the edges of the cluster of buildings that represented George Town's financial center, the rain pattered against the windows of one particular structure. An old but cheery thing of blue roofs and whitewashed balconies that had begun to fade only slightly with neglect, its three stories served as home to small businesses of all sorts.

One of those suites served as the offices—or at least the legal business and mailing address—of Charitable Endeavors Inc.

As CEI didn't get much walk-in custom, the front room was plain, consisting of little more than a desk and a handful of chairs.

Today it was also adorned with the battered, bruised, and groaning forms of three private security guards, lying sprawled on the floor or draped over the furniture in mimicry of so much dirty laundry.

Behind the desk, the door to the back office hung ajar. It had been locked, an obstacle that had impeded Gilad not at all. He stood in the doorway now, Cassandra behind him.

Across from him, at a much smaller desk flanked by massive filing cabinets, which loomed like temple columns, stood a thin, balding man with a phone raised halfway to his ear.

"You're probably calling the police," Gilad said. "Or more of your security. Funny for a place like this to even *have* private security, wouldn't you say?" he asked over his shoulder.

"Funny," Cassandra confirmed.

Gilad looked back at the man, whom the plaque on the door identified as Keven Tibbett, Chief Financial Officer. "There, you see? Funny. Either way, you probably figure you can stall us long enough for help to arrive. I mean, you don't even know what we want, so talking us through whatever it is has got to take some time."

Without changing his expression, Gilad kicked the door shut behind Cassandra. He stepped to the nearest filing cabinet, put a hand on either side of it, and pulled.

The entire cabinet, with all its contents, slid across the carpet. Tibbett and Cassandra stared in almost equal degrees of shock as Gilad pushed what must have been a quarter-ton load into place to block the door.

"How does that enter into your calculations?" Gilad asked.

Tibbett slowly put the phone down on the desk.

"Wise man."

"N-now see here," Tibbett stammered. "I've no idea what it is you're after, but we keep no valuables here. No cash, no bonds, no wealth of any sort. We're just set up for anonymous charitable donations, it's all electronic, we don't—"

"Mr. Tibbett, we're not here to rob you. We're here for your records."

"I . . . records?"

"Yes. Everything you've got, on paper or in your head. Clients. Shareholders. Subsidiary companies. *Parent* companies. Basically, if it's not public info, we want to see it."

"You can't!" His voice practically squeaked. "Our clients have a right to privacy! We've done nothing wrong, and you have no legal authority to . . . to . . ."

"I'm sorry, have I done something to give you the impression that I'm remotely interested in legal authority here?"

"But . . . but . . ."

I don't have time for this. Gilad advanced toward the desk, smirking darkly as Tibbett backed into the wall and seemed very much as if he were trying to continue through it. Gilad removed the backpack that hung over his shoulder and began removing its contents.

Blades. A lot of blades.

Not weapons proper; he'd never have gotten those through customs. No, he'd stopped in the city to pick these up. A couple of steak knives. Filleting knives. A pocketknife. A box cutter. Even a small hacksaw.

Tibbett made a sound not entirely unlike a cat about to bring up a hair ball, and his face turned color enough that Gilad wondered if he would vomit.

"Yes?" Gilad asked casually.

"What, uh . . ." The CFO pasted on a sickly smile. "What records did you say you wanted again, sir?"

As Tibbett began pulling files from various cabinets, with many a sideways glance at the cabinet that had been relocated, Cassandra pulled Gilad to the far corner of the office. It wasn't much of an improvement, so far as privacy went, but they should at least be able to whisper freely.

"You weren't really going to . . ." She glanced at the knives.

"Just to scare him. I knew that would be enough."

"And if it hadn't been?"

Gilad squelched a flash of anger. She didn't know him, not well. "Some things," he told her, thinking with revulsion of the days long gone when he would have considered such activities to be quite normal, "I've gladly left in my past."

She said nothing, only nodded, but he saw what had been a rising tension drain from her shoulders.

While he may have assuaged her worry, however, he could see questions still lingering in her expression.

"Something else?"

"Yeah. How the fuck did you do *that*?"

He didn't have to follow her gesture to know she was asking about the filing cabinet.

"I already knew you were Connor MacLeod," she continued, "but when did you turn into Steve Rogers?"

"This is what you want to talk about?"

"As opposed to?"

Gilad shook his head, but Tibbett was still gathering folders and forms, so . . .

"I don't get tired, I don't suffer minor injury, and I've had five thousand years to train myself out of some fundamental instincts."

"Uh . . . okay?"

"The human body is literally incapable of functioning at its hypothetical full potential. Muscles grow fatigued or tear. Bones give. Instincts slam on the brakes. But mine don't, so I can."

"So you're not technically 'superhuman,'" she mused, "you just . . . human better than we do?"

"Something like that."

"Hardly seems fair."

"I'll be sure to pass that along to the management."

The *thump* of papers on wood preempted whatever else Cassandra might have said. "This should be more than enough to get you started, sir," Tibbett announced.

Gilad and Cassandra approached the desk, pausing only long enough to put the various knives away before dividing the stack between them.

After the first half hour or so, Gilad cleared the door long enough for their "host" to lean out and instruct the battered security guards to go home and to keep their mouths shut about what had happened.

After another three hours, he and Cassandra had everything they thought might be helpful.

As they'd anticipated, this office wasn't home to Charitable Endeavors alone. It served as a combination address and clearinghouse for a dozen or more tiny companies, shell corporations within shell corporations. Many were linked in chains of ownership or partnership, though others simply happened to be run by the same service. It was hardly uncommon for a group of investors or officers to make their money this way, serving as a legal address and rubber stamp for any number of corporate entities.

That Charitable Endeavors and Diversified Services—the owner of the Melidarishe church—turned out to be owned by the same umbrella shell came as absolutely nothing of a shock.

A more detailed perusal would take far more time than they could reasonably spend here, barricaded into this tiny office.

After Gilad made it very clear to Keven Tibbett how unpleasant things could get if anyone on either side of the law came after them for the missing files, the pair retreated to yet another hotel room, booked under one of Gilad's false identities.

Whereupon, fortified with a large meal and enough coffee to drown an aurochs, Gilad and Cassandra dove headlong into the fascinating world of shell companies and corporate ownership.

It took the better part of a day, and by the end of it, even Gilad felt as if his brain were on the verge of bleeding out his ears, but they finally had an intricate webwork of other corporate entities linked to Charitable Endeavors or Diversified Services—linked, in other words, to Raymond Pfinster. The files were spread out all over the floor, connected by strips of tape, forcing them to carefully pick their way across the hotel room, but they formed, if not a complete picture, at least the bulk of one.

Too bad that was only phase one. Now they had to get back online and find out, whether through public records or through whatever strings Cassandra could pull, what each of these other companies was up to, and hope that one of *those* avenues actually led them somewhere.

"*This* is what you do for a living?" Gilad demanded. "Today feels like a century, and that's coming from a man *who knows what a century feels like.*"

Cassandra snorted something unintelligible and remained focused on her laptop.

Still more hours passed, and then . . .

"I've got them!"

Gilad was instantly at her shoulder, staring at what appeared to be a page of numbers, times, and locations. "Tell me," he said.

"Do you want all the intermediate steps or just the bottom line?"

"Dear gods, the latter."

Cassandra smirked. "All right." She pointed at one set of digits. "That's the tail number of a private plane. Not near as nice as the one you're currently paying for, I should point out. It's owned by a company that's owned by a company that's owned by the company that owns Charitable Endeavors."

"Okay, but that doesn't necessarily mean—"

"It left the country a couple days after Pfinster was killed."

"Still, it—"

"And touched down at Kuwait International."

Gilad's jaw snapped shut. He saw the look Cassandra was giving him, with no remaining trace of her earlier grin, and knew she'd already had the same thought that was now coming to him.

Assuming one wanted to land outside Iraq in order to hide one's true destination—which one might well prefer to do, if being pursued by an enemy like Gilad Anni-Padda—then Kuwait International was the closest major airport to . . .

"Nasiriyah," he said. "It's all coming back around to Nasiriyah."

"Yeah." Cassandra sounded apprehensive, perhaps even afraid, but no less determined. "Yeah, that's what I . . . It almost feels like fate, doesn't it? You, and me, and . . . there."

Gilad, who had any number of thoughts on the subject of fate, many bitter and unpleasant, said nothing.

When he didn't answer, she said, "But I mean, we don't *know* the Melidarishe were on that flight. It *could* be coincidence."

"It could. But you don't think so any more than I do."

"No." She sighed. "No, I don't. And we have to check it out, to be sure, either way."

"Yes."

"Why?"

He knew she wasn't asking why it was important to be sure, but beyond that he didn't follow. "Sorry?"

"Why go back now? What are they after? Those tablets . . . They got those already, right? The, uh, the ritual?"

"Those, and probably anything else they found at the time that might've been useful to them. But there are other repositories, hidden caches of old magics. And there are the historians I mentioned, like those three old men, who study and watch over them."

Gilad rose and began moving around the room, packing. "If we're lucky, they're only trying to figure out a way to further modify the Thief of Yesterdays rite, so they can learn more—either from me, or maybe from Halba and Aradlugal."

"Uh, okay, and if we're *not* lucky?"

He stopped in the middle of shoving a pair of jeans into a satchel. "Do you know where Ur was, Cassandra?"

"Not that far from Nasiriyah, right?"

"Which means Nasiriyah is also not too terribly far from—"

She got it before he said it. "From the portal!" Then, "You think they already know how to find it?"

"I think he probably doesn't. And I think I'd very much like to find him before that changes."

Cassandra, too, began to pack.

"Still," she added as she worked, "it could be worse."

"Oh? How do you figure?"

"*I* could be on the hook for what this charter's going to wind up costing you."

TWENTY-FOUR

Through a battered neighborhood at the outskirts of Nasiriyah, nearly a village in its own right, which had seen far, far too much violence already, the sounds of gunfire burst and echoed. Smoke lay thick over the earth, acrid and choking.

From behind parked cars, from nearby windows, and within the halls of the target building, the attackers fired, advanced, fired again. Melidarishe soldiers, reinforced by local mercenaries acquired through Nathan Wheeler's few remaining connections, seemed half invading army and half intrusive swarm. Anything that moved was fair game, and those who had fallen before them included not just armed defenders but harmless civilians, men and women, girls and boys.

The bulk of those defenders, now holed up in a few sporadic apartments across the uppermost level—the only one they still held—had no idea what they battled. They just happened to live here and took up arms against the sudden violence. Standing at their side was a handful of local police, equally unsure of what the hell was happening. Most, to their credit, wouldn't have abandoned the people here even if they could have—but as they had no viable exit, even those who might not have elected to stay and fight still found themselves doing exactly that.

A very few who fought, however, were not so ignorant of their enemy. A smattering of men and women in traditional Iraqi garb, people who did not much stand out from their neighbors, counted themselves among the inheritors of a very old tradition and even older lore. They alone knew what was at stake here tonight. Knew what the faithful of Nergal sought from them—not in specifics, not the precise secrets, perhaps, but certainly the gist.

They knew it was better everyone in the building, everyone in the neighborhood, should perish than the invaders should have what they desired. And they knew, if they were to lose, that it was *far* better they die in the process than linger on to experience what the victors would do to them afterward.

It was mostly due to those few, then, that the firefight still continued, even though the Melidarishe had already taken most of the structure and the surrounding block.

The main hallway of the second floor was a balcony, with multiple rooms on one side, overlooking a central courtyard on the other. Aradlugal strode along the balcony, stepping over bodies and leaving bloody footprints behind him. Halba, Wheeler, and several Melidarishe soldiers followed in his wake.

Two of the cultists, Halba had long since noticed, seemed to make a special point of sticking close by her. Not, she suspected, for her own protection.

A number of the building's inhabitants knelt at the hall's far end. They faced the wall, hands on their heads, frightened sobs and grieving screams adding a spectral chorus to the night's proceedings. Every sound was an ice pick in Halba's gut.

The loudest of the sounds, however, was Wheeler's furious ranting, a constant diatribe that finally drew Aradlugal to a halt.

"Do you really think," he demanded, turning on his heel, "that I'm unaware of any of that?"

Wheeler looked ready to burst. "It sure as fuck seems like you are! Jesus fucking Christ, Nasiriyah never looked like this even back during the war! There were a hundred quieter ways we could have—"

"We're still looking to identify the scholars among the populace. I needed to see who fought hardest, and for *them* to see how hard *we* fight. I needed to give them no time to hide. The time for quiet is over."

"You're insane! It won't be just cops responding to this kind of violence! We're gonna have Iraqi military coming down on us any minute! Maybe even US forces!"

"I have people dug in at every neighborhood access point," Aradlugal said, kneeling to examine one of the fallen defenders. "And we've rigged most of those intersections. They'll come in slow, careful. We'll have plenty of notice to be out of here."

Wheeler threw his hands in the air. "You're insane!" he repeated. "You won't listen to my warnings. You won't listen to my advice. You've *barely* even listened when I pointed you toward the kinds of people you're looking for. Why the fuck are you even paying for me to be here?"

"Because if you weren't, I couldn't do this." Aradlugal rose, lifted the Tariq pistol he'd taken from the dead man, and fired twice. Both shots struck Wheeler above his body armor, one piercing his throat, the other smashing through his chin. The mercenary dropped in a shower of blood, bone, and teeth, spasmed, and lay still.

Ignoring the gasps, the cries, and the stares, Aradlugal carefully placed the weapon back in the dead Iraqi's hand.

"Care to explain?" Halba asked, hoping she sounded calm and unbothered.

"Now the inevitable investigation has a villain to point to. Wheeler was behind this, along with a team of hired guns, but one of the poor souls he attacked took him out before dying. Given his court-martial and discharge, and how he's made his living since, nobody should have trouble believing it."

"And he did this why, exactly?"

"He was after the insurgent stockpile of weapons and cash I've currently got people hiding in one of the rooms. Relax, Halba. I've covered everything. It won't hold up indefinitely, but it'll have the authorities looking in the wrong direction long enough for us to do what we have to."

What we have to. Halba shivered despite the heat. He'd finally told them what they were here for, what the Melidarishe would accomplish under his leadership. The unprecedented glory they would bring to Nergal's name.

Most now followed Aradlugal out of sheer zealous awe. Halba was nearly sick just thinking about it.

Because of that distress, it took Halba an extra moment to follow Aradlugal's scheme to its logical conclusion. The idea that Wheeler had been in command here, that the attackers had been a mercenary force looking for stashed cash, would only work . . .

With no witnesses left behind to contradict it.

As if on cue, Aradlugal raised his voice so all his nearby followers could hear. "Gather the survivors. *Everyone's* coming with us."

"That could be a problem, my priest," said the Melidarishe soldier called Sura. They'd all taken to calling Aradlugal "priest" since his takeover, despite his having no liturgical claim to the title. "There are a lot of prisoners, and many of the faithful have fallen. We may not be able to control so many."

"Then whittle them down to more manageable numbers." For all the emotion in his tone, Aradlugal might have been discussing a grocery list. "Just remember the ones we're looking for are scholars, so don't kill anyone over . . . let's say, forty."

The world around Halba seemed to slow. Half a dozen gun barrels rose and took aim at the hostages against the wall.

One of the Iraqi men shot to his feet, hurling himself backward and knocking the nearest gun aside with his shoulder. He whirled on the startled cultist, yanking the AK-47 from frozen hands.

Even as the first of countless bullets struck him, as his balance wobbled, the brave civilian shouted a final prayer to Allah—a prayer for his own soul and the souls of the men and women and children he had to know he couldn't save—and opened fire on the Melidarishe.

Most of the cultists were in no real danger; only one fell before the rest had shot the man down in a hail of lead. In those seconds, however, half a dozen more hostages rose and ran, some throwing themselves at the enemy, others making for any possible escape.

One of them, a middle-aged woman in slacks and an orange hijab, grabbed the little boy beside her, holding him to her chest as she ran. He wasn't even her child, just a neighbor, yet she clutched him as though he were the most precious thing in the world.

In the chaos, the Melidarishe on the second-floor balcony seemed unsure what to do first, but one of the weapons turned the sprinting woman's way . . .

For an instant, the face of the boy was visible beneath the woman's arm, only he didn't look like himself anymore, but like Timeus: young son, millennia gone, of Gilad Anni-Padda.

Halba snapped.

If the two cultists beside her had indeed been tasked with watching her for misbehavior or betrayal, they were down before they could do anything about it. A perfect elbow strike landed against the base of the first man's skull, cracking bone and separating spine from brain stem. Halba would realize only later that it was a level of precision of which she'd never before been capable—because it wasn't *her* precision.

The second lived a few seconds longer. Halba kicked back as she threw the elbow, catching him just below the kneecap. He toppled, crying out.

She yanked the rifle from the dead man's hands as he fell, putting a round through the head of a Melidarishe soldier down the hall, the one who'd been about to shoot the fleeing woman. Halba then stepped back, stomping on the skull of the wounded man to ensure he never rose again. It was a favored move of Gilad Anni-Padda, and while she might have lacked his strength or his weight, she was more than skilled enough to do the job.

The older woman threw herself over the courtyard balcony, twisting so her precious burden would take none of the coming impact, but so far as the Melidarishe were concerned, she was already forgotten. Drawn by the commotion, the gunshot, and Aradlugal's enraged shouting, they'd turned all their attention to the traitor in their midst.

Halba dove desperately around the nearest corner, bullets ricocheting off stone behind her, and scrambled for the stairs. Although ranks of her former brethren still waited between her and escape, she had no conscious thought for her own well-being. She could only pray—though she had no real notion to whom or to what, only that it was no longer, would never again be, Nergal—that the fleeing woman and the child might find safety.

And that, if she survived, she could possibly find forgiveness for all the others she had no choice but to leave behind.

Oppressive as the early-afternoon heat might be, it could not compete with the weight of sorrow, of fury, of bitter resignation that smothered the neighborhood.

The black-and-blue camouflage uniforms of the Iraqi Federal Police, along with the plainer blues of local law enforcement, continued to comb over the apartment complex and walk the surrounding streets. A few clusters of citizens still gathered at the intersection or in the entryway of the building, watching the proceedings. Yet for all the activity, it was a smaller and less intrusive affair than the people of many other nations might have expected, and the bulk of the neighborhood's citizens went about their daily lives, interrupting their routine only where they were required to maneuver around an investigator or official vehicle.

The people of Nasiriyah—indeed, the people of Iraq—had grown far, far too accustomed over the preceding decades to sudden and often inexplicable surges of violence. All they could do was continue living.

Gilad, studying the aftermath of what had occurred some four days prior to his arrival in the country, had gotten to within a quarter mile of the block of the tenement before someone barred his path. "If you have no official business here, sir," the man told him in Arabic, "I must ask you to leave."

He was a police officer—one of the city's force, not federal. Probably in his fifties, his hair and mustache both going gray, and developing something of a gut that the uniform couldn't hide. His back and shoulders were straight, however, his eyes alert, and the clench in his jaw suggested an ongoing grief and an intense anger over this newest horror.

A man local not only to Nasiriyah, Gilad calculated, but to this section of the city. Perhaps not this precise neighborhood, but near enough.

"Perhaps you can tell me what happened here," Gilad said,

also in Arabic. He carefully modulated his tone, making the question sound official rather than like idle curiosity. Not sufficient to learn anything that wasn't public knowledge, but enough that the officer wouldn't dismiss him as some entitled tourist.

What followed was the same tale Gilad had heard from half a dozen others already that day. An American mercenary and his men. A stash of money and weapons, hidden by insurgents in the apartments. A prolonged firefight and bloodbath. Dozens dead, as many more missing, taken hostage. The authorities still waited for some manner of demand or ransom.

The same tale, but he told it just a bit differently than the others. Not in detail but in demeanor. It would have been easily missed if Gilad hadn't been watching for it, but this was a man reciting the party line, not one who believed what he was spouting.

Between that and the near certainty that he was indeed a local, Gilad decided to take a chance.

"Tell me, Officer . . ."

"Fayad, sir," he replied, preoccupied and ready to walk away.

"Tell me, Officer Fayad, are you certain this was about cash and not something more? Something involving the scholars who live here and the secrets they keep?"

From anyone who had no idea what that meant, that would have drawn puzzlement or an impatient dismissal. When Fayad's head snapped around to stare at him, it told Gilad all he needed to know.

The officer might not have been one of the small sect who studied and guarded the old relics, the old magics, here in the heart of what had once been ancient Sumer—but he absolutely knew of them, even if only as neighborhood folklore and urban legend.

"Who are you?" Fayad demanded.

I wonder what else he knows of local folklore . . .

"My name is Gilad Anni-Padda."

Well, he thought as Fayad rocked back a step, *I guess that answers that.*

"*Muharrab al Azly!*"

"Some have called me that." Then, as the other remained gawping, speechless, "The missing may not have a great deal of time, my friend."

"Of course." Fayad pulled himself together. "But I don't know how I can help you. I've heard rumors and gossip. Many of us have. Most of the neighborhood knows of the wise men who live among them, and you're not the first to suggest that this . . . this evil might have been directed at them or the relics they keep. Yet we've found no evidence to prove so, and the federal authorities don't want to hear it. Most think us superstitious fools, and the few who don't would rather not get involved. There's just nothing for me to tell you, sir."

"Are you certain? Think! It might not be anything obvious. It might not even seem related to what happened here. *Anything* out of the ordinary might be useful."

Fayad frowned—and then nodded. "There have been a few other violent deaths in the past few days, incidents we've been unable to investigate deeply due to . . ." He waved a hand at the damaged tenement. "Murder is not nearly so uncommon here as we might wish, but these four . . . all foreigners, all stabbed to death despite being armed, all found in back streets or alleys. And all of them, or least all we've heard of, occurred *after* the attack here. Does that help?"

"It just might. If you could tell me *where* . . ." Then, after Fayad recited several addresses for him, "Thank you, my friend." Gilad began to turn away.

"You were meant to be a myth." Fayad sounded almost dreamlike, and Gilad wasn't sure he knew he spoke aloud.

"Yet you didn't doubt when I told you who I was," the immortal said.

Fayad offered a sad smile. "If you are lying to me, nothing I've said puts the hostages in any *worse* danger, and if you are delusional, you will never find them. But if you truly are who you say, those people might still be saved. Given the options, I choose to believe."

Gilad briefly clasped him on the shoulder, then walked away.

He met Cassandra, as they'd arranged when they split up, in front of a nearby café. It was closed for business, allowing the proprietor time to grieve the cousins she'd lost in the attack, but as a local landmark it still made a good rendezvous point. As the patio was readily accessible, and already sporadically occupied by pedestrians looking for a break from the sun, they settled themselves at an empty table.

Cassandra grumbled something under her breath and reached a finger under her hijab to scratch. Gilad smirked.

"You've only had that on for a few hours."

"It's hot, I'm sweating, my hair's sticking everywhere, and *you* don't have to wear one, so shut up!"

"You didn't have to, either," he pointed out, then smirked wider at her glare. It had, in fact, been Cassandra's idea. Gilad could easily pass as a local, but Cassandra had neither the complexion nor the features for it. Anyone who came near, let alone spoke to her, would recognize her as a foreigner instantly, but dressing the part at least kept her from standing out in a crowd.

"Here," Gilad said then. "In case something comes up."

After a quick look around to make sure nobody was watching—or at least nobody official—he slid something wrapped in a rag across the table. Cassandra curiously folded back the cloth to reveal a .38 snubnose revolver.

"What in . . . How did you . . . ? Where . . . ?"

"One of the first things I did after we separated. One of the federal police is going to be really confused when he gets home later and discovers his ankle holster's empty."

"You took it off a cop?!"

"It's his backup piece. You need it more than he does." When her expression failed to change, he continued, "What? You thought combat was the *only* thing I picked up in five millennia?"

"How the fuck do you pickpocket an *ankle holster*?"

"Carefully." Then, "What about you? Learn anything?"

"I . . ." Cassandra dragged herself back to more immediate subjects. "Only a little, but it's interesting. There are a few of our boys—uh, US troops—hanging around the edges of this. Officially they're advising, making sure this isn't going to spread, the usual."

"And unofficially? Wait, let me guess. Since the 'mercenary leader' was American, they want to be seen helping out. Wouldn't do to let this inflame anti-US sentiment."

"Got it in one," Cassandra said. "What I was getting to, though, is that a couple of them were willing to shoot the shit with a former soldier."

"And interesting shit was shot?"

"Yeah. They weren't about to tell me anything too secret, of course, but I heard a name that's probably not meant for public ears." Her expression shifted as if she'd stepped in something soft and squishy. "Our mercenary? Would you believe it was one ex-Major Nathan Wheeler?"

Gilad leaned back in his chair. "Well. Given the timing, and who he was working for last time he was here, I think we can say this confirms the Melidarishe were behind the attack."

"Weren't we already figuring that?"

"We were, but always better to be certain." He dusted his hands off on his pants and stood. "Come on."

"Uh, okay. We're going where?"

"Nasiriyah's a city of more than half a million. We'd never find the Melidarishe on our own. At least not in time to do any good."

"So . . ."

"So," Gilad said, striding off along the sunbaked street, "we're going to acquire the services of someone who can."

TWENTY-FIVE

"I guess I just figured you had a plan beyond 'wandering random streets for hours on end,'" Cassandra grumbled.

"Oh, I do." Gilad took an abrupt left at the next intersection, nodding to an old couple walking the other way as they passed.

"And that would be . . . ?"

"Wandering *specific* streets for hours on end."

Night had fallen. With it, the blazing heat of the day faded to a dull weight that lay over everything, and the pedestrian traffic on the back roads began to thin. Gilad's course took the pair ever further into more decrepit neighborhoods, where the pavement held more cracks than concrete and even the stone walls seemed to sag. Passersby grew more and more sporadic until the byways seemed almost empty.

Gilad and Cassandra both recognized that impression as false. Like any major city in any nation, Nasiriyah had its neighborhoods where one did not walk alone at night unless one was exceedingly foolish or exceedingly dangerous. So far, the pair of pedestrians had been left alone only because the watchers weren't yet sure which category they fell into.

"Gilad, enough. What are we doing?"

"Armed foreigners all stabbed to death," he said. "What does that sound like to you?"

"Like you're about to jump to a conclusion that's not really supported by evidence."

He halted, turning to face her. "Someone's killing Melidarishe, and I've got a pretty good idea of who."

"Gilad . . ."

"Every murder took place in this general vicinity. Either she was hunting them, in which case we're near their hideout and one of their lookouts will eventually spot us. Or they were hunting her, in which case we're near *her* hideout and *she'll* eventually spot us. Either way, we should be able to get some answers."

Cassandra pinched the bridge of her nose as if trying to ward off a headache. "Gilad, even if you're right about who those victims were, you don't know it's her killing them, and if it *is*, you don't know *why*. I know you feel like you've got some sort of responsibility to her—"

"I do."

"You *don't*! You didn't shove your memories into her head, she *stole* them! She's a murderer. She joined the Cult of Nergal eagerly and willingly. You have no idea how much she's changed, and you have no idea how long it'll last. She's walked you into a trap once already. Assuming she's anything but another hostile is idiocy!"

"How about it, Halba?" Gilad asked loudly. "Are you just another hostile?"

A moment of confusion, and then Cassandra reached for her revolver, cursing. Halba, worn and tired, her clothes dirt smeared and sporting countless tiny rips, emerged from the shadows where Gilad had spotted her tailing them long before.

Gilad stepped between them, blocking any potential shot either might take at the other. Cassandra's cursing continued.

"She's probably right." The former cultist sounded exhausted; more than that, bitterly resigned. "Whatever you did to me, it—"

"What I did?" Gilad challenged, without anger.

Halba shrugged. "Whatever was done to me, you have no idea if it's permanent. The smart thing to do would be to put a round through my skull."

"Is that what you want?"

"Doesn't matter."

Gilad wasn't about to accept that answer. "What do *you* want?"

"I don't know! Not *this*!" She took a single aggressive step toward him, then seemed to deflate, stumbling against the corner of the nearest building. "I don't want to *care*! I was . . . It was so much easier . . ."

"You always cared. You just convinced yourself otherwise."

"You don't know that!" Halba's protest was petulant, even childish. "You don't know me."

Almost between one breath and the next, Gilad stood only a couple of paces from her. Cassandra remained silent, still watching from a short way down the block.

"You and Aradlugal got different selections of my memory," Gilad said, "but it's not as if my past was neatly divided into good and bad. You should both have gotten more or less equal amounts of each."

"So?"

"So the difference in how those memories have changed you . . . is you. Everything of mine that you feel, you still had to be *able* to feel. He doesn't, at least not enough to matter. You do."

Halba's hand shook where she steadied herself on the stone. "Why do you care? Why does it matter to you what I feel, or who I am? Or what happens to me?"

Gilad could have told her, again, that he felt some responsibility for her. That even if he hadn't volunteered them, it was his memories—a part of him—that had set her on a new path. And it would all have been true, but it wouldn't have been a real answer. It wouldn't have told her *why* that sense of responsibility mattered.

"I've spent five thousand years fighting," he said, "and I will probably spend thousands more doing the same. I love it, whatever that says about me or the world I was born into. I revel in it.

"But I never meant it to be *all* that I am, and every now and again . . . When it's all over, however long from now that might be, and I'm telling my story to my family in the world beyond, I'd like to be able to say that, every now and again, I fixed a life rather than taking one."

Something inside Halba, some tension that had been pulling against itself ever since the Thief of Yesterdays ritual, gave way. She collapsed, shuddering, weeping for years lost and innocent blood shed.

Gilad caught her as she fell. Cassandra appeared from across the street, the suspicion that had clung to her now washed mostly away in a torrent of sympathy, and together they supported the young woman until she could stand once more.

"Of course I know where they are."

The strange trio no longer huddled in the open street. Rather, Gilad had led them to a small electronics store, an establishment that, thirty years prior and halfway around the world, would've been an off-brand RadioShack. The shop was thoroughly locked up for the night, but Gilad had pulled a loose brick from the back wall, revealing a hollow containing an old grit-coated key. With it, he'd unlocked the rear entrance, which led directly into the manager's office.

"I know the family," was the only explanation he'd given.

Now they sat, Gilad and Halba in the cramped room's two scratched and battered chairs, Cassandra perched on the edge of an equally abused desk. She seemed physically pained by the computer beside her, which was so old it still had an integrated CD-ROM drive.

It was more than a little claustrophobic, but at least it offered them privacy.

"I left the woman and the little boy at a nearby mosque," Halba continued, "and then I doubled back."

"Not the safest choice," Cassandra pointed out.

Halba studied her. Probably, Gilad guessed, trying to decide if Cassandra's comment contained any lingering distrust. When she didn't find it, she said, "No, it wasn't. But I didn't have any other way of keeping tabs on them, except to follow when they pulled out of the tenement. Some of them must have spotted me, though. I've killed too many of them to think they don't know the general area I'm staying in."

Gilad seemed oddly intent on studying the carpet, though he was clearly listening. "You can't have meant to take on the Melidarishe yourself."

"No, but it didn't take shared memories to know you'd probably show up sooner or later." Halba's brow furrowed, as if she found her own words startling.

"And if I hadn't?"

"I . . . don't know," Halba admitted. "But they . . ." She sighed and gave in, acknowledging what had driven her no matter how foreign it felt. "They have to be stopped. But I don't know how we can do it without potentially giving them what they want."

Now Gilad gave her his absolute attention. "How do you mean?"

"Aradlugal still needs knowledge only you have. Or maybe me, somewhere, but either way . . ."

"Either way, we risk being taken if we go after him and lose." Then, at her nod, "But some of the people he's taken, or who he seeks, might also know what he needs. Or at least know of ancient relics that might include those teachings."

"Yeah."

"Then there's really no choice, is there?"

Halba sighed, acknowledging yet again what she'd already known.

Cassandra cleared her throat. "That sort of brings up a pretty big question . . ."

"What are we stopping them from doing, exactly?" Gilad concluded for her. "Somehow, I don't think this is just about someone wanting to be immortal."

"No." Halba shook her head. "That's what Namenzida was after, or at least that's how Aradlugal tells it. But he . . . he's a lot worse."

The others waited while she gathered her thoughts.

"He wants to understand the portals to the Faraway," Halba said finally.

"Tactical use?" Cassandra asked.

"No. And he wants to understand the Boon—but not for immortality. He needs them both."

Halba was far from finished, but she might as well have been. The many thoughts and theories that had swept through Gilad's head calmed enough for one to emerge. It crashed over him like an avalanche (an event he'd actually experienced more than once).

"He wants it as a weapon," Gilad growled.

The former servant of Nergal nodded. Cassandra looked puzzled.

"I told you my tale," Gilad reminded her. "Including what happened when my brothers improperly activated the Boon."

"Oh, fuck. You said it killed . . ."

"Every living thing in Ur, and for miles around."

"Then if . . . if he turned it on near a portal, while others were open . . ."

"Or in the Faraway itself," Halba interjected.

"Yes." Gilad's fist clenched on the arm of his chair, shattering the wood. "I don't know enough to say for sure the effect would even travel through the portals, but if it did? Depending on which portals were active and where they are, he could kill millions across the globe. Multiple cities snuffed out at once."

Cassandra looked as if she might vomit. "That's just the start. Millions more would die from what follows. Supply chains would crash. Economies disintegrate."

"People would have no idea what had happened," Halba said, "or why. Or whether it could happen again. Panic. Probably war. Aradlugal . . . he's even more fanatical than he used to be, he . . . said he's going to tear down civilization itself. That should be an empty boast, but . . ."

"But this," Gilad said, "might actually do it."

The silence stretched on. In the distance, they heard the rumble of a car engine.

"It could even be worse than *that*," he continued after a time, thoughts once more racing. "I still have no idea what sorts of magics the Keepers of the Timeless Word might control. What relics other than the Boon they've created. What sorts of creatures and wonders can be found throughout Utnapishtim. If Aradlugal wreaks this sort of havoc *there*, I can't begin to guess what the mystical or metaphysical consequences could be."

More silence.

"I, uh . . ." Cassandra gave a tense smile. "I guess we should get started?"

"We should." Gilad rose. "Starting with tearing this carpet up."

The two women stared at him.

"Right here." He pressed his foot down on the spot he'd been studying, grinding the fibers down enough to mark it. "A square yard at least, please."

Confused, Halba handed Cassandra one of her akinakes. Using the daggers, they cut away a swath of the carpet as Gilad searched through the small office. By the time they were done, exposing the concrete beneath, he'd found a small hammer.

"I don't think the owners are going to be thrilled with this," Cassandra said.

Gilad waved a dismissive hand. "They knew this might happen someday when I paid for the building. They'll deal with it." Preempting any further questions, he knelt, raised the tool, and struck.

For most people, a hand hammer would never have been enough to break through the concrete, at least not anytime soon. Even Gilad, strong and tireless as he was, took long minutes.

In the end, however, though the hammer was bent and mangled, he had a pile of rocky chunks where solid floor had been. It took but a few moments more to clear those away, revealing a hollow containing an old box—a box like so many others he had stashed in a myriad of cities across the globe.

This one he had moved here after his last trip to Nasiriyah, twenty years before.

Gilad ignored the cash and the myriad of false IDs within. He removed a Glock, clipping the holster to his belt; several knives, which he secreted around his person; and an M4 carbine. The latter he passed to Cassandra, along with several spare magazines.

She raised an eyebrow.

"Your army lost countless weapons in the early years of the war. I'm only responsible for a tiny portion of them."

She said nothing, just set about checking the gun.

"I assume you've still got your own?" he asked Halba, who grunted an affirmative.

Gilad collected a small bag containing more "borrowed" military equipment, then reached in one last time for one last weapon. He had no idea if he'd need it or not—but considering where he was, and the sorts of places Aradlugal might well be digging into, taking it was a wise precaution.

Carefully he hefted the tightly wrapped parcel, folding back the cloth to reveal an ancient axe with a blade of chipped bone.

He felt Cassandra appear behind him. "Is that . . . ?"

"The same one, yes. Made from the scapula of a . . . Well, the Caral didn't have the concept of a 'saint' as you understand it, but a comparable holy figure."

"That's why it could hurt those, uh, those creatures?"

"One of the few things that can." He hefted it once, then slung it over his shoulder by a strap that clearly wasn't as old as the weapon itself.

"All right, Halba. Show us to your old friends."

TWENTY-SIX

The warehouse was a newer structure, perhaps a decade old. No light shone through the windows; no sounds escaped its heavy walls. Like everything else surrounding it, it appeared shut down for the night.

Yet a handful of armed men wandered the property, and a handful more loitered around the loading dock. To anyone happening by, it would appear something of value must be stashed within. Curious, perhaps, but hardly suspicious.

Gilad knew better. He knew who the guards really were.

He did not sneak. He did not charge. He waited, in fact, until the patrolling sentries drew near the ones stationed by the entrance, until every one of them stood between him and the door. Then, as casually as if he were on a moonlight stroll, he stepped from the gloom and walked toward the warehouse.

The first saw him coming, tapping his nearest companion on the shoulder to alert him, that one then calling to the next. All of them watched as the stranger drew near.

Then he was near enough, even in the dark, for them to recognize him.

Cries of shock and shouts of alarm shattered the silence. Half a dozen weapons rose, barrels or bolts coming to bear, while the rest of the sentries reached for cell phones or radios.

Gilad walked on.

Blades whirled in the gloom from *behind* the Melidarishe. Halba struck, a specter of shadow. Akinakes carved through flesh. Blood sprayed and bodies fell—two, three. The cult soldiers hesitated, their focus ripped from Gilad's approach by the threat suddenly in their midst.

Gunshots echoed across the neighborhood, not from the startled sentries but from behind a car parked dozens of yards down the block. Cassandra fired short, controlled bursts from the M4, selecting targets on the opposite side of the loading dock from Halba's attack. More Melidarishe dropped, most without ever returning fire.

Between the two women, the bullets and the blades, every sentry was dead in moments.

His stride never wavering, Gilad walked on.

Beside the dock's garage door was a smaller entrance, which was probably locked. Gilad didn't bother to check.

A brutal kick with every bit of his preternatural strength ripped bolt from wood and wood from hinge. He strode through the mangled shape of what no longer fully qualified as a door, Halba and then Cassandra slipping in behind him before spreading out to either side.

It took only a couple minutes of scouting (Gilad and Halba on the ground floor while Cassandra covered them from a walkway above) to confirm that the warehouse was clear. Crates of various sizes filled less than half of it, none of which concealed any of the enemy.

That was fine. Gilad wouldn't have expected them here, even if Halba hadn't already warned him the real threat lay below.

Below, in the ancient passageways, hidden and forgotten beneath the city since the days of Sumer. Just as it had been twenty years ago.

Halba had never seen the method for opening the secret door, but Cassandra and Gilad had both experienced a similar situation, and while this was neither the same structure nor the same section of underground ruin, they managed to locate the mechanism quickly enough. One of the cargo crates, tucked back in a far corner, turned out to be no crate at all but an extension of the wall constructed to look like one. One of the knotholes in the wood contained a switch much like the one a younger Cassandra had found beneath the stairs—and that switch, in turn, triggered a portion of the floor to slide aside, revealing a narrow stone staircase leading down.

Again Gilad would have known, even if he hadn't been told, that this concealed passage had seen recent use. The dust wasn't thick enough, nor the escaping air stale enough, for it to have been sealed for long.

"No alternate routes and no cover," Cassandra said as she appeared behind them. "If anyone's stationed near the base of the stairs, we're going to be easy pickings."

"I'm aware." Gilad reached into the bag he'd removed from his emergency cache. When he withdrew his hand, he clutched a pair of US Army–issue grenades.

"Fire in the hole," he said casually, yanking the pins and almost nonchalantly tossing the explosives down the steps.

The detonation was more a sharp *crack* than a *boom*. Gilad was pounding downward at full tilt before the echo faded, Halba and Cassandra hot on his heels.

The time for stealth was past. Even if the enemy had not heard the gunfire from outside, they'd certainly heard *that*.

Gilad took the stairs three at a time, all but flying between the narrow walls, drawing his pistol as he went. At the bottom, scorched and shrapnel-pocked stone bore witness to the pair of grenades almost as dramatically as the shredded corpse he stepped over. Beyond gaped a broad chamber carved from the desert rock—not so massive as the one in which Gilad and Cassandra had met long ago, but enormous enough in its own right. Pillars covered with faded Sumerian patterns supported the high ceiling, from which a mosaic of bronze lions and strange winged beasts gazed down upon them.

In the room, a squad of Melidarishe guards was already waiting. From the ornate archways that led to multiple side passages, many more flowed into the chamber, weapons raised, drawn by the sound of the twin explosions.

Flowed into the chamber and died.

Twenty years ago, Cassandra had been badly wounded, terrified, bewildered by the chaos and the impossible creature that menaced her and her companions. Days ago, in George Town, the only "enemy" had been a handful of hired security guards, a nonthreat easily subdued.

For Halba's part, though she shared some of Gilad's memories, they were scattered, fragmented, often unclear. He had not been himself during the raid on the Callahan Ranch, and he'd been badly injured, recovering from prolonged torture, during his escape from Namenzida's church.

Before today, neither woman had ever witnessed Gilad Anni-Padda at his peak. After today, neither would ever forget.

Even as he passed through the entryway, Gilad threw himself downward, sliding across the floor on one shoulder before flipping to the other, firing as he spun. The two men who'd stood in either corner, ready to mow down whoever entered, died without getting off a single shot. Melidarishe bullets crossed the room from the far end, only to flatten and ricochet from the stone walls.

He was still firing as he came back to his feet, pushing off with one foot so he jerked back and to the right, the momentum of his roll reversed in a single thrust. More of the enemy's shots passed harmlessly through the empty space where he'd been; more of his own were anything but harmless.

Eighteen rounds in the Glock 17, including the first in the chamber. Two rounds in each target: center mass, then head. The pistol was empty in mere seconds, and nine of the Melidarishe lay dead. Never holding still, under a withering barrage of return fire, Gilad hadn't missed once.

Only years of experience kept Halba or Cassandra from stopping in the doorway to gawk.

By then Gilad had closed the rest of the distance in a sprint that would have put Olympians to shame, and he was among the first cluster of the foe.

He spun the pistol in his fist, flipping it so he held the barrel. The grip landed like a hammer against a collarbone, shattering it hard enough to drive fragments into surrounding tissue. He thrust back with the other arm, his elbow splintering the ribs and rupturing organs of a second man, even as he stomped down and cracked the shin of a third.

Three more still surrounded him, but for the moment that was fine: It kept the other groups of Melidarishe from opening fire on him. He heard the swift bursts of Cassandra's own weapon and the brief aborted cries that meant Halba's daggers did their job as well.

It was nice to have the backup, though he didn't need it.

He ducked beneath the blow as an opponent swung their own M4 like a club, raised a leg to take an incoming kick on the thick muscle of his thigh rather than to his crotch where it was aimed, and turned slightly into the attack as the third man struck with a brutal hunting knife.

That thrust he caught, trapping blade and forearm between his own arm and his ribs. Gilad dropped to one knee, dragging his attacker down with him, then released the hold and struck down with a palm, driving the falling man's face hard into the stone floor. Cartilage flattened, bone cracked, teeth scattered, blood flowed.

From there he kicked back, shattering a nearby ankle, even as he lunged. His empty hand closed on the groin of the last standing member of this first group, twisted, and yanked.

The resulting scream was physically painful to hear.

Now the rest of the Melidarishe in the chamber, already scrambling to take cover from Cassandra, opened fire on Gilad. If they cared at all that some of their comrades around him were only wounded, not yet dead, it was no longer concerning enough to stay their hands.

As the man he'd just horribly wounded doubled over, collapsing, Gilad caught him, rolling to put his body between himself and the incoming fire.

The human shield thrashed and spasmed as the first bullets hit, but quickly fell still. Flesh, bone, and body armor absorbed most of the rounds. A few penetrated, striking softer, unarmored spots, but by then they'd been slowed enough that their impact on Gilad was shallow. For a normal human, they still might have been debilitating, but he shrugged them off. The bleeding would stop in a matter of moments.

Gilad took an extra half second to drive his fist into a man's temple, finishing off another of the wounded. Yet another twist and he grabbed the last survivor, the man whose ankle he'd mangled—and whose body armor remained undamaged. Ignoring the soldier's screams, Gilad rolled to his feet and, holding the struggling body before him as a brand-new shield, charged the next nearest cluster of Melidarishe.

He reached them in seconds, their fusillade scarcely slowing him down. A few strides away, he hurled the now-deceased body at their legs, bowling most of them over like pins. This time, just before hurtling into their midst, he drew two of the small blades he'd secreted about his person.

He struck, spun, struck again, his arms twinned serpents with fangs of steel. He was everywhere at once, except where the enemy's own desperate counterattacks tried to find him; he saw everything, no matter which way his back might be turned. The Melidarishe might as well have thrown themselves into a Cuisinart. The ones who'd fallen never got back up; the ones who hadn't fallen joined them swiftly enough.

Gilad stood atop a dune of carnage, soaked to the elbows and spattered in gore.

The third and final group of sentries lay dead as well, taken down by Halba and Cassandra, both of whom stared at Gilad in awe and shock and perhaps a tinge of fear.

Gilad nodded at them, shook the worst of the mess from his arms, and moved toward the nearest archway.

"Have you ever—" Cassandra began in a stunned whisper.

"No," was Halba's only reply.

Having dropped his pistol, Gilad retrieved a Škorpion from one of the fallen before continuing. A quick check at each archway, just a glance around the frame, revealed that most led into further tunnels, while a few opened directly into smaller adjoining chambers.

From one of the latter, an array of filthy, pain-filled, and tear-streaked faces gazed back at him.

Gilad didn't know who among them might be part of the same informal group he'd dealt with before, the scholars who kept the secrets and studied the relics of the region's past ages. He'd only ever met a few, many years ago, and three of those had died the last time he and Cassandra had been here. Most of the hostages had been taken, even tortured, not for anything they knew but solely to draw out those Aradlugal wanted, to convince them he was not to be taken lightly. Gilad saw the many sloppy bandages, soaked in blood and caked with dirt; the agony not only of pain but of grief and loss; the smattering of corpses scattered among the living, left as rotting reminders.

He saw and he hated—hated Aradlugal and the Melidarishe far more than he already had.

"Cassandra!"

Other than to whisper reassurances in Arabic that their ordeal was at an end, Gilad didn't so much as move until Cassandra, and Halba as well, appeared at his side in the archway.

"What do you . . . Oh, God . . ."

He heard her voice break, though she tried hard to swallow it. He heard, too, a faint hitch in Halba's throat, a stillborn gasp.

He heard it, and he almost raged. *You've seen worse than this! You've* done *worse than this! Why aren't you proud of your associates' handiwork now?*

But he quashed the thought even as it formed, long before it could turn into speech. He'd already known what she'd done, what she'd been part of, and he genuinely believed in her change of heart. Wherever it had come from, however tormented she'd been over it, he'd read it in her voice, her posture, her eyes, and she'd proved it in her actions.

Beating her over the head with it now, shattering her budding trust in him, would serve no one but the enemy.

"Get them out," he said.

Cassandra hesitated a second or two, then nodded. The brief straightening of her posture, the twitch of her arm, suggested she'd almost reverted to old battlefield habits and saluted. "Wait a second, though . . ." She turned to face the assembled prisoners. "Do any of you speak English?"

Several spoke up or raised their hands. She waved sharply at Gilad and Halba, indicating they should go, then asked, "Do any of you know your weapons and feel strong enough to use them?"

It was probably unnecessary—there shouldn't be any living Melidarishe between them and safety—but a wise precaution nonetheless.

Gilad and Halba crossed the chamber. Disturbed dust on the floor and the occasional scratch in the rock suggested that one passage had seen more use than the others. Moving almost in sync, they slipped inside.

With one last glance over his shoulder, Gilad saw Cassandra and several hostages moving among the fallen foe, collecting guns and ammunition, before a bend in the tunnel blocked them from his view.

TWENTY-SEVEN

Few if any side passages branched off this tunnel, but it was far from straight. Multiple curves and a few sharp bends would all have made excellent ambush points.

Yet not one of them concealed a single enemy. Gilad would frankly have felt better if they had, and to judge by the growing clench in Halba's jaw, she felt the same.

"Could he be running out of soldiers?" Gilad asked, not even so much a whisper as a breath.

"It's possible," she replied, almost as softly. "I don't know how many were lost in the firefight at the tenement. But . . ."

Yeah. *But.*

But he had to have heard the massive battle in the entry chamber.

But he should have put anyone he had left in position to take greatest advantage.

Aradlugal might be a bitter, rageful fanatic, but he was not remotely a fool.

By unspoken agreement Gilad and Halba separated further, now creeping along opposite walls of the tunnel.

They needn't have bothered. By the time the passage finally came to an end, opening into a chamber as large as the entry hall and replete with even more etched columns, they still hadn't met with a shred of resistance.

The room was lit by lanterns, fire and electrical both, scattered without apparent rhyme or reason. In its center—probably the *precise* center, though Gilad would have had to measure to be sure—sat an old metal bed frame. It held no mattress, leaving the coils and wires exposed. Manacles hung from all four posts, anchored by bolts and thick chains.

Against the nearby pillars leaned large stone tablets. Some Gilad recognized from his ordeals in the church: the modified texts of the Thief of Yesterdays. Others, however, were unfamiliar. These were smaller and still partially coated in the dust of ages.

On their knees beside yet another column were two men and a woman, all elderly, all dressed in traditional old Iraqi style. They knelt motionless, without sound or sign of what they must be feeling. These, Gilad knew, must be some of the scholars for whom Aradlugal had been searching. He wondered what secrets they'd already been forced to give up.

Two Melidarishe soldiers stood by them, one to either side, weapons trained on the prisoners.

"I'd prefer not to kill them. They can still teach me so much."

The voice emerged from the darkness of the chamber's far end. Gilad listened intently as Aradlugal spoke, but the faint echo of the underground vault made it impossible to pinpoint him by sound alone, and he seemed uninterested in stepping out into the light.

Pity. Gilad had fully intended to just shoot the man. He could tell by the sounds, however, that Aradlugal wasn't alone. At least two more Melidarishe lurked along with him.

Off to his left, Halba disappeared into her own pocket of shadow.

"Maybe you should have thought of that before you murdered the man with all the occult experience, Aradlugal," Gilad called back.

"Oh, he didn't have *all* of it, and I'm a quick study. And it's just Lugal now."

Gilad burst out in mocking laughter. "I've refused to call any man 'king' in my native tongue since before the birth of most modern religions. You *certainly* aren't about to be the first . . . Benjamin."

"Halba, you traitorous bitch!" Aradlugal's wrath rebounded through the chamber.

When she answered, the echoes cloaked her own position as effectively as they did the enemy's. "From you, that's a compliment. And my name is Jada."

The brief surge of pride—not quite fatherly, but almost—startled Gilad with its intensity.

Aradlugal's voice shook with fury as he shouted, "Do it!"

The two men guarding the trio of scholars had barely raised their guns when they died, cut down by four impossibly swift and accurate shots from Gilad.

Unfortunately, he couldn't stop the soldiers he couldn't see. More gunfire erupted from across the chamber, first aimed at Gilad himself, forcing him to dive for cover. Then it swept to his left, cutting down the three helpless prisoners. Even as they died, they made no sound or motion.

Gilad's stunned disbelief sang even through the maelstrom of his own rising anger. Aradlugal had *just said* he could still learn from them, that he didn't want them dead—yet he'd ordered their murder without hesitation for no other reason than the pain and frustration the failure to save them would cause Gilad.

And he'd forced his men to give away their positions in the process.

Could even Aradlugal be that petty?

Pondering didn't stop Gilad from returning fire. Precision wasn't an option, so he settled for a sequence of bursts, beginning where he knew they'd been, where their own shots had come from, and sweeping outward.

A shout, a gurgle, and a sodden *thump* suggested he'd caught one of them, but that left at least one more along with Aradlugal himself.

From the darkness came another cry, a burst of shock and pain. The second Melidarishe soldier collapsed into view, akinakes protruding from his chest. Halba—*no, Jada*—followed him down, yanking her weapons from the newly made corpse with a wet slurping sound.

Aradlugal appeared behind her as she sprang back to her feet, spinning to meet him. Blade clashed against blade, her Persian daggers against the Japanese tantos in his fists. To anyone without Gilad's extraordinary speed and experience, it would've been a mind-boggling display of skill.

He considered taking a shot, but their steps and thrusts and parries carried them back and forth so unpredictably, in and out of the illumination of the nearby lanterns, he couldn't be certain of his aim. He knew, too, that the Škorpion had only a few rounds remaining.

Instead he dropped the gun, drew his own knives, and charged. Aradlugal was good, but he'd have had no chance facing Gilad alone, let alone against Jada as well. This would all be over in—

Aradlugal shouted in words even Gilad couldn't understand, though he recognized the language. It was an ancient tongue, a slightly younger contemporary of Gilad's native Emeĝir, but from the other side of the globe. The tongue of the long-dead Caral civilization of the Andes.

Two thoughts flashed instantly through Gilad's mind.

First, Aradlugal could not possibly have known that tongue—unless he'd literally stolen the knowledge from the mind of one of the rare occultists who still had access to texts and proto-writing the entire archaeological community thought long lost. *That* must explain the strange lethargy that had wrapped all three captive scholars prior to their execution: They had not yet recovered from being subjected to the Thief of Yesterdays rite.

And second, Gilad could come up with only one reason Aradlugal would *want* to master that extinct tongue.

Gilad raised both arms in a blind and desperate block, but it wasn't enough. A furious blow, inhumanly strong, struck from the side, bruising to the bone, lifting him off his feet, and hurling him back to land in an aching, rolling heap on the unyielding stone.

Throughout the chamber and the many winding passages beyond, it echoed. The unholy mixture of a whistling kettle and a wailing infant—a piercing, hissing scream he hadn't heard in twenty years and had hoped he would never have to hear again.

Standing beside the entrance to the claustrophobic stairs leading to the warehouse, to the street, to freedom, Cassandra froze. Around her the last group of hostages, those who hadn't yet made their way up and out, cried out in fear at the dreadful sound, but in that moment she was no longer aware of them.

The people around her were no longer Iraqi civilians but her squadmates: Kolowitz and Daniels and Nash and the rest. Her heart pounded and her head thickened with a terror simultaneously alien and all too familiar. Sweat coated her face and her neck; her hands shook.

On her left arm, the old burn scar throbbed.

Suck it up, Private!

She had to smother a brief grin as she snapped back to herself. Sarge's bark was so clear, she expected to feel his breath from behind her.

Two decades ago, she'd watched her friends die at the talons of something unnatural, profane. She'd almost joined them.

The man who was the only reason she hadn't now faced that same threat again. She had no reason to expect he couldn't destroy it today as readily as he had back then.

But if he couldn't, just maybe it was her turn to make the difference.

When she turned back toward the last of the civilians, several already faced her, their expressions deeply serious. One, a middle-aged man clutching a heavy pistol taken from a dead cultist, offered a deep nod.

"We will be fine," he told her in thickly accented English. "Go."

Cassandra clasped his hand, raised the M4 to her shoulder, and proceeded back into the winding complex.

TWENTY-EIGHT

"Do you recognize it, Gilad?"

Taking advantage of Jada's momentary distraction at the attack on Gilad and the creature's howl, Aradlugal disengaged and stepped back. He'd bought himself room not merely to maneuver but to taunt. For every step she advanced, he retreated, preserving the distance between them.

Gilad also backpedaled, circling the chamber, watching for the faintest glimmer of light or shifting of the gloom that would serve as his only warning of the entity's next attack.

"It's the only survivor of your last little excursion beneath the streets of Nasiriyah!" the young cultist continued. "When I offered it another crack at you, it was only too happy to bargain. You think *I* can hold a grudge . . ."

A glint that might have been a mote of dust in the lantern light. A scrape on the rock barely louder than a crawling beetle. Gilad hurled himself into what at first seemed a backflip, letting the near-invisible talons pass harmlessly by. Then, with strength and agility only he could accomplish, he shoved off the floor with both hands. His momentum halted, reversed; rather than continuing, he instead launched himself forward to land back where he'd started.

A violent shrug dropped the strap over his arm, letting the axe fall neatly into his waiting hand. Gilad spun it slowly, ready to strike from any angle as soon as—

There.

He saw it coming again but couldn't fully dodge the blow. Though he avoided the raking talons that would have shredded skin and muscle, the heel of whatever passed for the creature's palm slammed hard into Gilad's shoulder, staggering him. His arm went briefly numb, and he couldn't quite swallow a grunt of pain.

Bruised, badly strained, but no dislocation. It would be fine shortly, or at least fine enough that it wouldn't impede him.

Hopefully it also wouldn't matter by then.

Gilad turned the stagger into a backstep and a spin, bringing the axe in low. Even if he couldn't see his foe clearly, even if it appeared as nothing more than reflection and shade even this close, he knew from experience that its shape remained roughly humanoid. His weapon struck hard at where he calculated its forward leg—which had to be bearing its weight for it to lunge as it had—must be.

He was right. The axe struck, the haft vibrating with the impact.

And the blade of bone shattered into a hundred fragments.

For the first time in years, perhaps a generation or more, Gilad froze in bewildered shock, unable to absorb what he'd seen. It lasted a mere fraction of a second, but long enough it nearly cost him his life. Those murderous talons plunged at his chest, and had he not caught the entity's hand with both his own at the last moment, had he not braced against the blow so that it threw him up and back rather than punching through him, he'd have found his spirit once again in the company of his family beyond, while his corpse lay waiting for the tender ministrations of Aradlugal or his pet.

The bones of his arms screamed at him, quivering at the impact; when he slammed against the nearest pillar, his back and shoulders joined in that agonized chorus. He slid to the floor, nearly falling before he steadied himself, while stars burst at the edges of his vision.

Aradlugal laughed almost hysterically, though he kept his weapons raised before him and his gaze forward, in case Jada should take advantage of his seeming distraction.

"I guess nobody would know better than you, Anni-Padda! They just don't make *anything* like they used to!"

It doubtless wasn't his foe's intention, but Gilad's confusion dispersed like ashes and embers before his taunting. He understood fully what had happened, what *must* have happened, as surely as if Aradlugal had sat him down and explained it.

The bastard had known about Gilad's stash, had pulled the knowledge from among his stolen thoughts and memories. He'd been *days* ahead of them in getting to Nasiriyah; plenty of time to dig up the stockpile, engage in a bit of subtle tampering, and set everything back as it had been. Carpet could be pulled up and refastened, and while fresh concrete wouldn't have had time to fully cure, a layer that thin would have dried enough to do the job. Maybe, if he'd been actively looking for sabotage, he might have noticed . . .

I should have been, damn it!

Whether Aradlugal had done something to weaken the blade, perhaps a touch of acid, or had ordered some artisan among his ranks to craft a duplicate, Gilad didn't know, and ultimately it didn't matter. The result was the same.

I have no way to kill this thing.

If he'd been alone, with nothing and nobody else at stake,

he might have been able to find a way. Perhaps the entity's neck could be broken with enough strength, or it could be crushed beneath the stone of a collapsing chamber, or . . .

But that would take time he did not have, and would risk far too much on a desperate roll of the dice. Here, now, today, though the very notion galled him to his core, he had only one option.

"Jada! *Run.*"

It should, at least, have bought them time.

As they pounded back along the winding tunnel, footsteps echoing ahead of them like an uninvited herald, Gilad had every reason to believe the enemy wouldn't closely follow. The unseen entity would be forced to struggle and squeeze through the narrow space, assuming it could fit at all, and Aradlugal would never be so foolish as to pursue them on his own. Gilad and Jada should have a clear shot to the outside, where they could reunite with Cassandra and decide their next move.

They burst out into the entry chamber, leaping over the nearest of the strewn Melidarishe corpses, and had covered about half the remaining distance to the exit when something slammed into Gilad with battering-ram force.

Again, reflex and instinct, a last-second awareness that made him take half a step to the side, saved him from the worst of the blow. No bones broke, nothing ruptured. Still he flew, carried on a wave of stunned agony for several yards before he crashed to the ground and skidded to a stop, leaving a trail of blood and scraped skin across the rough stone.

A faint distortion passed between him and one of the pillars, warping the engravings out of shape, and something that was almost a foot pressed into the partially drying blood of a dead sentry.

Aradlugal's mocking tones drifted from one of the archways—*not* the one Gilad and Jada had used. "By the way, Anni-Padda, there are a *couple* of routes to the inner chamber. I just made sure my people only used the longer one. I knew you'd track them once you arrived."

Again he chuckled, while Gilad cursed internally. "I really have," the bastard continued, "prepared for everything."

He flew from the entryway, blades flashing. Jada twisted to meet the attack, parrying with her own daggers, but the sheer ferocity of the attack forced her to retreat.

The beast lunged at the same moment, howling its head-splitting cry. Gilad scrambled upright, but he wasn't quick enough to dodge the unnaturally swift entity. He managed to bat one grasping hand aside, but the other closed tight around his ribs, squeezing painfully and lifting him from the ground. Pain shot through his back, and he felt the spreading warmth of blood as clothing and flesh tore.

He felt, too, the entity's supernatural venom pumping obscenely into his body. Gilad knew from painful experience that his system could fight off the corruption that consumed mortals from within, but the process was as excruciating as any torture, and spiritually filthy besides.

Whether it wanted to torment and toy with him, or because Aradlugal's bargain required it to keep him alive, it hadn't driven those talons as deep as it could. Still, Gilad was in trouble. Without a weapon that could harm this creature, anything he did now would only prolong the inevitable, and even if Jada managed to defeat Aradlugal—an outcome far from guaranteed—she'd be just as helpless before this unholy . . .

"I really have prepared for everything."

The echo of those words pierced the fog of pain trying to smother his mind. Fanatical and impulsive as he was, Aradlugal had proved over and over that he wasn't a fool. No matter what his captive scholars told him or what knowledge he gleaned from their relics, he couldn't have been *completely* certain the entity could be bargained with. For a man who'd thought to sabotage the axe before Gilad himself even knew he was coming here, who'd deliberately laid a trail down the longer passage to keep his enemy ignorant of the shorter one, it would be unthinkable to leave himself helpless should this ancient, inhuman creature prove uncooperative.

With a shout and a surge of every bit of strength, Gilad threw off the misshapen digits wrapped invisibly around him. He dropped and rolled just beneath the thing's desperate grab, then launched into a mad sprint. The entity followed close behind, its endless wail and the slapping of its feet announcing its proximity as surely as if Gilad could see it.

Gilad couldn't keep ahead of it long. Even his speed could at best match the thing, not exceed it, but that was okay. He didn't *need* long.

A partial circuit of the chamber carried him briefly behind the other pair of combatants. Aradlugal spared him only the briefest glance, otherwise unwilling to take his attention off his clash of blades with Jada. And why should he? Gilad wasn't near enough to interfere, and any change of course would grant his pursuer the fraction of a second it needed to catch him.

But as much as he would have liked to assist Jada—and to feel Aradlugal's life ebb from his body—Gilad wasn't *trying* to interfere. He was trying to *see*.

And there it was. Strapped at the small of Aradlugal's back in a makeshift sheath, a bulky, thick-bladed thing that could only in the most generous and general terms be called a "dagger."

The blade might be hidden by the leather wrapping, but Gilad knew what it must be. Bone—the bone of a holy man of Caral.

He took a chance, juking abruptly to the right, trying to make a dash for Aradlugal. Just as he'd anticipated, he took a jackhammer blow to the ribs for his trouble, once again launching him off his feet.

"Jada!" he shouted as he twisted in the air and landed in a ready crouch. He hated to let the enemy know that he knew, but so long as the entity was on him, he'd never be able to lay hands on the weapon himself. "The dagger! On his back!"

Aradlugal's glare was pure murder, and the cult's newly anointed leader redoubled his furious attack on Jada, driving her back. She parried, dodged, weaved in a desperate defense she could not afford to break. Any grab at that dagger would cost her fingers at best and quite possibly a mortal wound. Unless her rival stumbled or tired before she did, that blade of bone might as well have been miles away.

The translucent creature streaked after Gilad, winding like a serpent. He retreated before it, juking and dodging. A desperate handspring avoided what would otherwise have been a crushing bear hug. He ducked, letting a talon pass overhead. Once he even dove toward it and kicked off its bent leg, letting it pass through the space he'd occupied and winning himself an extra few yards of breathing room.

But it was all he could do to keep ahead of it. He had no means of counterattacking, and every time he tried to close on the other combatants, to come anywhere near Aradlugal and his dagger, the entity interposed with a speed Gilad could barely match.

Jada cried out in pain. She stumbled, nearly falling to a knee as one of her akinakes clattered across the stone. Blood pumped from a deep gash in her upper arm, instantly soaking her sleeve. Aradlugal watched her stagger, smirking, spinning his crimson-drenched tanto. Snarling, Gilad tensed for a mad dash at the man before he could close again to finish Jada off, even though he knew his own inhuman opponent would never allow him to reach them in time . . .

From somewhere in the chamber thundered a three-round burst of gunfire.

Blood misted from Aradlugal's shoulder, now little more than a mess of shredded muscle and shattered bone. His scream, shock as much as pain, drowned out the clatter of his falling blades and his own *thud* as he hit the floor.

His words pinched tight with pain and choked with tears, he shouted something in that foreign language. Gilad felt the shift of mass in the air before him as the thing moved to answer that call, likely to protect its fallen partner.

Oh, no, you damn well don't!

Now it was Gilad's turn to lunge. He struck, his arms spread wide to catch a target almost too broad to miss. He tightened his grip instantly, squeezed, and with every bit of strength, *heaved*.

Like the mythic heroes of the lands to which he'd been born, Gilad hefted the unseen thing—nearly twice the height of any man and far, far more than fivefold the weight—clear off the ground, and then slammed it down upon the stone.

With a driving shout of her own, breaking through the pain with a furious will, Jada dove upon her enemy. Aradlugal scurried backward, pushing himself along with his heels and one working arm, but he wasn't quick enough.

They grappled, the two horribly wounded rivals who had once been closer than friends. A flailing backhand caught Jada across the chin, snapping her head around and knocking her away, but not before she'd accomplished her goal. Letting herself fall painfully on her wounded arm, she used the other to hurl the leather-sheathed weapon across the room.

Howling, hissing, the entity shot upright from where Gilad had thrown it down—and Gilad let it. More, he went with it, snagging a glint from its shadowed skin where he guessed its shoulders to be. At that speed, from that height, it took only an acrobatic marvel to most, but a mild effort coming from him, to propel himself through empty space and snatch the weapon out of its flight.

He flipped and twisted, drawing the bone blade in midair and landing to face the creature. He swung in lightning-fast slashes—two, three.

Lines of dark and almost gelatinous gore, as much oil as blood, appeared across the otherwise invisible carapace, gleaming dully in the lantern light. The thing fell back, nearly colliding with the far wall, its painful wail not of predatory fury but of fear and pain.

Gilad did not pursue. Instead he raised the dagger, holding it up before him as if displaying it, and then—still presenting the weapon like a crucifix to a vampire—made his way toward his wounded companion.

"What are you *doing*?" Jada called to him.

"That's deep. It needs bandaging or you're going to bleed out."

"What about—?"

"I don't know if it understands our words," he said, loudly enough to echo. "But it knows *this*. And in a moment it's going to realize . . ."

The pained howl turned once more to rage, and the shadows once more streaked through the chamber. Gilad readied, just in case, but as he'd suspected, the beast no longer came for him.

Aradlugal shrieked one final time as talons tore through his chest, just beneath his one remaining shoulder. Even as the flesh began to fester and blacken, as that terrible scream began to turn wet, he vanished back into the darkness of the far corridors, dragged away like the toy of an angry, sadistic child.

". . . who carried that weapon," Gilad finished, his tone matter-of-fact. "And what it implied about the man it chose to bargain with."

TWENTY-NINE

"What . . ." Jada winced, biting back a groan as he wrapped a length of torn cloth tightly about her wound. "What if you'd been wrong?"

"I'd have had to kill it. Which would probably have taken longer than you had left."

"Oh. Uh, I'm glad you weren't wrong."

"As am I." Then, "Are you coming out? That can't be a pleasant place to hide."

Jada cast him a bewildered look, but he hadn't been speaking to her.

"Just . . . making sure it wasn't coming back."

The pile of dead Melidarishe nearest the entry shifted, one of the bodies sliding aside as a blood-smeared Cassandra emerged from beneath. In her hands she still carried her M4.

"*You're* where those shots came from?" Jada sounded almost accusatory.

"I'm sorry it took so long. You were too close to him until you were wounded and fell back. I didn't have a clean angle of fire."

After she ran to gather the satchel of supplies Gilad had carried in with them, then helped to treat Jada's wounds with more suitable materials, Cassandra went on to tell them how she'd heard the entity's hunting cry. How she'd just returned to the chamber when she heard it and Aradlugal approaching from their shortcut, and had leapt for the first hiding place she could think of.

"I could've taken him then," she concluded, "but that would've just exposed me to that . . . that thing." She shuddered with twenty-year-old memories. "Wasn't any point in it until—"

"Until you knew about the dagger and had a clean shot." Jada still sounded miffed that she'd had to be wounded before that could happen—or maybe it was just the pain—but she gave a stiff nod. "I get it."

Gilad helped her rise, steadying her until it was clear she could stand on her own, if only just.

"We'll get you stronger painkillers as soon as we can," he assured her.

She could only grit her teeth at him.

"That's it, then?" Cassandra asked, taking a few steps toward the exit. "We're done here?"

Gilad looked around, checked what remained of his own supplies, and then began searching the bodies of the dead cult soldiers.

"Almost . . ."

He'd sent the two of them on ahead so that Cassandra could find more help for Jada. It wouldn't have been fair to ask her to wait, not in that degree of pain. His task hadn't been a brief one.

In the end, it almost hadn't been possible. He had few grenades remaining in his supplies, and only a handful of the dead cult soldiers had been carrying explosives of their own. Still, he'd scavenged up enough, if only just.

He'd placed them deliberately after careful study of existing faults and cracks. With the equipment and other weaponry lying about, he'd jury-rigged a detonator. Now he stood across the street outside, leaning casually against the corner of a nearby building, waiting for . . .

Wump!

It didn't sound much like an explosion from above ground. The warehouse shuddered almost invisibly, shaking free a layer of accumulated dirt. Slowly, a few streams of smoke leaked from the windows, having climbed their way up the hidden stairs.

And Gilad knew, far below, that several stone tablets now lay shattered.

His gut twisted at the thought of having destroyed knowledge more ancient than he was, and he knew the surviving neighborhood scholars would have been horrified had they known. Yet he could not risk anyone else following in the footsteps of Namenzida and Aradlugal, and even he wasn't strong enough to cart the massive stone carvings away by hand. Destroying the Thief of Yesterdays ritual, as well as select portions of the other mystical writings, was the only wise choice.

As it was, he lacked sufficient explosives to do a thorough job. He wished he could obliterate them all, perhaps even bring down the chamber, but he had at best managed to shatter a few of the most essential tablets. He could only hope it would be enough to stymie anyone who might come after them.

He stood, watching the trickles of smoke dissipate in the night air and imagining them as the dim and unpredictable paths his own future might follow, until he heard the approach of emergency workers. Then, like those tendrils of fumes, he, too, vanished into the darkness.

Valerie Coswell leaned back in her chair, idly swirling a glass of wine, and pondered all she'd just been told.

Cassandra had obviously been through the wringer in the weeks she'd been away. She was exhausted and clearly troubled by what she'd seen—or perhaps done. Val didn't doubt that her report about taking time to help an old friend with a serious personal problem was more or less true—but it sure as all hell wasn't *complete*.

When Val asked, Cassandra hadn't even been willing to tell her why she'd called in so many favors or made use of so many of the agency's connections, citing a promise of confidentiality. Val could have fired her for that alone, and indeed Cassandra had seemed almost surprised that she hadn't, and that she hadn't pressed harder for answers.

The reason, of course, was that Val didn't *need* answers. Her broodmates had already filled her in on almost everything Cassandra Reyes had been up to from the moment they'd picked up her trail. Like the Melidarishe and Cassandra herself, they'd recognized Gilad Anni-Padda when "Jack Eren" made the news, and they'd been watching the Callahan Ranch when Cassandra showed up.

And now . . . now they had eyes on Anni-Padda himself, something none of their kind had managed in centuries.

This wasn't the time to act, nowhere near it. But they would keep watching, so they would know where to find him when it was.

Tonight had been a close thing, though. If Cassandra had shown up just a few minutes earlier . . . well, she'd have had to die, and that would've been a shame. She could still prove useful, too.

Valerie Coswell rose and stepped over to the mini fridge, opening it to reveal a desiccated husk of leathery flesh and crumbling bones—all that remained of the *real* Valerie Coswell. Putting the wine aside, she knelt to drain the last bits of life and memory from the woman she was becoming. No telling how long she'd have to maintain this facade, and she had to work with an entire business of people who made a living by spotting lies. It wouldn't do to leave some vital recollection behind . . .

—

"How long, do you think?"

The old pickup bumped and clattered over the haphazardly maintained highway—the same road on which they'd first begun getting to know one another, even if he'd scarcely begun to remember and she'd barely begun to figure it out.

Gilad, one hand on the wheel and the other hanging out the window, grunted as he gave it some thought. "A few days, probably. Definitely no more than a couple weeks. 'Jack Eren' is blown. There's no telling who's connected him to me by now. But we should have a bit of peace, at least long enough for me to fully transfer everything into Henry's name. I figure he'll be too stunned and overwhelmed to ask *too* many questions."

Jada chuckled. "No, you don't."

"No, I don't. But he'll have to live without getting any answers."

"And then what?"

He was surprised only that it had taken her this long to ask.

"Then I have to reconnect with Tama. See what she's been doing the last two years, make up for disappearing. Find out if there's anything she needs me to do—either as the Geomancer, or just as a young girl trying to figure out her life." It was his turn to chuckle. "I seem to be collecting those."

"Why?"

"Why am I collecting them? I'd already gotten all the good stamps."

"No, you . . . !" She flexed as if to hit him lightly on the shoulder, but the pain in her heavily stitched arm, and the sling that held it, drew her up short. "I mean, why . . ." She floundered for the words.

Why have I taken you into that collection? I haven't had family in centuries, Jada. You may not be blood, but sharing memories has to be close enough.

If he was responsible for shaping who she'd become—and he already was, thanks to those memories—then he would damn well see it through. He'd been a father more than enough times, even if he wasn't hers, to take that duty seriously.

He said none of that aloud, though. Until she could find the question, he wasn't sure she was ready to hear the answer.

Instead, what she finally came out with, even though they both knew it wasn't what she'd meant to ask, was, "Why are you so sure she'll accept having me around?"

"I wasn't really planning on asking. But she'll trust you when I tell her *I* trust you."

Gilad saw the protest in her expression before she choked it back. She didn't trust *herself*. No matter how many times he told her that his memories didn't *make* her feel anything, only reminded her how to feel—that even if they faded, she wouldn't turn back into Halba unless she *wanted* to—she hadn't yet been able to make herself believe it.

That was okay, though. She'd get there. And he'd help.

He knew how to treat even the oldest of wounds.

"Tell me," he said softly, "about you and Ben. Tell me how it all started."

Her breath caught. Her jaw, her shoulders, her fists, all tightened. A full minute passed in silence.

Then, in a voice thick with over half a decade of unshed tears, "It started at a party. Just like a hundred others we'd been to, and mostly couldn't even remember . . ."

Gilad turned off the highway and onto the Callahan Ranch private road as the rotting knot of denial and guilt and pain that had given birth to Halba of Nergal, that had nearly strangled Jada Lowry, finally began to unwind.

ACKNOWLEDGMENTS

Brendan, for invitation and collaboration.

The wonderful folks at Valiant, for inspiration and cooperation.

Moustafa Chamli, for translation and education.

And, as always and forever, George, for everything else that doesn't end in "-ion," as well as a few that do.